Love
and other
Dangerous
Chemicals

Anthony Capella

CORVUS

Page 170,171, 178: *Lady Chatterley's Lover* by D. H. Lawrence published by Penguin and Cambridge University Press. Reproduced by permission of Pollinger Limited and the Estates of Frieda Lawrence Ravagli.

First Published in the United States of America in 2009, by Touchstone.

This edition first published in the UK in 2011 as *Chemistry for Beginners* by Corvus, an imprint of Atlantic Books Ltd.
Copyright©Anthony Strong, 2009.

9 8 7 6 5 4 3 2

A CIP catalogue record for this book is available from the British Library.

Paperback ISBN: 978 0 85789 025 2
E-book ISBN: 978 0 85789 026 9

Printed in Great Britain by CPI Group (UK) Ltd, Croydon, CRO 4YY

Corvus
An imprint of Atlantic Books Ltd.
Ormond House
26–27 Boswell Street
London WCIN 3JZ

www.corvus-books.co.uk

LOVE AND OTHER DANGEROUS CHEMICALS

An\ ￼ny Capella was born in Uganda in 1962. He was educated at \ eter's College, Oxford, where he graduated with a first in En\ h Literature. He is the bestselling author of *The Food of Lo\ * Richard and Judy Summer Read), *The Wedding Officer*, an\ *e Various Flavours of Coffee*.

For S.S., research assistant

Female sexual dysfunction: some research issues

by Dr Steven J. Fisher, Department of Molecular Biology, University of Oxford.

International Journal of Sexual Biology 2008 May; 29(3):701-50

ABSTRACT

BACKGROUND: Male sexual dysfunction has been well described in the literature. The compound sildenafil citrate, marketed by Pfizer under the brand name Viagra, has created a market estimated at over $1billion annually. This has led to speculation that a drug targeted at female sexual dysfunction or FSD will be "the big pharmaceuticals' next miracle cure" (*Newsnight*, June 2007). However, the existence of FSD, and therefore of a treatment to combat it, remains controversial.

METHOD: The author describes a project to investigate a possible treatment for FSD, and cautions that some previously unconsidered factors may affect clinical outcomes. He describes in particular the case of Miss G, a research subject.

DISCUSSION: This paper was first presented at the conference "Towards a Sexual-Dysfunction-Free Future 2008", sponsored by Trock Pharmaceuticals, where it provoked a lively response (see, for example, the correspondence pages of this journal, *passim*).

INTERESTS: The author acknowledges the generous funding of the Trock Pharmaceuticals Research Foundation. This funding has since been withdrawn.

Twenty-eight women have now participated in the sexual dysfunction research project here at the Department of Molecular Biology, Oxford University. Our approach is empirical: that is to say, the treatment, a synthetic enzyme codenamed KXC79, is adjusted in response to each set of results. All the participants are volunteers and are assessed by my colleague Dr Susan Minstock using a number of standard evaluations (the Derogatis Sexual Functioning Inventory, the Locke-Wallace Marital Adjustment Test, the Female Sexual Function Index, etc) before a decision is made as to whether they are suitable for inclusion. It is always explained to the volunteers exactly what the study will involve; to date, thirty-one potential subjects have subsequently declined to take part. Nevertheless, early results have been encouraging (see, for example, Fisher, S.J and Minstock, S, 2007: *KXC79 and female sexual dysfunction: some encouraging early results*).

Miss G was slightly unusual in that she was a postgraduate student here at the university who heard about the project from one of our research assistants.[1] Strictly speaking, this was a breach of our selection protocol. However, Miss G worked in a completely different field, English Literature, and in all other respects fulfilled our criteria: she was anorgasmic and had previously consulted a doctor "to make sure it wasn't just a virus". (Notes were kept from initial and subsequent interviews: in addition, like all our volunteers, Miss G was encouraged to keep a record of her subjective responses during the trial.) She had also experienced relationship problems:

---

[1] The research assistant has since been terminated.

It wasn't just that I couldn't have orgasms – it was the fact that sex was such a big part of his life, and I couldn't share that. I simply had no interest in it. Almost as if I were going out with a football fan, but was bored by sport.

Based on this discussion and the questionnaires, Dr Minstock made a provisional diagnosis of Hypoactive Arousal Disorder and accepted her onto the study.

I myself met Miss G for the first time when she came to the lab for her induction. As this meeting, apparently so ordinary, was in some ways the beginning of the whole fiasco, I suppose I should at this point pause to note my initial impressions of her – as a person, I mean. The truth, though, is that I did not really have any. If I may be allowed a small subjective observation of my own, what I recall most is being somewhat annoyed she was there at all: my understanding was that the data-collection phase of our study was completed, at least for the time being, while I prepared our findings for publication. This was work that required a great deal of concentration, and when Dr Minstock showed someone into the lab I did not, at first, look up from my computer.

"This is where the hands-on part happens," my colleague was saying. "When I say hands-on, of course, I don't necessarily mean that literally. We've got toys to suit every taste."

Needless to say, I did not respond to this, either. Dr Minstock's jocular manner, which she frequently assures me is simply a psychological stratagem to put test subjects and co-workers at their ease, on occasion strays – it seems to me – into flippancy. Great scientists of the past – men such as James Watson and Francis Crick, when they were engaged in their revolutionary work on DNA – never felt the need to be flippant. But Dr Minstock, as a sexologist, does not have quite the same regard for scientific method that I do.

"That's Dr Fisher, who's in charge of the biochemical side," she added in a deafening whisper. "Working away, as usual! Don't worry, we won't disturb him if we're quiet. Over here's the photoplethagraph – basically it's like a little light we pop inside so we can see what's going on –"

"Photoplethysmograph," I said, still without raising my head.

"What?"

"That is a photople*thysmo*graph, not a photople*tha*graph. It calibrates reflected light. The darker the flush, the greater the vasodilation."

"Oh, yes," Dr Minstock said brightly. "Photoplethysmograph. Of course."

"What's 'vasodilation'?"

I did look up then. There was something about the voice that had just spoken – something wry, ironic even; as if the speaker were somehow mocking herself for not knowing the answer.

Or – it occurred to me a fraction of a second later – as if she were somehow mocking *me* for knowing it.

In short, I thought I had discerned in the way our visitor had spoken a spark of real intelligence, an impression only partially dispelled by her appearance. I did not at that point know Miss G was an arts graduate, but I could probably have deduced it. She was attractive; strikingly so – I might as well make that clear at the outset. But she was striking, if this makes sense, in an entirely unremarkable way. A pleasant face, torn jeans, a cashmere pullover, a book bag, a knitted cap; and, spilling out from under the cap, a fine mass of chestnut-brown hair, as squeaky-clean and glossy as a freshly-peeled conker. One could imagine that if one were to touch it, the hair would be expensive and soft, just like the pullover. Clearly, she was not part of the university I inhabit, bounded as it is by the Rutherford Laboratories on one side and the Science Parks on the other. Hers was another Oxford entirely, a city of drama societies and college balls and open-top sports cars roaring off for candlelit meals in country pubs. In that Oxford, which overlaps mine while barely impinging upon it, girls like her are… I almost want to say "two-a-penny", but of course they are considerably more expensive than that: their cashmere pullovers, their poise, and even their places at Oxford are the products of costly private educations.

So I glanced at Miss G and immediately thought that I knew her type; a type which was both as familiar and as alien to me as if she were a member of another species.

In this, as it later turned out, I was quite wrong.

"Vasodilation," I said, "relates to blood flow. Specifically, engorgement of the surface capillaries due to physiological stimulation."

"Anything you want to know about the technical stuff, Steve's your boy," Dr Minstock said, with a little roll of the eyes which clearly suggested that knowing about the technical stuff was a long way down her own list of priorities.

"Actually," Miss G said, "there was something…"

"I just need to check that file," my colleague said quickly. "Back in five." As she left it seemed to me that she gave the other woman a pitying look, as if to say "I warned you".

I sighed as I turned back to our visitor. "What did you want to know?"

"This treatment of yours," Miss G said hesitantly. "It's something like Viagra, presumably?"

I regret to say that even before she had finished this question I was smiling slightly at its naivety. "Not in the least, no. Viagra would be completely the wrong approach for any problem you might have."

"Why's that?"

"Well, I can tell you if you like," I said. "But I very much doubt you'll be able to grasp the answer."

She looked at me then in a rather level way, and I thought I detected a slight tightening of her jaw.

"Dr Fisher," she said carefully, "I have a double first class honours degree from Bristol University, an MPhil from Cambridge, and I'm three-quarters of the way to completing a DPhil here at Oxford. How about you try me?"

My explanation will undoubtedly seem rather simplistic to my present audience, but for the sake of establishing exactly what I said to Miss G, I will repeat it here. "The active ingredient in sildenafil citrate, or Viagra, is a specific inhibitor of phosphodiesterase 5," I pointed out. "This cleaves the ring form of cyclic GMP, a cellular messenger very similar to cAMP. The inhibition of the phosphodiesterase thus allows for the persistence of cGMP, which in turn promotes the release of nitric oxide into the corpus cavernosa of the penis."

She nodded slowly. "You're quite right."

"Of course. The mechanism is relatively well understood." I turned back to my computer screen.

"No, I meant you're right that I didn't understand. Not a word. Mind you," she went on, almost to herself, "it's got a sort of music to it, hasn't it, and I don't always understand a piece of Tennyson or Keats when I first hear it, either. Sometimes you have to sort of...*feel* the meaning before you can work out the details, don't you? So let's see...what you're saying is that once the phospho thingy, the phosphodiesterase, is taken out of the equation, and the cyclic GMP does its stuff, it's basically a question of nitric oxide, which must be a gas, so really it's just about hydraulics."

I must admit, I was quite intrigued that she had managed to work out the gist of what I was saying from so little actual knowledge. But that, I suppose, is one of the differences between science and the arts – they are positively encouraged to speculate beyond the realms of what they know, whereas for us, of course, it would be anathema. "Approximately, yes," I said. "Women's sexual responses are rather more complicated."

"Ah. Now there, perhaps, I can correct *you*. You mean 'complex'."

I frowned. "It's the same thing, surely."

She shook her head. "'Complicated' means something difficult, but ultimately knowable. 'Complex' implies something which has so many variables and unknowns it can only be appreciated intuitively

7

– something beyond the reach of rational analysis, like poetry or literature or love." And then, somewhat to my surprise, she recited what I took to be some lines of verse.

> "When two are stripped, long ere the course begin
> We wish that one should lose, the other win.
> And one especially do we affect
> Of two gold ingots, like in each respect:
>
> The reason, no man knows. Let it suffice,
> What we behold is censured by our eyes.
> Where both deliberate, the love is slight.
> Who ever loved, that loved not at first sight?"

"Marlowe, Christopher," she added. "1564 to 1593."

"Then I stand corrected," I said. "But even so, I still think I mean 'complicated'."

And then she asked the question that started the landslide.

"Oh? Why?"

1.3

I rarely get the opportunity to talk about my work. Because of the various irrational taboos surrounding the physiology of sexual response, and the even greater taboo surrounding scientific discourse, I find that when I try to explain to people what I do, either their eyes glaze over or they become embarrassed. So when someone asks me a straightforward question I take the view that the more I can dispel their ignorance with a straightforward answer, the better.

"What you call love," I said, "by which I assume you actually mean romantic attraction, is a relatively simple phenomenon – cascades of a

8

chemical called phenyl ethylamine gush through the central nervous system, inducing various emotional responses ranging from anxiety to a heightened need for touch. We know what it is, we know how it works, and, crucially, we know what it's *for*. Evolutionary theory, Miss G, teaches us that everything in the human body has a purpose. Our feet are shaped the way they are so that we can walk upright on the grassy savannah. Our thumbs work the way they do so that we can shape simple tools. Our hair is sleek and soft and glossy so that our sweat glands can work effectively. The male orgasm is another case in point. It has one purpose, and one purpose only: the continuation of the human race. Any pleasure we feel is simply the bribe by which nature induces us to spread our genes more widely.

"If you hook a man up to a scanner during climax, you see a localised, muscular spasm lasting about six seconds: highly functional, but with little variation. A woman, on the other hand, gets pulled into it gradually, building up her orgasm in a series of waves." At this point, I believe, I crossed to a whiteboard and sketched a brief illustration of the process, something along the lines of figures 1 and 2.

"First comes the excitement stage," I explained. "*Here*. There's a reddening of your face, chest and neck, akin to a measles rash. A feeling of warmth pervades your pelvis. Your genitals engorge with blood; your pulse races, your limbs relax; you find it difficult to keep your mouth closed or control the sounds you make. A cocktail of stimulants,

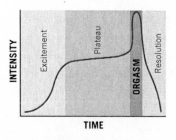

Figure 1: Typical male response.

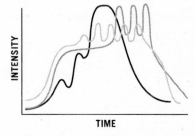

Figure 2: Three different female responses.

including dopamine and serotonin, are flooding your bloodstream, sensitising your nerve endings and giving you a rushing sensation. Round about *here*," I indicated with my dry marker, "your breathing becomes fast and shallow. Your capillaries dilate further, flushing your skin, which simultaneously becomes damp with perspiration. You are now at the stage scientists call 'the plateau', in which you feel as if you are being swept along on a rushing current of sensations. Synapses start firing in the right-hand side of your brain, the creative side, creating a flickering storm of electrical activity. Your nipples swell like berries. *Here* a chemical called oxytocin gushes from your pituitary gland, inducing an overwhelming feeling of euphoria. You gasp, you bite your lover's neck, you shudder uncontrollably and your lips contort.

"Yet all this has just been the curtain raiser for the main event. *Here* your whole body stiffens. You have reached the point of no return, a feeling sometimes described as like being suspended at the top of a very high swing. You take a gulp of air and hold your breath, or grab your ankles and bellow. A pronounced frown – the so-called 'orgasm face' – is a testament to the myotonic tension now building in your muscles."

I glanced at Miss G's face. She was frowning with concentration as she tried to follow what I was saying, but I could see that she was more or less keeping up, so I continued. "At around this point, *here*, the long tissues of the arms and legs also contract in involuntary spasms. A shower of electrical signals twangs up and down the vagus nerve, like vibrations bouncing along a tightrope. A fiendishly intricate chain of biochemical reactions, only recently understood by science,[2] lights up your brain like a switchboard. The central nervous system goes into overload; patterns dance behind your eyes; you feel yourself propelled, judderingly, as if travelling fast over rough ground in a flimsy vehicle.

"But only now, *here*, do you finally abandon yourself to what is happening. A cascade of muscular contractions, each one exactly 0.8 seconds

[2] Fisher, S.J: Neurotransmitter cascades during climax of human females, *NuMed Chem III*, 2006.

long, pulses from your genitals, pushing outwards, until there is no part of you, from the centre of your hips to the tips of your fingers, that isn't dancing to the same primeval beat. And then at last, *here*, it finally lets you go, although you may find after-shocks occurring up to half an hour later. For around thirty seconds, Miss G – perhaps for as long as three whole minutes – you have been in the grip of a sensation more intense, more extraordinary, than any male has ever felt."[3]

There was a brief silence. It occurred to me that the use of the word "you" might not be strictly accurate in this instance, since Miss G would presumably not have been there in the first place unless she was having difficulty with some or all of this process.

"That is the how," I continued. "But the interesting question, the question which has perplexed scientists ever since we started looking at this area, is the one you asked just now."

"'Why?'"

"Exactly. *What is it all for?* The clitoris appears to be the only organ in the body which has no function other than pleasure; the female orgasm the only physiological mechanism for which we can find no evolutionary purpose. It isn't necessary for conception; it isn't needed for eating, or sleeping, or raising young; it confers no advantage that can be passed on to the next generation. According to all the principles of natural selection, it shouldn't exist. But it does. And – even more fascinatingly – it sometimes goes wrong, for reasons we still can't entirely fathom either.

"That is the great mystery – and the great prize. In an age when we know almost everything there is to know about almost everything, the

---

[3] I should probably clarify that I was referring here only to the male and female of our own species. Amongst other mammals, the picture is more complex. Coitus between mink lasts approximately eight hours, though it is unclear how much of that is taken up by orgasm, as mink are notoriously irritable when sexually aroused and prone to biting researchers. However, it is known that a pig's orgasm lasts around thirty minutes, while the orgasms of the female bonobo are so frequent, and of such duration, that two or more can sometimes overlap. Fisher, S.J: Multiple orgasm amongst the higher primates. *Journal of Endocrinology* 74 June 2002: 91-121.

female orgasm is one of the few remaining puzzles. Your genitalia, Miss G, are the final frontier of scientific knowledge, the last great unexplored territory. Indeed, I would go so far as to say that scientists know more about the woolly mammoth than we do about your climaxes – and the woolly mammoth is extinct! But that's changing now. Little by little, the bright light of research is illuminating the dark recesses of ignorance, and soon there will be no problem or glitch caused by Nature for which Science does not have an opposite and equal solution."

I stopped, aware that I had spoken at rather greater length, and possibly with rather more passion, than I had intended to.

"Goodness," Miss G said, and once again I had the feeling that she might be mocking me, just a little. "You make it sound so much fun, as well. So, when do I start?"

1.4

I explained, of course, what the actual tests would involve – that she would be connected to instruments measuring blood flow, muscular activity, pH and so on. In order that she would fully understand what I was talking about, I even took her to the testing room and showed her the couch, with its hygienic paper cover, its lines of tiny plastic crocodile clips and its electro-conductive pads. It is at this point that many potential volunteers back out. Miss G, however, took it all in her stride, asking several intelligent questions about the different pieces of equipment, such as the Schuster balloon and the Geer Gauge, and even – somewhat to my surprise – observing that the software which linked them was not Windows or Apple but Linux.[4]

"I'm a part-time programer for the Tennysonline project," she

---

[4] Miss G, quite unusually in my experience, even pronounced the name correctly, ie "Linnucks", not "Lie-nux". See www.paul.sladen.org/pronunciation/

explained. "The coding would be a nightmare if we didn't use open-source."

I noticed her looking rather anxiously, though, at the array of devices by means of which arousal is induced. These range from a small monitor on which we can play video clips, to various kinds of transcutaneous electromechanical apparatus. The latter are necessarily rather more industrial in appearance than their high street equivalents, something which our subjects can find rather daunting (*Figure 3*). I tried to reassure her by explaining that the difference was partly because we had to be able to vary the input from the control room next door.

"So you control what's happening to me? Just by pushing some buttons in there?"

"Indeed. That way we can standardise the experience, and determine whether the treatment is working."

"And how many times will I have to do all this? Before I'm cured, I mean?"

Figure 3: Some high street stimulators (top) and their laboratory equivalents (below).

"I don't think you quite understand," I said. "This is a research project, not a doctor's surgery. There are no guarantees of improvement."

"But you've seen some encouraging results? Or was that paper you published last year over-stating?"

"Ah." I had never before been confronted with a research subject who had actually read up on the research in question, and for a moment I was at a loss as to how to respond in order to avoid any possibility of a placebo effect. "The paper was sound. But the science is highly advanced. I very much doubt whether you understood it correctly."

This seemed to satisfy her – although she opened her mouth as if to comment further, she closed it again without speaking. I turned to indicate Dr Minstock, who was by now loitering ostentatiously. "Now, unless you have any more questions, I will leave you in Susan's capable hands. I should explain, by the way, that she is a sexologist, while I am a neurobiologist. But we get along perfectly well." That, of course, is a joke, though admittedly not one which many people outside the fields of sexology or neurobiology would appreciate. As they left the room Susan said something to Miss G, something too low for me to catch, followed by a barely-suppressed cackle of witchy laughter. Generally I am immune to my colleague's so-called "empathy-building" remarks at my expense, but on this occasion – I suppose because, somewhat unexpectedly, I had actually quite enjoyed my conversation with Miss G – it annoyed me. I went into the control room and poured myself a beaker of water until I had regained my composure.

1.5

When I told Miss G that Susan and I get along, that was true, generally speaking. When I was first given funding by Trock – really substantial funding; funding that transformed my little theory about primates into a full-scale human research project almost overnight – the pharmaceutical giant imposed only one condition: that I was to bring a female sexologist on board. It wasn't easy, at first, sharing my project. But eventually Susan and I got used to each other – one of our research assistants remarked that it was almost like a marriage, but with rather more sex – and in any case, excitement about what we were doing helped smooth any difficulties between us.

I need hardly tell this paper's audience that, in the great race to bring a successful treatment for female sexual dysfunction to market, a race currently taking place in clinics and laboratories all over the world, our little team is widely considered one of the frontrunners. Oh, others may have reached the clinical phase before us; some may even have filed patents. By comparison, our progress has been slow but steady. While our rivals rushed to publish wild conjecture masquerading as research, we preferred to test and refine: methodically exploring every avenue, no matter how unpromising; eliminating every false trail, no matter how seductive; checking and replicating every tiny success, in order that our method would eventually be seen to be as sound as our results. And now the prize was almost within our grasp. I don't mean money, of course, although for our backers that must surely follow. I mean *acclaim*: the chance to have our names spoken in the same breath as those of the great scientific pioneers, people such as Chadwick, Townes and Koch; even – I may dare to believe – James Watson and Francis Crick. Under that sort of pressure, a few small personality clashes are almost inevitable.

But there have also been occasions when I have become aware that Susan thinks I am – how can I put this? – somewhat *staid*. I suppose this shouldn't have come as a surprise: sexologists are by the nature of their profession a rather wilder bunch than us neurobiologists. There was one occasion in particular, at last year's Sexual Endocrinology conference, when I had to go to her hotel room to collect some papers I wanted to look at before the following morning's session. I had already got ready for bed, so rather than get dressed again I simply put a hotel towelling robe on, over my nightclothes. I thought as I knocked at her door I could hear voices, but if I assumed anything it was simply that she had

15

the TV on. Then the door was pulled open. Susan stood there, dressed in a loose towelling robe herself – but she, I couldn't help but notice, was not wearing nightclothes underneath. In one hand she held a tumbler of drink. From inside the room drifted a herby odour which I took to be marijuana. On the bed behind her I caught a sudden, shocking glimpse of writhing naked bodies, and I heard a woman's voice – I am fairly sure it was Heather Jackson, a particularly attractive research student who had recently started working for us – laugh throatily. A man's voice, somewhat muffled, growled something in response.

Susan quickly stepped forward, blocking my view. I explained what I wanted and she went to get me the papers, closing the door again until she had returned.

Then, as I started to walk away, she called after me, as if on an impulse. "Steve?"

I turned.

"You know," she said, somewhat slurrily, "you should lighten up a bit."

I didn't reply. I took the papers back to my room but for once my mind was incapable of processing the formulae on them. I found myself realising, almost for the first time, that what I was reading – the complex interplay of neurotransmitters and secretions, hormones and platelets, desire and arousal, my life's work – was all about *sex*: actual, flesh-and-blood bodies, writhing together like that knot of naked sexologists cavorting on Susan's bed. It may sound odd, but it wasn't something that had ever really occurred to me before – or at least, if I had acknowledged it, it had only been on an intellectual level. And I was disappointed, too, with Heather, whom I had believed to be a more serious academic than her behaviour that evening had revealed her to be. That night I did not sleep well, and my paper next day on the climax of the female pygmy chimpanzee was one of the worst-delivered I have ever given.[5] I kept hearing that throaty female laugh coming from the bed, and the muffled deeper voice answering it.

[5] A pity, as it remains one of the very few studies of its kind.

Nevertheless, it was sensible of Trock to insist on my partner being a woman. Susan takes care of the difficult part, the interaction with our volunteers; attaching all the plastic clips, explaining how to use the mechanical devices, carrying out psychological counselling and so on. Now that I think about it, it was perhaps a good thing that the volunteers themselves were unaware – presumably – of the omnivorous nature of her own tastes, as revealed by that glimpse into her hotel room. But whatever her other failings, I really cannot fault her manner with our test subjects, with whom she never seemed less than totally professional.

The testing room, as I have explained, is separated from the rest of the lab, to foster an impression of privacy. In the control booth, I opened the microphone channels and heard my colleague's voice say, "So that one just eases in there – whoops – a little closer to the couch, if you could, the lead won't reach that far. That one's a snapper. Great."

I brought up Startle on my laptop. This showed a view of Miss G's left eye, magnified a hundred times. I adjusted the focus, and on my screen the giant disembodied iris also adjusted itself, the pupil opening and closing as Miss G settled (*Figure 4*). She had unusually-coloured eyes for a brunette – the bluey-grey-brown double-recessive must have been present in both her parents.

"So what happens now?" her voice said, breaking into my reverie.

I activated my own microphone. "We wait. KXC79 – the pill Susan

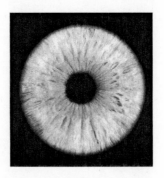

Figure 4: Miss G's left iris.

gave you – takes around fifteen minutes to pass into your bloodstream."[1]

There was a short silence, during which Susan joined me in the control room and we began going through the pre-test checks. Visitors have occasionally likened our little booth to the cockpit of a 747 before take off – crammed into the tiny space are over thirty different monitoring devices, all of which need to be primed and readied before the tests begin.

Out of the corner of my eye I saw my colleague looking puzzled. "This is odd," she whispered, pulling off her headset. "The vibration meter is showing quite intense activity, but my inputs are set almost at zero."

I looked at the readouts. Sure enough, they appeared to show that Miss G was oscillating at a steady 14hz. It was most perplexing.

"Whatever it is, it's not responding to any of my controls," Susan said, twisting a knob at random. "Could she have brought her own stimulator? I didn't think to ask –"

Then I realised what was causing the instruments to read as they were. For all her apparent self-assurance, the woman on the testing couch was trembling; trembling like a leaf. This, of course, was something of a problem – the data would be worthless if we were unable to distinguish between the different stimuli that had generated it. "Perhaps some music will help," I said, turning to the CD player.

Swooping, melodic sine waves and polytones began colliding in our headsets, re-emerging as something completely different and utterly beautiful – an extraordinary mixture of music and mathematics. "What's *this*?" Susan said, frowning.

[1] We have been criticised, I believe, for providing KXC79 in pill form, rather than as a faster-acting nasal spray. Our reasons for this were largely to do with patient acceptability – we believed that nasal sprays are inherently anerotic. Others disagree. According to one newspaper report, "Palatin, an American drug company, is in clinical trials of a melatonin-based drug that can be taken as a nasal spray before sex." Melatonin is the chemical responsible for changes in skin pigmentation during exposure to sunlight: its effect on libido is more controversial. "Researchers think it unlikely that such sprays would lead to people becoming tanned as they would not be used every day. However, those using the implants to get a tan could experience frequent sexual arousal." *Sunday Times*, 11/4/04.

"Tomita. *Pictures at an Exhibition*. I must have left it in the machine – I was listening to it earlier. Did you want the Barry White?"

"Well, this is hardly going to put her in the mood, is it?"

On the contrary," I said, indicating the instruments, where the trembling was already subsiding. "It seems to be having exactly the desired effect."

Susan shrugged and turned back to the controls. "Let's get on with it, then, shall we?" She reactivated her headset microphone. "Annie, I'm going to start a very gentle stimulation device. At this stage we're not looking to do any more than relax you. Later on you'll notice it getting rather more intense." By her elbow an oscillograph came to life, its flower-like pattern opening and closing in time to the neurostimulator's output.

There was a silence which lasted for almost the entire first movement of *Pictures at an Exhibition*.

"Dr Fisher?" Miss G's voice said.

"Yes?"

"Could you tell me a bit more about that pill? How it's going to affect me, I mean?"

"Don't you worry about that, Annie," Susan cut in. "You just lie back and enjoy the ride."

"It's a neurotransmitter," I said without thinking.

After a moment I heard Miss G's voice again. "Sorry, Dr Fisher. You're going to have to explain what that is."

On my left, Susan pointed urgently at the clock and shook her head, mouthing a silent "No" in my direction. Presumably she was fretting about losing KXC79's window of optimum effectiveness. But her anxiety, I noted, was misplaced: there was still at least another minute to go.

"Well, different parts of the body communicate with each other by sending messages through the cells," I said. "It's a bit like a computer network – each cell has a little wifi station, known as the presynaptic nerve terminal –"

Susan was by now waving one painted fingernail vigorously back and forth across her throat.

"So once a receptor site has been activated, you either get a depolarisation, which means it has what we call an excitatory postsynaptic potential –"

Susan threw up her hands, rolling her eyes at me in a soundless parody of bewilderment.

"– or hyperpolarisation, which means it has an inhibitory postsynaptic potential," I concluded (*Figure 5*). "And that's it, really."

"Finally!" Susan muttered, reaching for the controls.

"To put that in layman's terms…"

"Dear God!"

"…a depolarisation makes it more likely that an action potential will fire, while a hyperpolarisation has the opposite effect. KXC79 is just amplifying that natural process."

"And that's the end of the science bit," Susan said quickly. "Annie, we're going to move this up a notch. Try to think some nice erotic thoughts. If you can." She gave me a poisonous look, pushed some buttons, and the familiar background hum of electromechanical devices whirring into life began to crackle on the headsets.

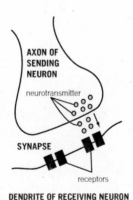

Figure 5: How a neurotransmitter works.

We sat in silence for a while, watching the readouts.

"This is looking surprisingly positive," Susan murmured. "I'm going to go to four."

The hum intensified.

"The KXC79 should just about be peaking," she added. "I'll see if we can't –" She pushed some more buttons. "And a bit more of *this*." She twisted a knob. "OK. Let's see what's cooking."

I switched to the heat-sensitive thermograph, looking for the tell-tale pattern spreading across Miss G's chest and neck that would indicate an arousal flush. So far, nothing. There was little I could usefully do to help now, so I got on with plotting the data from previous test subjects on a spreadsheet according to their ethnicity.

After another four minutes Susan pushed another switch. "We seem to be losing the… But perhaps…" She twisted a dial towards the maximum.

I glanced at Startle. The screen was completely blank. Then I saw that this was because Miss G's eye was in fact now closed. According to the respirometer, she was breathing deeply and regularly – almost, in fact, as if she were fast asleep.

A delicate snore began to make itself heard on our headsets.

"Is she *asleep*?" Susan said incredulously.

"It appears so."

"How extraordinary. Well, there's not much point in continuing with this." My colleague began briskly flicking switches to their off positions. "Annie? Annie, wake up."

"Wha? Soz. Was that OK?" Miss G's voice asked, a little groggily.

"It was fine. I'm just sorry it wasn't a bit more…*eventful* for you."

"Oh, it was nice," Miss G said. "Nicer than usual, anyway."

"Perhaps Dr Fisher made it all just a bit *too* relaxing. Or perhaps it's some little problem we haven't spotted with the treatment."

"I'm sorry if that wasn't much use, Dr Fisher," Miss G called.

I hastened to reassure her. "Oh no, that isn't the case at all. It isn't an experiment if you know the result in advance – that's the whole basis of scientific investigation. And anyway, that was only a very mild dose. I'm going to give you a skin patch to wear for a week or so. It's just like a nicotine patch, really, except that it'll be raising your background levels of KXC79. Hopefully when you come back we'll see a very marked difference in your responses."

2.3

Sometimes our subjects like to chat after a session, so Susan has evolved a debriefing procedure that gathers more feedback in the post-test period. In Miss G's case, however, there had been so little reaction it was barely necessary, and it was only a few minutes before my colleague rejoined me in the control room.

She picked up a readout from the EMG and began to cross-check the results. "Interesting girl."

"Yes."

"I wonder why she didn't –"

Suddenly we were both talking over each other. "You must have misjudged –"

"If you had prepared her properly –"

"You actually bored her to sleep. To sleep! I mean, that has to be a first. Even for you."

We worked for a while in a furious silence.

"That's odd." Susan was studying the printout.

"What is?"

"There's a small escalation about seven minutes in."

"What happened at seven minutes? Is that when we increased the stimulation?"

"That's what I'm checking." Susan was running her finger down the list of Stimulation Events. "No. According to this, seven minutes was before the actual tests had started."

"Play the tapes," I said. But Susan, ahead of me, was already winding the audio tapes back to the right place.

"Here we are. Six minutes fifty," she said, pressing Play. I heard my own voice saying: "*So once a receptor site has been activated, you either get a depolarisation, which means it has what we call an excitatory post-synaptic potential, or hyperpolarisation, which means it has an inhibitory postsynaptic potential…*"

Susan pressed Stop. "Must be an RAE."

RAEs – Random Arousal Events – are a recurrent difficulty in our line of work (*Figure 6*). Put simply, people sometimes react in odd ways, and at odd moments, for reasons neither they nor we can fully explain. We tend to exclude RAEs from our data, because if we didn't, nothing would ever make any sense.

"Another one?" I said. "That's the third this month." And we carried on packing up the equipment.

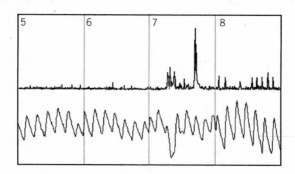

Figure 6: EMG showing Miss G's Random Arousal Event at 06.50 (top). The lower line is just me talking.

24

Time is an interesting phenomenon, isn't it? Normally, it flows from A to B, and thus to C and so on, in a pretty straight line.[1] And this, frankly, is the way we scientists like it. For all our talk of wormholes and relativity and the space-time continuum, we actually prefer our time quite classical. When we describe a discovery, especially, we tend to relate the events and experiments which led up to it in the order in which they happened, rather than in the order in which we became aware of them. Thus do we give the impression of a planned, methodical progression towards an inevitable truth, rather than the chaos of half-glimpsed solutions, blind alleys, false dawns and wild guesses that – if we are honest – actually occurred.

All of which is a roundabout way of saying that the document I am about to quote from is one with which I only became familiar much later. Needless to say, events might have proceeded very differently had I been made aware of its contents at the time.

Ladies and gentlemen, may I draw your attention to Appendix A: Miss G's private diary.

---

[1] I mean C as in the third letter of the alphabet here, of course, and not C as in the letter Einstein used to denote the speed of light (299, 792, 458 metres a second) in the equation $E=MC^2$, since that does all sorts of strange things to time. In fact, it would be completely untrue to say of Einstein's C that time goes from A to B to C and so on – one would have to say that time goes from A to B, approaches C, and then gets stuck.

Ugh! I still can't believe that I'm going to write a blog – sorry, *diary* – about my sex life. Or lack of it.

But apparently it's a necessary part of the study that I keep a record of how sexy I feel. Dr Minstock – Susan – says it's all part of learning to be intimate with myself and that it'll liberate my inner feminine or something. (Random question: why does "intimate" mean sexual? When "intimation" means a thought or idea? Must look that up later.) Susan, I suspect, would prefer me to pen this by candlelight in some scented leatherbound notebook scattered with rose petals. I told her no way am I putting anything on paper. Quite apart from the environmental cost, what if someone finds it? At least this computer is password protected. No one will ever read these words except me.

Another weird thought.

So here goes.

This whole thing started when Simon decided I had a problem. It seems my lack of enthusiasm in bed was making him unhappy.

"So do you want to stop having sex with me?" I asked.

"Of course not," he said, a little tetchily. "Making love to you is utterly sublime, my darling. I'm just wondering what we can do to make it even better."

"I wouldn't mind stopping," I said. "In fact, that probably *would* make it better, for me. Plenty of people are having celibate relationships now, you know. I read an article."

Wrong answer. Recriminations, shouting, followed by the mother (father?) of all sulks. Believe me, no one knows how to sulk like a male academic with a bruised ego. By the end of it I've a) had sex with him (again! That's the second time this month) and b) promised to go to the doctor to see if there's anything that can be done.

Basically, it's not enough that I do it occasionally. I have to enjoy it too.

26

The disloyal thought occurs to me that Simon would be perfectly happy with someone who faked it, so long as she faked it convincingly enough. Like that girl we used to call the Shrieker, who had the ground floor room at Bristol. After a year of keeping us awake with her screams of pleasure, she and her boyfriend split up. She confessed it had been a kind of method acting all along – if she gave a good enough performance, she was able to persuade herself she was getting something out of it.

Not that Simon would like me to shriek. That would be Distasteful. And Simon has very good taste. This is evidenced by the beautiful art on his walls, the beautiful clothes on his body, and the beautiful thoughts about the Nature of the Romantic Sublime in his head. (So heaven knows what he's doing with me, since I'm clearly not in his league beauty-wise. Perhaps it's just the forbidden thrill of seducing one of his students.)

Goodness, what a lot of disloyal thoughts seem to be spilling out. Maybe Susan's right after all – this is actually quite therapeutic.

More later, then.

UrlGirl67 ☺
"When the only tool you have is a hammer,
you tend to treat every problem as if it's a nail"

Anyway – to continue with the backstory – after we had the row I did what I usually do when confronted by a problem: I went on the internet. And, feeling faintly silly, typed in "female + can't have orgasms + can't seem to get excited about boyfriend + not sure if really fancy him".

No exact matches, but removing the quotes and some extraneous words brought up 200,964,237 results. Mostly stuff that I *don't* want to look at, thanks very much. So I added the magic words "peer-reviewed".

And this strange little paper appeared. Or rather, three papers appeared, but two were about monkeys. The one that wasn't was titled:

KXC79 and female sexual dysfunction: some encouraging early results.

Fisher, S.J and Minstock, S, 2007, Department of Molecular Biology, Oxford University.

In other words, just up the road. I'd never heard of an academic called Fisher, or one called Minstock, but arts and sciences tend not to mix much here, so that was hardly surprising.

There was a lot of science stuff I didn't fully understand, even with the aid of a dictionary, but the gist of it seemed to be that they were working on a treatment for female sexual dysfunction that was going to be as straightforward as popping a pill. It wouldn't be available on the open market for a while, because of the time it takes to get government approval, but reading between the lines they were pretty confident they'd cracked it.

Which started me thinking.

If I could solve all these problems with Simon, a little voice inside me was saying – if I could just take a pill and turn into the happy, orgasmic, randy little unit he so desperately wants me to be – wouldn't that be nice?

Well, no, actually, another little voice was saying. Who wants to be Simon's drugged-up sex puppet?

Ah, but that's the Female Sexual Dysfunction talking, another voice pointed out. (And it was pretty impressive, incidentally, to suddenly have a proper medical label for what I thought was just a low sex drive. Not to mention a whole chorus of voices popping up in my head to talk about it.) It's only because you have this problem in the first place that you aren't keen on the drugged-up sex, the voice said (that's the third voice, of course, not the second – try to keep up). Look at everyone else, at it like rabbits. That's what's normal.

In fact, the more me and my voices discussed it, the more we decided it was a pity I couldn't give something like KXC79 a go.

I mentioned the article to Simon. I hadn't meant to, actually, but he was getting grumpy again and I thought it might help if he knew that I had at least done a bit of research.

"Fisher," he said thoughtfully. "Fisher... I do seem to remember some ghastly pointy-head of that name skulking round the place. Not the most likely person to have solved your little problem."

(That is so typical of Simon, by the way – whilst he will happily tell you that he has an IQ of a hundred and fifty-eight and is therefore a near-genius, anyone who works in a different discipline is just a pointy-head.)

(And another thing I've noticed – he always talks about the discrepancy in our sex drives as being '"my" problem, not his. Of course, according to all the magazines, TV programmes, books and so on he's right, so I suppose it must be me. It's just that no one has ever really convinced me that sex isn't, well, a waste of good reading time.)

(Since I seem to be complaining about Simon rather more than I meant to, let me just say for the record that of course I do love him. Not in the he-makes-my-heart-beat-faster-every-time-I-see-him sort of way – because, let's face it, that doesn't really happen, or at least not to me – but I know I'm so lucky to have him. He's one of the cleverest, most amazing people I've ever met. And he's going to be a professor soon. And –

And he's my supervisor.

Which makes it rather hard for us to break up, actually, without causing a whole load of problems I'd rather do without. The Role Of The Mythical Feminine In *The Idylls Of The King* And Certain Other Poems By Tennyson is tedious enough already without having to explain it to a new supervisor who'd probably tell me to start again from scratch.

And after all, who wants to be single?

So basically, although I'm unlikely to end up as the next Mrs Frampton, this is fine.

For now.)

UrlGirl67 ☺

"When the only tool you have is a hammer,
you tend to treat every problem as if it's a nail"

The funny thing was that although Simon had initially been sniffy about Dr Fisher and his "dodgy little pills", as he called them, after he'd spoken to a couple of people in the Senior Common Room he came back quite excited. "Apparently the man's on to something. He's got backing from one of the big pharma companies – there's a whole laboratory up on South Parks Road stuffed full of strange buzzing little machines. Porn, too. They have a special dispensation from the university to store some of the most filthy film clips ever made." He paused significantly. "You never know, you might enjoy it."

"Enjoy what?"

"Being part of his study."

I stared at him. "What do you mean?"

"It's obvious, isn't it? You can't get these pills on the open market yet, but if you become one of his test subjects you'll get them straight away."

"What makes you think he's recruiting test subjects?"

"Oh, it's well known," he said evasively. "Actually, I think I might have spotted an ad. Where was it? Ah yes." And he handed me a copy of the *Oxford Mail* with a small ad circled in red pen.

"*Are you sexually dysfunctional?*" it said. "*Female? Would you like to earn extra cash by helping out with medical research?*" There was a phone number, and then, in smaller print, it said "*Oxford University is an Equal Opportunities Employer*".

"Come on," he said persuasively. "It might be fun."

I shuddered. "Fun? Fun? Normal sex is depressing enough. Why on earth would I want to go and have my bits poked about with by some weirdo scientist?"

Another tactical error.

"Because you love me, of course," he said stiffly.

And that was the beginning of Simon's campaign to get me to ring the number on the ad. Although he was pretending to be matter-of-fact about it, the idea of me being wired up to all the machines he'd heard about and made to watch dirty movies was clearly exciting to him – almost as if he thought it would somehow jumpstart me into becoming more enthusiastic in bed.

So what with his nagging on the one hand, and a nagging feeling that I really ought to do something about this missing piece I seem to have on the other, I thought I should probably give it a go. But I still wouldn't have done anything if I hadn't met this girl at a party. She was telling me about her supervisor, who she described as "a total goof" – but she said it with a fond smile on her face, and I could tell she actually liked her goof quite a lot. Then she said his name.

"You work for Steven Fisher?" I said. "The sexual dysfunction man?"

"That's right. He's a bit of a genius, actually. You know he was the youngest scientist ever to win the Nicholas Kurti Award?"

I didn't. Nor did I have the faintest idea what the Nicholas Kurti Award was, but I could tell it was something I should have been impressed by. The next day I phoned the number on the ad.

There was an initial interview with Susan, which I evidently passed, and then I had to come in for the first session. By this time it was seeming oddly normal to be discussing my orgasms, or rather the lack of them, with complete strangers, and I actually found myself becoming quite interested in what these people did. I mean, it's all very well to find traces of vegetation myth in the poems of Tennyson, but this lot were actually *discovering* stuff. Stuff that might change people's lives.

And then I met Dr Fisher.

Let me just say that I loathed him the moment I set eyes on him. I'd been expecting – oh, I don't know: some spotty, dandruff-ridden, odiferous technician. Like the person who comes to mend the photocopier, only smarter. But the person who I met in the lab was much, much worse than that. Because he was shy and good-looking and clever and just unbelievably, fantastically, condescending.

"What's vasodilation?" I say, just to make conversation – well, just to remind him that I'm there at all, actually: he was having some tetchy argument with Susan about whether they really needed any more data.

I mean, hello? The data is standing right here, and she has a name.

And he smirked – he actually smiled at the question! As if I were some dumb blonde asking what the carburettor did!

All right, smartarse, I thought, I'll show you. So I rather pointedly asked some intelligent graduate-student-type questions. You don't get to do a DPhil without learning how to deal with male academics and their overdeveloped egos. Tell me about your specialist subject, ooh please why don't you, while I open my eyes very wide and look impressed.

Unfortunately, he smirked even harder, and told me in so many words that there wasn't much point, as I couldn't possibly understand.

Try me, says I, through gritted incisors.

But the bastard was right. I realised too late I had simply demonstrated the appalling depths of my ignorance.

And then – a funny thing – instead of just giving up, I actually started to try to puzzle out what he was on about. He was talking about orgasms by now – why they're such a mystery, and how by studying them he hopes to find out more about other species or something – I couldn't follow it all. But I realised that for these people it isn't just about who's got more publications to their name, or being able to boast about your TV appearances like Simon does. These people are *driven*. They want to solve the big mysteries. And suddenly I wanted to be part of it. To be in the clever club, like them.

I even dropped into the conversation that I run Linux on my laptop. Talk about showing off! But I think Dr Fisher was impressed, just a little.

And then, once the tests had begun, the oddest thing happened. I found myself getting – no, I can't write this down. Oh, all right then, I'll try. (As it says on the login page: AUTHORISED USERS ONLY. If you do not have permission to access this information, please exit now…) To try to take my mind off what they were about to do to me, I started talking to Dr Fisher. And, suddenly, I felt myself reacting to the sound of his voice through the headphones. I mean *physically*. It was so ridiculous it was almost funny. There I was, trying to have a serious conversation (and trying to prove to Dr Fisher that I'm not just some ditzy Eng Lit airhead)

32

when – whoosh – my body starts behaving as if I'm some lovestruck teen-ager in the presence of a rock god.

Of course, I realise straight away that it must be the KXC79. But that doesn't make it any less embarrassing. I mean, Dr Fisher's hardly going to have any respect for me if I start gasping and moaning before the tests have even started.

Something else I start to think about: how come Simon has never made me feel like this?

Bugger.

Because the time to consider questions like these is probably not when you're hooked up to at least a dozen different measuring devices, including something called a napkin-ring myosograph which is positioned several inches beyond where the sun usually shines, and two pointy-heads are monitoring every aspect of your sexual responses.

I assume it's just some sort of reflex reaction – Dr Fisher being a man, and the KXC79 making me extra-responsive. But I don't really want to ask him if that's the case, because I know he'll just say I'm too dumb to understand.

All in all, it's easier just to do what I usually do when Simon gets amo-rous – ie pretend to be asleep. I seem to get away with it, too, so perhaps those machines aren't as sensitive as they make out.

UrlGirl67 ☺

"When the only tool you have is a hammer,
you tend to treat every problem as if it's a nail"

Simon, of course, wants details. He seems obscurely disappointed that I haven't been participating in some wild orgy.

"Look," I explain patiently, "it's the least erotic experience you can imagine. You're wired up, there are people scrutinising every sound, every movement you make – would you be able to perform under those conditions?"

He frowns. "Mmm. I see your point." Then he brightens up. "But they play porn clips?"

"Actually," I tell him, "they played music. To relax me." I've been humming Tomita's *Pictures* ever since, in fact, but I don't tell him that. Then something makes me add, "It's very hard work. I certainly won't be up to having sex normally until the study is over."

For a moment he looks furious. Then: "Well, I suppose if it eventually solves your little problem it'll be worth it," he says grumpily. "Perhaps you could remember to ask them about those film clips, though."

UrlGirl67 ☺
"When the only tool you have is a hammer,
you tend to treat every problem as if it's a nail"

The hands-on work with test subjects, although exacting, is only the tip of the research iceberg on a project such as ours. To help with the number crunching we employ assistants, usually postgraduate students who work in exchange for supervision on their theses. At the time of Miss G's inclusion in the programme there were just three of these: Heather Jackson, keeping a low profile after her uncharacteristic lapse at Sexual Endocrinology; Rhona Evans, a Welsh girl whose real passion lay in the genetic mutation of fruit flies; and Wulf Sederholm, a brilliant young theoretician whose work on sexual chaos theory was so esoteric and possibly so groundbreaking that I doubt whether there were more than three or four people in the world who were capable of understanding it.[1]

The week following Miss G's visit was an especially exciting one for our little team. After many delays my application for more equipment had been approved, and we took delivery of several new instruments, including a state-of-the-art Medoc genito-sensory analyser (*Figure 7*). As I

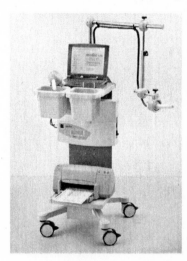

Figure 7: The Medoc GSA, a state-of-the-art genitosensory analyser.

---

[1] Unfortunately, neither Wulf nor I were among them.

had pointed out to the funding board, getting one of these was a clear sign that we were at last competing with the big boys.

Susan had also taken delivery of a new piece of apparatus: something called the Sybian, which she described as "the last word in stimulators". It was a fearsome-looking device, not unlike one of those bucking bronco machines that people try to ride at fairgrounds before the operator turns up the speed so much they get thrown off. I mentioned this to my colleague, who laughed and said "That's bucking with an F, Steve. And believe me, once you're pinned in place by the attachments on this baby, there's no way you're being thrown anywhere." She has a coarseness of expression, sometimes, that I find quite distasteful. And I particularly loathe it when she calls me Steve. However, I could see by the gleam in her eye that she too was excited about her new acquisition, so I left her to it and got on with installing the software for the GSA.

I was not so busy, though, that I didn't have time to think about Miss G. In fact, I found myself thinking about her quite a lot. KXC79 had never caused drowsiness in our test subjects before – rather the reverse. Although this was potentially a worrying development, I hypothesised that the problem was in all likelihood a simple anomaly, caused by a combination of Miss G's unfamiliarity with the process and a lack of engagement with Susan's stimulation programme.

At our weekly team get-together, where we talk over any issues that have cropped up, I raised this possibility and invited my colleagues' contributions.

"What about the stimulus materials?" Heather suggested.

"What about them?"

"Well…" she said hesitantly. "It's just that I was in the testing room recently, and I noticed that most of the videos seem to be girl-on-girl. What if she's not into that kind of thing? After all, a lot of women aren't." And it seemed to me that she glanced at Susan, a little defiantly, as she said this.

"It's a good point," I conceded. "It occurs to me in any case that as a literature student Miss G might prefer her stimulus in the written form.

I'll put some erotica on our account at Blackwell's. And I'll make sure it isn't girl-on-girl. Any more suggestions?"

There were none. So, finding myself outside the university bookshop later that day, I went in, with the intention of finding some appropriate – or should that be inappropriate? – material.

4.2

I was distracted from this mission, however, by the discovery that at long last my pre-ordered copy of Richard Collins' new book *Enzymes and Influences: How Biochemistry Built Our Brains* (Palaton Press, 2008) had arrived. Those of you who work in the fields of neurobiology and endocrinology will, of course, already be aware of Professor Collins' work, and indeed of my high regard for it. It is true that he is still a somewhat controversial figure. But to those who call him a "populariser", or sniff disdainfully at "media science", I say this: if a man can make evolutionary biochemistry so simple, so accessible, that almost anyone with a PhD or even a good degree in engineering can understand it, then where's the harm in that? I myself had the great good fortune to have Richard as my postgraduate supervisor, and to say that he inspired me is an understatement. I still remember that momentous day when I went to him with my thoughts on oxytocin and primate populations. His words of encouragement stay with me still, and whenever I read his books some of that idealistic excitement comes back to me: the heady sense that, by understanding science, we are understanding and changing our world. Sadly, he and I are in touch less than we once were – as well as his media appearances, there are his extensive teaching duties at the universities of Toronto, Adelaide and Harvard, not to mention his demanding schedule as the Trock Ambassador for the Physical Sciences. Some years, we only seem to bump into each other at the big international conferences. But I have his most famous saying – "For every human action there is a chemical reaction" – pinned up in my bathroom above the mirror, where it is the first thing I see each morning as I shave: it seems to me not only a witty aphorism about enzymes, but also a valid principle by which to live one's life.

It was with some reluctance, therefore, that I finally tore myself away from the pages of *Enzymes and Influences*, my head buzzing with excitement at the ideas and insights I had already discerned within its pages, and went in search of erotic literature. I had assumed that works in this category might prove hard to track down, but fortunately the shop had decided that sex warranted a bookcase to itself. (What determines these things, I found myself wondering – clearly there were no consistent principles at work here, such as the Linnean system, or there would also have to be separate bookcases for fiction about fruit, fiction about birds, and so on.) Erotica, for reasons which were not entirely clear to me, was positioned between Humour and Occult, and contained a substantial number of titles. But which to choose? The titles, in fact, were not much use. Was a book called *Dirty Laundry* (Birch, P, 2002) likely to be more or less erotic than one entitled *Punished in Pink* (Celbridge, Y, 2005)? It occurred to me that Miss G might prefer a book written by a woman. But that didn't make things any easier: almost every volume seemed to be the work of a female author. In the end I chose half a dozen at random, and was making my way back to the till when I saw her – that is, Miss G.

The university bookshop is one of those places which likes to pretend it isn't really a shop at all, but a cross between a library and a vast café, with armchairs scattered around the stacks and various drinks and snacks available. This hospitality is enthusiastically abused by the students, who go there to write their essays, consulting the books on the shelves without paying for them. (I say "abused", but I was recently informed by Wulf that a bookshop actually makes more profit from selling a cup of coffee than it does from selling a book, so perhaps it is simply a sound business strategy.) Miss G was sprawled sideways across an armchair, her legs over one of the arms and a pile of texts precariously balanced on her lap. In her right hand was a pen, around which she was idly curling a tendril of stray hair. She looked, if anything, even more striking than on the last occasion we had met. Unfortunately, as I looked at her another customer bumped into me, sending my own purchases crashing to the floor. Miss G glanced up.

"Oh, it's, um, Dr Fisher, isn't it?" She retrieved the copy of *Dirty Laundry* that had skidded under her chair and handed it to me. "How nice to see you."

"Hello," I replied. Unexpectedly, I found that I was blushing.

4.3

Blushing – or subcutaneous peripheral vasodilation, to give it its proper name – is actually a rather intriguing phenomenon. The physical mechanism is relatively well understood: the facial vein that supplies the small blood vessels in the face is responsive to beta-adrenergic stimulation, a property unusual in venous tissue. But the reason why some people blush and others don't is more obscure. Researchers in my own field have tried to link it to the vasodilation that occurs during sexual arousal, leading to the oft-repeated observation "After the blush, the orgasm". Personally, I think this a red herring – an early batch of KXC79, for example, which caused our subjects to blush furiously, had little effect on their sexual responses.

My own susceptibility to this functionless physiological quirk is, as you can imagine, a considerable inconvenience, given the nature of my current research. Over the past few years I have managed to train myself not to go red in the face whilst discussing female sexual responses in the laboratory – so much so that I had imagined myself to be completely cured. Yet it seems that if you put me in a bookshop with an attractive girl and a dropped pile of erotica, this is not the case.

Another curious thing about blushes: sometimes they can be contagious, just like yawns, sneezes, and, in certain circumstances, orgasms.[2] Certainly, this is what happened that day – no sooner had I greeted Miss G than it seemed to me that she too turned slightly pink.

"What are you up to?" I managed to ask. It was not the most imaginative question, given that there are only so many things one can be up to in a bookshop, but it got the conversation going.

"Oh, just reading some idiot who thinks romantic literature is inherently disposed to the semicolon. How about you?"

"I'm picking up some books," I said, demonstrating the literal truth of this as I plucked *Deviant Desires* (Anonymous, 2008) from the floor.

Miss G peered at the volumes scattered around her, and I felt myself going an even deeper shade of red. She ignored the erotica, though: it was the Collins she picked up, with an exclamation of "*This* looks interesting. What's it about?"

And then, somehow, without my even being aware of quite how it happened, we were sitting in the café with two cartons of steaming Fairtrade coffee in front of us, and I was telling her about Professor Richard Collins and his visionary insights into the biochemical basis of human society, the words tumbling out of my mouth as I struggled to explain as much as possible before she got bored – as surely she must – and left.

But she didn't leave. She sat there, her greeny-blue-brown eyes fixed on mine with an expression of furrowed concentration, interjecting occasional comments and questions as I described for her that mysterious, post-Darwinian bioverse where the enzyme, not the atom, is king, and where love quite literally makes the world go round.[3] Eventually I paused, and she looked at me with such fascination that I flushed again, this time with pleasure.

[2] This, of course, is a joke, though it occurs to me that my work would be very much easier if it were not.

[3] I was grossly simplifying Professor Collins' theories, of course, and refer the interested reader to the great man's own publications, where he or she will find them explained much better than I ever could. Also, I am aware that the world does not literally go "round", being an oblate spheroid.

"'Beauty is truth, truth beauty,'" she murmured. I must have looked perplexed, because she added, "Keats, John, 1795–1821. A poet."

"Oh," I said, considering. "Well, it's not an equation that's readily verifiable, is it? But it's a very compelling hypothesis."

There was a moment's silence.

"So what your professor – Richard Collins – what he's saying, basically, is that chemistry is inescapable," she said.

"Not just inescapable. Chemistry is *everything* – the whole world we live in. Take that coffee of yours." I indicated the carton in front of her. "Have you ever wondered why it doesn't stay hot?"

She glanced down. "Because they put more in the cup than any human being could feasibly drink in a week?"

"It's because the universe is dying."

Her eyes widened as she took in this statement.

"Entropy," I explained. "The second law of thermodynamics. Everything that exists – every person, every galaxy, every cup of liquid – is in a gradual transition from hot to cold, from unstable to stable, from disorder to order. In this brief interval of disequilibrium we have human life – and hot coffee."

She nodded thoughtfully.

"Or take this spoon." I picked up a plastic teaspoon from the table. "Just by rubbing it on my sleeve – like *this* – I can fill it with the building blocks of matter."

I held out the spoon and she peered inside. "But there's nothing there!"

"Isn't there?" I raised the spoon towards her hair, and one of the glossy chestnut tresses reached up to meet it. I moved the spoon, and the hair moved too, following my gesture. Like a snake charmer I made it dance – up, down, from side to side, adding more, giving her a fuzzy halo, then a wimple of stretching filaments…

"Oh!" she said, and there was a note in her voice that hadn't been there before.

"Negatively charged particles," I said. "The building blocks of matter."

Taking her hand, I placed it just above the table, where a few grains of sugar lay scattered around an open paper sachet. They jumped, attaching themselves to her skin like burrs on a glove. "You see? The attraction passes from me to you."

As she licked sugar thoughtfully from her fingers, I continued, "Chemistry can show you how to blow up the world, or it can tell you the best way to dunk a biscuit in your coffee. It can cure incurable diseases, or feed the hungry millions. Even the mysteries of sexual desire are now shown to be nothing more than the result of an endless series of evolutionary experiments. Friendship and love, our family life, the way we organise our society, our hopes and dreams – they are all the consequences of a billion irreversible reactions, and we, their by-products, are merely organic suspensions of salts and minerals in a temporary state of agitation."

"What an amazing thought," she said. A single rhomboid crystal, remaining on her upper lip, trembled as she spoke. The end of her tongue came out and licked it away.

"Yes." I tapped the volume on the table. "The words are Richard's, actually, from his book *God is a Biochemist*. But the sentiment is one with which I am in complete agreement."

4.4

And now I must come to the part of this encounter which, for a number of reasons, I find the most difficult to describe.

We were by now discussing the issue of evolutionary imperatives, as described by Professor Collins in his revolutionary first book, *The Genius of the Gene*. "But if that's the case – if reproduction is simply a delivery mechanism for the evolutionary advantage," Miss G was saying, "how do you explain sexual behaviours that *don't* give us any advantage?"

"Such as?"

"Well… Kissing, for example."

"Kissing?"

"Yes. I was just wondering," she said, fixing her eyes on mine, "why we sometimes get an urge to kiss someone. Even someone completely *random*. Where's the evolutionary imperative in *that*?"

"It's a good question," I conceded. "And one to which we don't yet have the full answer. After all, not all species kiss – there are even some human societies where it's unknown, suggesting it may not be an instinctive behaviour at all."

"Then it must be something we learn?"

I held up a finger to forestall her. "As it happens, there is a third possibility – the so-called histocompatibility theory. It hypothesises that kissing could be a way of exchanging invisible chemical messengers, in order to test the suitability of a potential mate. But many scientists think that's a somewhat sentimental proposition."

"Well, quite," she said.

There was a brief silence. For my part, it was because I found myself wondering what it would be like to kiss Miss G.

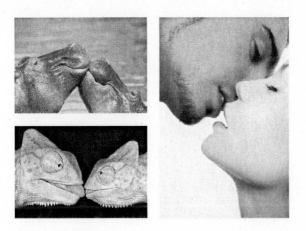

Figure 8: Three species which kiss. L-r: African Hippopotamus, *Chamaeleo jacksonii*, *Homo sapiens*.

While we had been talking, our natural wish to avoid disturbing those on neighbouring tables had caused us to lean our heads increasingly close together. Now, in this slight pause in the conversation, I happened to glance down from her eyes – her clear, intelligent eyes, each bluey-brown-green iris like a galaxy of gas and stars suspended in space – to her lips. She was, as I have already said, physically not unattractive, and her lips were no exception: rose-pink, plump, and slightly parted. I felt a sudden, extraordinary urge to press my own mouth against them. The feeling – the *compulsion* – was so powerful it was almost hypersensory: I could actually imagine the scent of her breath, the soft feel of her skin, and the taste of the sweet sugary residue still remaining on her upper lip.

And then something even odder happened. As – purely in my imagination – our lips touched, I had a sensation of vertigo, as if I were looking over the side of a cliff. The next moment, I was falling – falling through time. A series of unconnected images crashed into my brain. Two hominids, both covered in sleek brown hair, catching sight of each other across a grassy savannah. Two monkeys in a tree, tenderly grooming each other for mites. Two warthog-like creatures, early mammals, curled up together in a Mesozoic burrow with their hairless warmblooded young, while overhead the ground trembled from the stamping of a herd of diplodocus, and the sky glittered with falling meteor showers...

I shook my head, and the curious images receded. I must have betrayed my confusion, however, because the greeny-grey-blue eyes were now looking at me with a somewhat quizzical expression.

"Sorry," I said. "Miles away. Where were we?"

4.5

Soon after that Miss G said she had to finish her essay, and I realised that I had better be getting back to the lab. As we got to our feet she picked up *Enzymes and Influences*.

"Where would I find this? I'd love to read some more about – what did you call it?"

"Submolecular biosexuality? I'm afraid I had that copy on special order. And I very much doubt you'll be able to –" I caught myself. Miss G was looking at me in that rather level, steely way again. And although of course I had been looking forward immensely to reading Richard's book, it occurred to me that if Miss G *did* read it, and *did* manage to understand it, there was no one with whom I would rather discuss its contents. "Please," I said. "Why not borrow it?"

"Really? Well, if you're sure. I'll give you my contact details in case you need it back." She pulled out a pen. Not having any paper, I offered her the final page of *Over the Knee* (Locke, Fiona, 2006) and she scribbled something on it. "That's my hotmail. And my snail mail. Or I'll just bring it when I'm at the lab."

"Oh – yes. The lab." In the excitement of our conversation, I had somehow managed to overlook the fact that she was actually a research subject. I muttered something about hoping there had been no adverse effects after her last visit.

"Not adverse, no. But I'd say there's definitely been some kind of effect." She frowned. "Quite a marked one, actually."

"Good. Well, I suppose we'll find out on Thursday."

As I turned to go she said, "Oh, and by the way – I'd recommend *Lady Chatterley's Lover*, if you're after something erotic. It's much better written than most of that stuff."

I believe I may even have blushed again.

4.6

As you can no doubt imagine, I returned to the lab that day in a somewhat disturbed frame of mind. On the one hand, I had spent an enjoyable couple of hours talking about matters of science with an intelligent and attractive woman – an unusual, not to say unprecedented, occurrence. On the other, I had come dangerously close to having inappropriate thoughts about a research subject – thoughts, moreover, of a most bizarre nature. What had caused them? After all, I had conversed with attractive women before, often in circumstances far more intimate than my cup of coffee with Miss G, and nothing of the kind had happened then.

It is at this point that I need to reveal a small piece of personal information about myself. At the time I am describing, I was without a sexual partner. In fact, I had been without a sexual partner for over three years – almost as long as I had been engaged on the FSD project. And although it is true that I had been extremely busy, my single status was not entirely because of lack of opportunity. At various conferences and so on, one or two female acquaintances had hinted that they would not be averse to seeing me in a more informal setting, such as upstairs in their hotel rooms. But I had never followed these invitations up.

The real problem, if I am to be completely honest, is that I find women rather dull. This is not misogyny, I hasten to add: I find men dull as well. Compared to my work, having sex is just not very interesting. I am, of course, aware of the irony in this: I can be fascinated by the intricacies of a woman's pituitary gland or brain, while at the same time finding the prospect of actual intercourse with her somewhat mundane. Sex had been one of the many things which I had kept putting off until some unspecified later date.

In short, it was undoubtedly a build-up of simple physical frustration which had prompted those strange, almost hallucinogenic fantasies I had experienced in the bookshop. Fortunately I did not think Miss G had noticed anything amiss. As far as she was concerned, one could simply go on as if nothing had happened.

All the same, I made a mental resolution that I would not place myself in temptation's way again. When Miss G came in for her second session I would suggest to her that it would be better for all concerned if she were in future to seek help for her sexual problems elsewhere.

A couple of days after that first visit to the lab I have to go into college for a seminar group. I cycle over Magdalen Bridge and down the High, and there are the first Japanese tourists of spring grinning and snapping away at it all – at Magdalen Tower, and the Deer Park, and the Botanical Gardens, and the choirboys in their white surplices walking single file to chapel, and just for a moment I remember what it's like to see Oxford for the very first time and to fall in love with it. A couple of the tourists even raise their lenses and click at me as I pedal past, and I think how ironic it is that to them I'm part of this perfect tableau of English life, Student Girl on Bicycle, click click click, isn't she lucky.

After the seminar – at which I find myself being a little feistier than usual – the others invite me to The Trout with them, but for some reason I'm just not in the mood. Instead I go over to Blackwell's to check out a couple of groundbreaking new studies on Tennysonian punctuation Simon's suggested I look at (yes, really).

And I suddenly realise that I am completely and utterly bored. Bored with my thesis, bored with my subject, bored with my life.

I put *Sense and Sentences: the Semiotics of the Victorian Semicolon* back on the shelves and go up to Information.

"Excuse me," I say to the guy behind the desk, who looks as if he'd be more at home on a skateboard. "Where's science?"

He looks at me a bit strangely and says, "Downstairs, where it always is."

Turns out that underneath this tiny medieval bookshop there's a whole vast modern basement I didn't know anything about. It's like a spaceship down there – the hum of air conditioning, bright lights, modern stacks stretching away into the distance... I pluck a volume off the shelves at random. It's called something like *New Developments in Crystallography*. It's full of odd diagrams and strange formulae that mean absolutely nothing to me.

I glance at the guy browsing next to me. A spotty, odiferous smart alec. He's reading the same book with every sign of enjoyment. Christ, at one point he even *chuckles*.

Is he really any cleverer than me?

I think not.

I hunt along the shelves until I find something called *Chemistry For Beginners* and take it back upstairs.

UrlGirl67 ☺
*"When the only tool you have is a hammer,
you tend to treat every problem as if it's a nail"*

I'm on page fifteen when someone says hello and I realise it's Steven Fisher. A little embarrassed, I quickly drop *Chemistry For Beginners* behind my chair. Luckily he doesn't seem to notice – he's a bit embarrassed himself, I think, about the vast stack of dirty books he's buying. I think of telling him that, compared to the stuff Simon looks at on the internet, this is nothing, but instead I change the subject by passing a polite remark on the only book he's bought that isn't dodgy.

At which point he insists on buying me coffee and talking about it. And I realise that he isn't actually patronising at all, just incredibly passionate. For him, the world is an amazing place, and he wants to understand it. It's hardly his fault if everyone else exists on a lower level of knowledge than he does.

He even lends me the book. Though to be honest, it makes much more sense when he explains it. (In fact, when I'm reading the book at home later I keep imagining his voice speaking the technical passages, and somehow it helps.)

There's an odd moment when we start talking about why people kiss. I've always thought of kissing as a rather pointless thing to do, actually, but he tells me this theory that it's all about two bodies exchanging chemical messengers to see if they're compatible. And I find myself wondering what would happen if he and I were to kiss – whether our pheromones and molecules or whatever they're called would get on and pronounce us a match. In fact, the image of the two of us kissing is so vivid, and so nice, that it's all I can do not to swoon into his arms like some stupid Victorian heroine.

Of course, there's still all that KXC79 sloshing through my system from Tuesday's tests and the patch he's made me wear. So perhaps it's no wonder I'm getting these thoughts every now and again. It's not entirely pleasant – I mean, is this what normal women have to go through, women without FSD? Are they constantly imagining themselves kissing every attractive stranger they meet? That must be so weird... Admittedly it's only happened with Dr Fisher so far, but I'm clearly going to have to be careful.

UrlGirl67 ☺

"When the only tool you have is a hammer,
you tend to treat every problem as if it's a nail"

Back at the lab, I looked up "kissing" in the index of Richard Collins' book *The Evolution Revolution* (Palaton Press, 2004). There was only one brief reference:

> For another example of the terrible deception our genes play on us, we need look no farther than kissing. As men, we are all programmed to think we have to find the most beautiful woman in the world and make her fall in love with us – youth and beauty being nature's way of telling us we've hit on a nice healthy gene pool to mix with our own. But the truth is that the most beautiful woman in the world is already taken – or else, as described earlier, she's busy looking for the highest-status man. So, little by little, we learn to lower our standards. At some point, who we want and who we can achieve finally intersect. And at that moment, just to make sure we don't mess things up by taking a long, hard look at our potential partner and running a mile in the opposite direction, Nature helps us along by giving us a narcotic – a bit like having an epidural during the pain of childbirth, except that in our case we're blinded by the cocktail of aphrodisiacs, mood enhancers and other mind-altering chemicals we call falling in love. Kissing, along with all the other forms of mutual self-stimulation common in courtship, is just nature's way of slipping us the pill.

There was nothing about hypersensory hallucinations. Not that I had expected there would be – Richard, as a serious scientist, would hardly have devoted space to so subjective a phenomenon.

Meanwhile I decided I really must do something about my single status before it interfered with my work any further. The easiest solution, I realised, would be to join a dating website. After a brief search I found one that only took eight minutes to register with: I simply had to complete a short personality profile and upload a photograph, and then I was done. It was actually rather fascinating – I could immediately see how the data from such an enterprise might provide an interesting basis with which to substantiate a number of Richard's more controversial theories – and although it has to be said that none of the women the computer initially offered me as potential dates seemed like people I would want to meet, let alone have a physical relationship with, there were at least plenty of them, including one or two who looked a little bit like Miss G. I became so absorbed in looking through the profiles, in fact, that I lost track of time, and it was only when a phone call came through from Julian Noble's secretary that I remembered I was meant to be elsewhere, at a meeting with him and Kes Riley.

6.2

Professor Noble, I should explain, is our Head of Department. Scientists are not much given to jokes, but I sometimes think whoever appointed him must have had a sense of humour, since a less likely leader in an exciting field like experimental neurobiology you could hardly imagine. Nor is he even much of a scientist. Many years ago, as a young man, he made some interesting observations about wing mutations in Malaysian Moon Moths that garnered him a Fellowship and, in a lean year for discoveries, even a prestigious medal or two. Since then he has clung on, limpet-like, to both his tenure and his reputation. As he has never been distracted by the demands of any research worth the name, he was gradually handed more and more of the administrative responsibilities no one else wanted; the Department, and a Chair bearing the name of some equally fusty and forgotten forebear, eventually fell into his lap as well. Retirement, and even greater obscurity, now beckon, but in the meantime he runs the Department as if it were a small British preparatory school and we a group of troublesome school-boys, instead of the internationally-renowned cutting-edge think-tank that we actually are.

Kes Riley is also no academic. But I sometimes think Trock's Inter-national Director of Marketing is smarter than almost anyone I have ever met – it is simply a different kind of intelligence: a drive to succeed. Kes is no older than I am – and to be on the board of one of the biggest pharmaceutical companies in the world at his age is just as remarkable as anything I have achieved. There is absolutely no doubt that were it not for him, and the vast research budgets he scatters around the world seem-ingly on a whim, there would be no KXC79 project.

"Steven!" Kes got to his feet and gave me a complicated handshake. We sat down around Julian's ancient desk, and the professor made us instant coffee in mismatching tannin-stained mugs. I saw Kes take a sip and put his to one side.

"Steven!" he said again. He had the most recent draft of my results in front of him. "What can I say? I'm speechless." He tapped the pages. "Are we sure? The numbers work? No side effects? No psychotic episodes or feelings of depression? And – most important of all – no acne? The occa-sional psychosis we can live with, but nobody wants a sex pill that gives you bad skin." He smiled, but his eyes remained fixed on mine.

"No acne," I said firmly. "Absolutely none. As for other side effects – well, we'll have to wait for the data from a proper clinical trial, of course, but I'm reasonably confident. Twenty-seven sexually dysfunctional women have taken part in the study: twenty-seven women are now sexu-ally functional again."

Nodding, he picked up the paper and began to leaf through it. I saw that the margins were covered with his annotations. "Remarkably thor-ough," he said at last. "Steven, I salute you. You've done a brilliant job. As ever."

"Of course, it's only preliminary," I said modestly. "There are months

52

– possibly years – more work still to be done."

Kes slapped the papers back down on the table. He seemed expectant; excited, even.

Julian Noble sighed.

"Tell him," Kes said impatiently. "Or shall I?"

Julian waved his hand and gazed out of the window. Kes leaned forward. "Steven, it's great news. Thanks to your results, we're giving the Department preferred partner status on the FSD project."

"Really?" I said. "But what about Tokyo? The Higachi programme?"

"You hadn't heard?" His face clouded. "As you know, Professor Higachi's treatment is – was – derived from the testes of the sperm whale. Supplies have been difficult to come by – it was always a worry for us, frankly. Anyway, it seems last week the professor was on board a Japanese research vessel when they finally caught one. In his excitement, and his efforts to direct the whalers where to cut, he leant too far over the safety rail. He was crushed against the ship's side by the creature's death throes... He's alive, just, but it seems unlikely his project will survive."

"I see. Poor Higachi. As you know, I disagreed with his approach, but there was no doubting his commitment."

"Yes. But still – science marches on." Kes picked up my paper again. "Can you have this ready to deliver at the conference?"

I stared at him. I did not have to ask which conference he was referring to. In a little under two months' time Trock were sponsoring a major symposium in London. All the big players in FSD would be flying in to take part.

"I'm talking about a keynote address," he added. "Quite apart from anything else, it'll help bury the Higachi fiasco..." He slapped my paper with the back of his free hand. "And 'Oxford University' still looks good on a press release, at least to the general public. Why not? It will look as if we planned the whole thing – stage-managed it to launch Desiree to the world."

I was so astounded that, of the many responses I could have given to this proposal, I selected completely the wrong one.

"Desiree? What's Desiree?"

"Well, we can hardly go on calling it KXC79 now we're going public, can we? I've had my team brainstorming some ideas – Desiree's the current favourite."

"But it sounds like –"

"It's a name, Steven," he said impatiently. "*This* is what matters." He pointed at my paper. "Well? Can you be ready? I need hardly tell you what an honour it is."

He did not. To give such a paper, to such an audience, and in such circumstances – the launch of my discovery to my peers, with the support of my backers plain for all to see! I have read many accounts of the first readings of famous papers, from *On the Origin of Species* to the Watson–Crick paper on DNA.[1] For a moment I dared to think that the first reading of the KXC79 study might rank alongside them. In my mind's eye I could almost picture it: my colleagues rising to their feet, row upon row, applauding me. *Acclaiming* me...

"But it's so sudden," I said. "Are you sure? I really ought to double-check –"

"According to *this*," he held up my paper, "you've already triple-checked."

"Quadruple-check, then."

"Steven," he said impatiently, "it's very simple. Are you 100% confident in this paper or are you not?"

"Oh, yes. The science is unarguable."

"Well, then." His eyes narrowed. "Unless there's something you haven't told me? Something that's been niggling you – some result that didn't look so good, so you quite reasonably decided to omit it...?"

---

[1] Waton, J.D and Crick, F.H.C 1953: A Structure for Deoxyribose Nucleic Acid, *Nature* 171, 737-738. "It has not escaped our notice that the specific pairing we have postulated suggests a possible copying mechanism for the genetic material," they wrote. When they walked into The Eagle pub at lunchtime, they were less circumspect. "We've just found the secret of life," they announced. But it is the former statement, surely – in all its elegant understatement – which deserves its place in the annals of science.

I shook my head. "Of course no –"

And then I remembered Miss G.

6.3

The paper which I had sent in draft form to Kes – *KXC79 and Female Sexual Dysfunction: More Encouraging Results* – had been written, of course, long before Miss G walked into my lab. There was not a word or a figure in that paper which was not true. But, more importantly, there was a particular tone of voice which spoke, to those able to decipher such things, even more eloquently than the data. It was a kind of scientists' code: despite all the possiblys and the mights and the should-be-investigated-furthers my tone was one of quiet, understated triumph. And why would it not be? I had developed a treatment for a distressing disorder which afflicted, according to some reports, up to 56% of all women.[2] I had tested it, refined and reformulated it, then trialled it on twenty-seven volunteers – and in every single case it had worked. My success rate was 100%.

But then a twenty-eighth woman had walked into the lab, and it had not worked on her. Indeed, it appeared to have sent her to sleep.

Kes Riley and Julian Noble had moved on and were now negotiating budgets. So far as I could tell Trock were offering to pay 150% of the costs of the project, as well as the salaries of everyone involved, along with various bonuses and royalties. I continued to agonise. Should I say something or not?

The fact was, twenty-seven women is not actually a very big sample, and in the early days of the study we had experienced some fairly disparate results. To begin with, for example, our subjects experienced at the

---

[2] I am of course aware that, to a statistician, this means FSD is not actually a "disorder" at all, since by definition a disorder must affect less than half the population. I do not propose to get into that debate now, which seems to me to be principally a matter of semantics.

crucial moment instead of an orgasm an overwhelming desire to sneeze. It was massively encouraging – it proved that KXC55, as it was then, was doing *something* – but our efforts to replace the sneeze with a more appropriate reaction were initially unsuccessful. We were very pleased when two participants, instead of sneezing, suffered from violent nosebleeds – again, it proved we were able to stop the sneezing – but the rate at which we were now losing our volunteers was, as you can imagine, quite rapid, and it was some time before an opportunity to test a new formulation presented itself. Then came the phase when our subjects started blushing furiously. After that we had a difficulty with hiccups, and although on several occasions they were also accompanied by orgasms, the EMG data showed that the hiccups had been, if anything, more eventful. We managed to cure that problem, but the unexpected side effect was that our subjects experienced extreme arousal every time they got an attack of the hiccups. And so on.[3]

It was one balmy Oxford evening the previous summer, whilst strolling on the water meadows, that I hit on a radical way of reformulating the treatment – KXC79, in other words. So far, as I have said, the results from that formulation had been nothing short of spectacular. But twenty-seven good results, statistically speaking, means almost nothing, particularly if accompanied by another result you can't explain.

"Actually, there is just one small problem," I said reluctantly.

6.4

Wrapped up in their discussion, at first they didn't hear me. I cleared my

[3] At least we never had the problem recounted by Chuang et al in *Seizure*, Vol 13, Issue 3, April 2004: "We report a 41-year-old woman with complex reflex epilepsy in which seizures were induced exclusively by the act of tooth brushing. All the attacks occurred with a specific sensation of sexual arousal and orgasm-like euphoria that were followed by a period of impairment of consciousness."

throat. "I'm afraid I'm not going to be ready to launch this treatment at SexDys after all. Sorry."

Startled, they broke off and stared at me. Julian Noble gave a drawn-out sigh of exasperation. Kes Riley frowned – but it was Julian, not me, to whom he turned. "Now wait a minute, Julian. If Steven Fisher is telling me there's a good reason why this paper, which is apparently so watertight and which only needs a few little grammatical and stylistic corrections – and, if I may so, Steven, a few more colour illustrations and rather fewer equations and footnotes and so on – if he says there's a reason why it can't be ready in time, then I personally think we ought to hear him out. Because although it may sound colossally dumb to let such an opportunity go by, and although it may well have knock-on effects in terms of your Department's preferred partner status – we might even have to devolve the funding into next year's fiscal – those sorts of issues are secondary to the science, right? Whatever happens, we at Trock always want to do good science. And if this opportunity has to be let go, and the whole project sinks into obscurity, and some other approach gets into trials first – well, that's just too bad. The important thing is that we never, ever make our scientist partners do anything they aren't completely comfortable with. At Trock, scientific integrity is always our number one, two and three priority."

Then he turned and looked expectantly at me.

I said hesitantly, "It's just that there's another research subject. One who isn't in the paper."

6.5

"The issue," Kes said, "is not the bloody paper."

It was twenty minutes later, and we were still going round in circles.

"We're all agreed we should exclude this woman's results, yes?" he demanded, looking from one of us to the other. "After all, she's a student.

An *arts* student. For all we know, she simply stayed up too late the night before the tests partying and doing Class A drugs. In fact, it would probably be more irresponsible to include the dopey cow than it would be not to put her in."

I frowned, and he held up a finger. "That's the public line, anyway. But – privately – neither can we afford to ignore her. Are there side effects we hadn't anticipated? Interactions with other medications? Steven, I know you're confident you've got the depression angle covered, and I'm very reassured that you say this girl's got good skin, but this is completely new territory for Trock – there could be angles to this stuff that we haven't even thought of. It'll all come out in the clinical trials, sure, but the bottom line is, I don't want to go to clinicals and spend a shedload of cash just to end up with egg on our face. Or acne, for that matter." He shuddered. "So we proceed, but with caution. We continue to prepare Desiree for launch at SexDys, just as if nothing had happened. But we also prepare a plan B – another paper, something bland and noncommittal, that we can present in its place."

"And what, pray, decides whether you go with paper A or paper B?" Julian Noble enquired.

"It's obvious, isn't it?" Kes said. "If by the time of the conference this girl's problem is sorted, then so is ours. Equally, if we know what the issue is and it's something we think we can deal with, fine – we can quietly omit it from the data and no one will be any the wiser. But if in, say, six weeks' time we're still in the dark, we'll have to present paper B. And in the meantime we'll keep talking up the Higachi programme, just in case."

There was a long silence. There seemed to me to be a flaw in this plan somewhere, but my head was spinning and I could not for the life of me think what it was.

"Steven – is there anything you need to get this sorted in time?" Kes demanded. "More funds, more equipment, more people?"

"There are a few things, yes. Another genitosensory analyser would be useful. Perhaps even some Axiom brain mapping software… And Susan's always on about some new stimulator or other."

"Whatever you need. I've gotta go," he said, looking at his watch. "But I'll leave it with you, yes? We have a plan?"

Julian nodded. Kes zipped his papers into a small black case. "One other thing," he said as he got up from the table. "Now the launch is live, our competitors are going to start sniffing around. Pfizer, Carvel, Glaxo – they've all been working on their own treatments for FSD, and that means they'd be happy to see ours come a cropper. I want no hint of these little…glitches to go outside this lab. Get your team to re-sign their confidentiality agreements. And make sure those pills are kept securely locked up. Understood?"

With a wave he was gone.

6.6

There was another long silence. Julian Noble was staring out of the rather grimy window at the small square of grey Oxford sky it revealed.

"Perhaps we shouldn't do it," I said.

Julian snorted faintly.

"I mean, I'm still not 100% convinced that this plan is good science," I added.

Sighing, he reached into the top pocket of his tweed jacket and brought out a small tin of mints. He popped one in his mouth and replaced the tin, without offering it to me.

"I could phone Kes back," I said. "Tell him KXC79 needs more time."

Julian swivelled his gaze at me. His eyes were rheumy and liquid, as brown and threadbare as his jacket. "You will do no such thing, you fucking little fool."

"I'm sorry?" I said, taken aback.

"For twenty years," he said, "I have managed, by hook or by crook, to prevent the university from closing this department down. I did this, not in the hope that any useful research would ever get done here, but because it was the only department I was ever likely to get. When I arrived, it was the Department of Applied Zoology. Now it is the Department of Molecular Biology. I did that – I changed the name. And do you know why?"

I shook my head.

"I did it in the hope that one day some idiot sponsor would come along, be impressed by the humiliatingly trendy moniker, and throw some money at me. It didn't work, of course. Not at first. I had to watch charlatans – media scientists like your friend Collins – getting all the attention and the budgets. I even took on his cast-offs." He stabbed a long finger, as bony and emaciated as the end of a Malacca walking stick, at my chest. "It wasn't until after I'd agreed to give you house room that I discovered what you were really up to – that my department was now effectively a knocking shop."

I opened my mouth to protest, but he ignored me. "They laugh at me, you know. The other Department Heads. I'd give up going to High Table completely, if I could afford to. 'Afternoon, Julian. Anything to report from the love lab?' 'What news from your nymphos?' 'Nice of you to swing by, Julian.' All the bitchy remarks, day in, day out. And now – finally! – the years of biting my tongue have paid off. It couldn't have come at a better time, as it happens. Lowther on the first floor has just produced some very promising work on the varying lengths of earthworms. No funding, of course: the world isn't interested in worms. But that doesn't matter now, does it? Your orgasms are going to pay for his *lumbrici*. Not to mention my retirement home in the Pyrenees. So let me tell you this, young man: when you sit there and squeak that you aren't sure whether your sordid little project is good science or not – frankly, I couldn't give a monkey's."

"Ah," I said.

He nodded, and popped another mint in his mouth. There seemed to be no more to say.

"And I want those pills in my safe," he said as I got to my feet. "Every last one of them. If those are Trock's conditions for getting Precious Partner status, or whatever they call it, then we follow them to the letter. Do I make myself understood?"

6.7

I did not give him the satisfaction of seeing how angry he had made me. I went back to the lab. There I mixed up a hundred grams of chalk powder with twenty cc of water and put the mixture into the pill press, along with a little coloured food dye.

One of the ways we double-check our findings is to periodically substitute the real treatment – KXC79 – with a placebo, an imitation pill made of nothing but chalk. I therefore had all the ingredients for making imitation pills to hand – in fact, the only difference between the dummies and the real thing was a few drops of concentrated KXC79.

Leaving the real pills locked in my own fridge, I took the dummies upstairs and placed them in Julian Noble's safe.

Once I had done that, I gathered my team together in the lab.

"I have good news," I said. "Kes Riley of Trock has just informed me that, thanks to the work you have all done on KXC79, we are now gaining preferred partner status."

There was a smattering of polite applause.

"Which means, amongst other things…" I paused, "that in six weeks' time I will be making the keynote presentation at SexDys, to which, of course, you will all now be invited."

This time there was a moment's stunned silence before they applauded wildly. I called over the noise, "I need hardly tell you how much has to be done before then. And on top of everything else, we have a small anomaly with one of our research subjects to clear up." I explained briefly about Miss G. "The upshot is that we're going to have to go back over every single test session and look for indications of drowsiness. Heart rate, blood pressure, but especially Startle – check them all. If we spot anything at all, we'll get the subject in and retest."

"Even the Ukrainian prostitutes?" Rhona asked.

"*Especially* the Ukrainian prostitutes," I said firmly. Looking around the room, I could see they understood how much I was asking of them.

As they dispersed, talking excitedly amongst themselves, I found Susan hovering at my shoulder.

"Yes, Susan? What is it?"

"These new tests. I was just wondering… Will they involve Lucy?"

"You know perfectly well that's out of the question."

"But Lucy's available. And she's more than willing," she argued. "Tracking down the other test subjects could take forever."

"Susan, how many times do I have to tell you – that's exactly the kind of slipshod thinking that could cause problems when our results are scrutinised. There can be no cutting of corners."

"Very well," she said calmly. "In that case, can I take it she'll be leaving us soon?"

I hesitated. "It's not quite as straightforward as that."

"Steve – last week she threw a radio at one of the cleaners. The poor woman was frightened out of her wits."

"I heard about that incident. Lucy had simply run out of batteries. She needs company, that's all."

"And who's going to give it to her?" she demanded. "We're all busy – and we'll be even busier now. Steve – isn't it time we sorted this out? You say we mustn't cut corners, but in that case, what's she doing here?"

I sighed. "I understand what you're saying. Look, I'll go and have a word with her. Maybe I can do something."

Susan nodded, although I could tell she was unconvinced. I took a deep breath and headed for the staircase.

7.2

I followed the stairs down to the basement. As I pushed open the heavy rubber door I heard the sound of people arguing. There was a shout, gunfire, then dramatic music. I looked at my watch. *Emmerdale*. Lucy never missed an episode.

Down there, amongst all the outmoded scientific junk that had somehow never been thrown away – the jars of Victorian foetuses preserved in formaldehyde, the boards of pinned butterflies, the moth-eaten civet cats and the rusting Tesla coils – down there, the smell of perishing rubber and evaporating formaldehyde was overlaid by another smell: the faint but pungent scent of urine on straw. At the back of the room was a line of built-in cages, their rusting bars running all the way from ceiling to floor. Most were empty now, their concrete floors swept bare, only a few stains and discoloured patches remaining as evidence of a scientific past that was either glorious or shaming, depending on your point of view.

When Lucy saw me she bared her teeth and made a rude gesture.

"I know, I know," I said. "Far too long. But something came up."

For a moment she sulked. Then, springing to the bars, she rattled them forcefully and signed 'tree.'

"I'm sorry," I said reluctantly. "I don't have time to take you out today."

She chattered angrily and gestured at the door.

"Sometime soon, I promise."

She turned her back on me, even more sulkily. I had been expecting that, and in any case it was no more than I deserved. I checked her food and water and made sure she had some toys to keep her amused. But in my heart I knew that it was all completely inadequate. The simple truth was that Susan had been right. Lucy should not have been there.

Bonobo, for any of you who are not familiar with these remarkable primates, are an offshoot of the chimpanzee family – *Pan paniscus*, to be precise (*Figure 9*). In the wild, they survive only in one small area of the

Figure 9: A bonobo.

64

African Congo, in an area devastated by civil war, poaching, illegal logging and climate change. It seems almost certain that at some point this century we will drive them to extinction. The loss of any species is a catastrophe, but in the case of the bonobo it would be a terrible genocide.

What makes bonobos so special is that their society is organised almost entirely on sexual lines. Unusually amongst primates, they have sex for pleasure as well as procreation, but it goes much further than that: they trade sexual favours amongst themselves in a kind of barter economy, and use sexual prowess as a way of establishing pecking orders. Their simian flexibility helps, of course, but an exuberant willingness on the part of every bonobo to throw themselves without hesitation into the nearest gang-bang counts for even more.

When I first acquired Lucy she lived in the basement with nine other bonobos, doing what bonobos do best – eating, sleeping, and having energetic sex of every hue and description. For two years I studied them, writing up my observations in a succession of papers that, amongst other things, helped to establish my own reputation.[1] Then the ban on laboratory experiments with apes was introduced.

Whatever you think of this ban – it is still a subject of great controversy amongst scientists – its motives were undoubtedly honourable. And yet its effects were disastrous. Almost overnight, in Oxford alone, hundreds of animals – those too old to be returned to the wild, or those bred in captivity – were put down. Amongst those scheduled for termination were the bonobos – all of them. Imagine it: a species that was almost extinct, whose natural environment was inaccessible because of war, whose numbers were in freefall…and we were going to kill them.

By then Lucy had become a favourite of mine – she was easily the most intelligent primate I had ever met, able to communicate in simple

---

[1] *Singultus and the orgasm of the female bonobo: a possible mechanism for future investigation*, winner of The Peter Beaconsfield Prize for the Most Outstanding Postgraduate Thesis; *Neural pathways of the female bonobo*, which won the Nicholas Kurti Most Promising Young Scientist Award, etc.

sign language and almost house-trained. I asked the authorities if I could keep her. They said no – regulations were regulations. So, the night before the bonobos were due to be put to sleep, I smuggled Lucy out and hid her.

My life has been spent in the service of the scientific method. Logic and reason are my watchwords – but what I did that night was scarcely rational. To this day, I still don't know if it was the right thing to do. I was taking a highly social animal, an animal for whom sexual interaction with her peers was the greatest happiness she knew, and condemning her to a life of solitary, sexless misery. Perhaps, if Lucy herself had been able to say what she wanted, she might even have told me to leave her with the others.

All I knew is that I could not abandon her to die. For once in my life I didn't stop to think. I acted on instinct, and I have half-regretted it ever since. One day, I knew, I would have to deal with the consequences of my actions. But for now, Lucy would have to wait, while I readdressed myself to the more pressing problem of Miss G.

That night in bed I read some more of the book Steven Fisher lent me, with Simon tossing and turning beside me – well, more turning than tossing, actually, which might be the problem: I'm seriously thinking of giving him a blowjob just so he'll go to sleep and I can get on with *Enzymes and Influences*. This stuff is dense – you need to concentrate on every line, or you miss some vital piece of information and whole chapters become incomprehensible.

Eventually Simon says, "What on earth are you reading?"

"It's a science book."

"Science!" From the way he says it you'd have thought I was reading Jilly Cooper. He grabs it from me and flicks through the pages with a supercilious sneer on his face. "Well, well," he says, handing it back. "I always thought you were a bit of a geek."

And I know he's just being catty because he's pissed off about the whole no-sex thing, but for some reason this remark makes me so cross that I mentally withdraw the offer of a blowjob, even though it means I lie there pretending to turn the pages but actually unable to concentrate at all.

Am I a geek?

Well, it's true I like making lists. Such as:

Five signs you're a geek

5. Think Leela is cooler than Lieutenant Uhuru.
4. Know who Leela and Lieutenant Uhuru are.
3. Know my computer's IP address.

2. Know everyone else's IP addresses in the Department, can solve most network problems quicker than the system administrator – admittedly not difficult because Bruce, the sys admin, is Really Not That Bright.
1. Make lists the correct way, ie descending order.

Five signs you're not a geek
5. Have First Class Degree, MPhil etc, in English Literature.
4. Female.
3. No spots.
2. No dandruff.
1. No BO (God, I hope).

On the minus side I should probably mention that I'm the secretary of the college S & S Society. But being into S & S doesn't make me a geek. It just happens to be something that a lot of geeks are into. Coincidence.

Hmm. Is it possible that, as Dr Minstock would say, I'm blocking something here?

UrlGirl67 ☺
"When the only tool you have is a hammer,
you tend to treat every problem as if it's a nail"

I don't mind admitting that I spent the days leading up to Miss G's next visit in a somewhat apprehensive state. In addition to two new genitosensory analysers, the testing room now contained a stack of the paperbacks I had purchased, plus half a dozen scented candles; but the fact remained there was little I could do other than run the tests again and hope that this time the outcome was different. If it was, I would be able to dismiss Miss G from both the study and my thoughts, writing off her previous results as an unexplained but allowable blip. The launch could go ahead, and triumph and acclaim would be mine.

I wondered if Miss G might mention our chance meeting in the bookshop to Susan, and it was this, as well as my own nerves, which prompted me to keep one ear on their conversation via the intercom as I prepared the tests.

"So, Annie. Anything to report?" I heard Susan's voice ask. "Any erotic feelings, fantasies…?"

"Um," Miss G said hesitantly.

"Go on," my colleague demanded.

"Well, yesterday I did have a sort of daydream about – it's a bit embarrassing, actually."

I heard Susan laugh. "I'm a professional sexologist, Annie. I can assure you there's nothing you can tell me that I won't have heard many, many times before. Spit it out."

"All right – it was about snails."

"Snails?" Susan said doubtfully. "That is a bit… So what happened in this fantasy of yours?"

"I'd been reading about these snails, you see," Miss G said. "Giant

African snails. Which are huge – almost as big as guinea pigs. And I was just drifting off when I began imagining about six of them, slithering all over my body." (*Figure 10*)

"And this was…erotic?"

"Just for a second. Then I felt really stupid."

"Nothing's stupid in fantasy, Annie," Susan said sternly. "You have to go with the flow. Even if it's…snails. Anything else?"

"Not really. There was someone I – but that definitely doesn't count."

"OK." I heard the sound of Susan snapping shut her clipfile. "Annie, last time you got a little too relaxed, so today we're going to sit you on this piece of apparatus here." I heard a thump as she patted her new stimulator.

Miss G sounded doubtful. "Do I have to? It looks a bit…daunting."

"It's certainly a powerful machine. But that may be just what we need, wouldn't you say? Now, let's see if Dr Fisher has managed to find his little pink pills."

I turned the microphone down. By the time Susan entered the control

Figure 10: *Achatina immaculata.*

room I was busy measuring the correct dosage of KXC79 into a plastic cup, and trying to remember where I had come across a reference to African snails before.

9.2

While we waited for the treatment to do its work I put on Jean Michel Jarre's electronic classic *Oxygene Parts 1-6*. Miss G, meanwhile, leafed through *Dirty Laundry* (Birch, P, 2002) briefly, before putting it to one side with a sigh.

"Dr Fisher?"

I leant forward to the mike. "Yes?"

"Sorry I didn't bring your book back. I haven't quite finished it."

Susan's head swivelled to look at me. But I had no intention of explaining which book Miss G was referring to. "Are you enjoying it?"

"Very much. Though I wish I could get my head round the difference between a hormone and a pheromone."

"That's an easy one," I said. "In fact, I'm teaching this to the second-year undergraduates this very term. A hormone is a chemical messenger within the body; a pheromone is a chemical emitted by the body, usually as an odour, which has a specific effect, such as sexual excitement, on another body."

I suddenly remembered where I had heard a reference to giant African snails before. Richard Collins used them as an illustration of this very point.

"As it happens," I said, "there's a very simple example of pheromones at work in the case of the giant African snail, where the slime one snail leaves behind contains a substance that inhibits sexual activity in other snails."

"Well, if she wasn't sleepy before…" Susan muttered.

Miss G's voice interrupted, "OK, except by your definition I can't see there's much difference between a hormone and a neurotransmitter."

"Exactly!" I said. Miss G had put her finger on one of the most important points in neurobiology. It is an insight second-year undergraduates often fail to grasp – and she had understood it almost intuitively. "We call them pheromones when they travel from one organism to another, hormones when they're released into the bloodstream, and neurotransmitters when they're released from a cell. But essentially, they're all the same process."

"I thought so," Miss G said excitedly. "I thought – those snails are like great big cells –"

"Firing their slime at the next cell along," I agreed.

Miss G sighed. "It must be great to be a scientist," she said, a little wistfully. "You know all this incredible *stuff*."

"I need you both to stop talking now," Susan said firmly. "Annie, try to concentrate on sexy thoughts. If you can." She twisted a knob on the control panel in front of her.

9.3

We waited, studying the machines. I was particularly interested in the output from the GSA, which was giving me a level of detail I had never had access to before. I pushed a button, and brought up Miss G's face through the heat-sensitive camera. Her lips were almost black; the lobes of her ears were dark purple, and her exposed, thrown-back throat was a shifting vermillion (*Figure 11*).

I cross-checked with the graphical information from the GSA. This is excellent, I was thinking – real-time comparison of data streams.

Suddenly there was a little tremor in the readout, like the first shivers of an earthquake. I switched back to the thermograph. Before my eyes, orange shaded through to yellow as warmth spread up Miss G's throat.

I went to Startle. Her eye was blank and unfocused. But the GSA

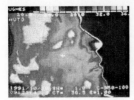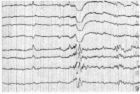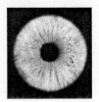

Figure 11: Real-time comparison of data streams.

readout was flickering insistently, a scribble of tiny but persistent zigzags that, as I watched, grew in intensity.

"Go on," I found myself whispering under my breath. "Go on…"

Like a kite taking off in the wind, the line suddenly shot up… peaked…dipped…peaked again, but higher this time…hesitated…then finally soared into a series of dizzying, undulating peaks and troughs, almost touching the roof of the graph, before drifting back towards the baseline in a long, lazy decline. In all this time Miss G made hardly a sound, but what I was seeing left no room for doubt. KCX79 had done it. Miss G was anorgasmic no longer.

I let out a long, relieved exhalation, and a knot of tension in my shoulders, previously unnoticed, eased perceptibly. The paper…the conference…triumph and acclaim… Everything was back on track.

Susan's voice cut across my thoughts. "Annie? Are you getting anything from this?"

I stared at her. Hadn't she noticed what had just happened? I opened my mouth to say something, but Miss G's voice forestalled me.

"I – uh – no, not much," she said, rather breathlessly I thought.

"Oh." Susan flicked a switch, and the hum of the machines died. "In that case…"

I leant towards the mike. "Annie?"

"Yes?"

"Did you feel *nothing at all* just now?"

"Well, it was perfectly pleasant, but – no, nothing special."

I didn't answer. I knew for a fact that Miss G had just experienced an orgasm (*Figure 12*). How could she not be aware of it? It just didn't make any sense.

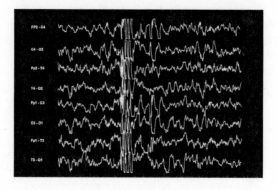

Figure 12: It doesn't look like "nothing special" to me!

…The big embarrassment is that when I go back to the lab for my next appointment I only have to hear Steven Fisher explaining the difference between a hormone and a pheromone and I just seem to *melt*. And when they rig me up to their machines – well, let's just say something happens that hasn't happened for a very long time.

My God, that KXC79 must be powerful stuff.

But for some reason they don't spot what's happened to me. And I don't tell them. Don't say a word, in fact.

I decide I'll tell them next time, instead.

After all, I wouldn't want them to think it's got anything to do with my meeting Steven Fisher in Blackwell's. Or talking to him about pheromones. Because it hasn't. And – since it hasn't – it would actually be more accurate, and more useful to them, if I left it for another day. Just so it's absolutely clear that it's nothing whatsoever to do with that.

Besides, what if it's just a one-off?

I think Susan may suspect something, though. I tried to throw her off the scent with some random stuff I made up about snails. But I ask you – snails? Where the hell did that come from?

UrlGirl67 ☺

"When the only tool you have is a hammer,
you tend to treat every problem as if it's a nail"

It is my habit, when confronted by a particularly difficult problem, to mull it over during my weekly attendance at the university's Campanology Society: that is, while bellringing. Whether it is the noise – a sound so massive it seems to reverberate through your very bones – the feel of the woollen sally as it slips through your hands, the venerable smell of cassocks and candle wax, the way all eight of us stand in a solemn circle, our only communication nods and smiles as the Tower Captain ritually bellows the changes – "Eight to two: four to one" – or the simple mathematical elegance of the ringing patterns themselves, I don't know, but I find that bellringing is an activity especially conducive to thought. I have unravelled some of the most complex difficulties of sexual function whilst ringing a Clifford's Pleasure, Plain Bob Minor or Cambridge Surprise, and on the rare occasions when the Society is able to pull a complete peal of five thousand and forty changes I almost always gain some new insight or understanding of my work.

That night, at our midweek practice, I once again found my thoughts returning to Miss G. Clearly, resolving the mystery of her anomalous results was now both crucial and pressing. Yet the mystery seemed only to be deepening. I could conceive of no biochemical reason why she should suffer from drowsiness on the one hand, or be unaware of having an orgasm on the other. I could not even be certain whether they were two separate problems, or if there was a link – some connection between them I was currently unable to discern.

It was exactly the sort of problem which, in my postgraduate days, I would have taken to Richard Collins. He has a remarkable ability to cut through the complexities of a situation. I can still hear the advice he gave me when one of my bonobos started to behave strangely. "Every problem of science," he pointed out, "is ultimately a problem of logic. And every problem of logic is ultimately a problem of biology. The world is physics, Steven, but brains are biochemistry."

It was exactly that sort of inspirational steer I needed now. I had already tried emailing him, but there had been no reply. So I did what I sometimes do in these situations: I tried to imagine what he would suggest, if he were with me.

And I seemed to hear his voice, quite clearly, saying: "Don't guess: investigate. Stick to the science, Steven. First establish the facts, and only then develop your hypothesis."

As ever, he was quite right. I decided I should not jump to any conclusions until I had double-checked my findings.

II.2

On the following Tuesday Miss G returned to the lab for her third test session. Unfortunately on this occasion there was a delay in the proceedings caused by a computer incompatibility between Susan's new state-of-the-art programmable neurostimulator and her laptop. What the incompatibility was did not become clear for some time, owing to the fact that Susan's response to any software problem is to press all the keys at random, causing her machine to lock up completely. Miss G was already wired up to the measuring devices, so the delay was ill-timed to say the least, but after re-routing the biothesiometer to my laptop and – Miss G's suggestion, this – running a workaround by porting Susan's laptop to my slave drive, we were able to proceed.

Susan was by this time rather flustered, and muttered to me that we should probably abandon the session altogether. But Miss G said she was happy to continue, so we did.

At four minutes twenty, a series of thirty-eight internal muscular contractions at 0.8 second intervals commenced. This was accompanied by an increase in skin galvanicity of ±6.5*u* and a rise in temperature of 0.8°. During this time Miss G did not make any sound, although admittedly if she had done it might have been drowned out by the music she herself had chosen (*The Well-tempered Synthesiser*, Wendy Carlos).

At five minutes ten, the contractions subsided.

At seven minutes thirty Miss G said through the intercom, "You know, we could also have tried checking for an IRQ conflict on the LAN ports." I agreed that this would indeed have provided an alternative solution.

At nine minutes eighteen, a series of twenty-four internal contractions at 0.8 second intervals commenced. This was accompanied by a similar increase in galvanicity and temperature.

It seemed to me that Miss G twice moaned involuntarily, but on both occasions she quickly turned it into a cough.

At nine minutes forty the contractions subsided.

At twelve minutes exactly, Dr Minstock asked Miss G over the intercom, "Annie, is this doing anything for you?"

On receiving a negative response, she terminated the test session at twelve minutes twenty seconds.

What on earth was going on?

Another session. Similar result. TWICE. That's never happened in my life.

OK, so here's the thing: I really, really do not want Dr Fisher to know what is happening to me at the lab.

First, because it's only a teeny-weeny stupid physical attraction for someone who – let's face it – I barely know from Adam.

Second, because he is very clever and may work out what effect he is having on me. In which case I think I will die of embarrassment.

Third, because once I tell him that his treatment has worked, and I'm cured...well, that'll be it: there won't be any reason for me to go back to the lab after that. And – oh, admit it – I quite enjoy it. Not just in the obvious way (though that has been a revelation – just as he described at the beginning) but also because –

Because of him, I suppose. Talking to him. Seeing him. Just being in the same building as him.

And fourth, because – Oh God – what if my reaction wasn't only down to the KXC79? What if I never really was anorgasmic, or whatever they call it, after all?

What if I'm just with the Wrong Man?

Gulp. Don't go there.

UrlGirl67 ☺

"When the only tool you have is a hammer,
you tend to treat every problem as if it's a nail"

"Ah, Wulf," I said, catching up with Dr Sederholm on the stairs of the Department building next day. "I need to pick your brains about this girl on the study. I think she's having orgasms but she's saying she isn't and I don't know why."

My colleague considered this for a while. "The first time Rhona and I slept together," he said thoughtfully, "she was not having orgasms either. But she did not want to seem rude. So she pretended that she did have them. Now, there is no problem, and she doesn't need to pretend any more."

"How do you know?"

"Know what?"

"That she isn't pretending any more."

"Oh." He shrugged. "She told me."

"Unless she's just saying that because she thinks you might be asking yourself if she's still pretending, and saying that she was pretending before makes her pretending now more believable," I pointed out. Something else occurred to me. "The *a priori* of this, I cannot help but observe, is that you have slept with Rhona, and on more than one occasion."

"Oh. Yes. It's been almost two months now. Didn't you know?"

Now that I thought about it, I had seen the two of them together on several occasions, holding hands, although I had not drawn any specific conclusions from this. I shook my head.

"Anyway,' he continued, "what I am suggesting is that it doesn't really matter if someone is having orgasms or not. Not in the long run."

"Although it does make our results rather problematic," I said. "The whole point of our research being to establish whether or not KXC79 actually *works*."

"Hmm." He pondered for a moment. "Perhaps you need to think of your experiments as being like Schrödinger's Cat. You know, the hypothetical cat shut in a box which would eventually be killed by a radioactive molecule. Schrödinger's point was that at any one moment the cat would be either alive, or dead, but on *average* it would be half dead and half alive all the time. This is the whole basis of my own work on submolecular chaos, actually."[1]

"Wulf," I said, "I am familiar with the conundrum of Schrödinger's Cat. I'm just struggling to see how it helps. In this particular instance."

"Or there's the 'tomato effect'."

"What's the 'tomato effect'?"

"When the tomato was first introduced to North America, scientists thought it must be poisonous, owing to its coming from the same family as deadly nightshade. It was only when people started cooking with it that they began to reconsider. So we use the phrase 'tomato effect' to describe phenomena which are obvious to everyone except scientists." He brightened. "Perhaps you even have a Schrödinger's Tomato. That would be very interesting, actually. Something very obvious, but also incomprehensible."

"Wulf," I said, "I think I see what you're getting at now."

"You do?"

"You're telling me I shouldn't jump to any conclusions until I know much more about her."

"Exactly," he said, sounding a little relieved. "On a submolecular level, that's almost certainly what I'm saying."

[1] Dr Sederholm has asked me to point out that this is in fact a very approximate summation of his work, in which he is attempting to bring together Schrödinger's Cat, Godel's Undecidability Theorem, fuzzy logic, chaos theory, Quantum Incompleteness Physics and Heisenberg's Uncertainty Principle into a Unified Theory of Bafflement.

I got out Miss G's file, hoping some simple explanation would leap out at me.

She was, as I had surmised, extremely well-educated. At school she had acquired a large number of A-levels in the arts subjects, subsequently taking up a place at Bristol University. Graduating with a First in English Literature, she had moved to Cambridge to do her Masters, and then to Oxford for her doctorate, for which she was being supervised by Dr Simon Frampton.

After this brief CV came the standard questionnaires – standard for our line of research, that is. Miss G had her first sexual experience at the age of seventeen, an event she described as "satisfactory" (we were into a multiple choice format by now, so perhaps she simply meant more "satisfactory" than "excellent" or "unpleasant", those being the other two choices). In all she'd had six sexual relationships. One of these she rated as "excellent", though under "duration" she had selected "one night". One was "unpleasant"– that, oddly, had lasted a year. The others were mostly "satisfactory", although in one case I noticed she had ticked both "excellent" and "unpleasant".

Then came a section relating to current relationship. From the choices ("Are you a) single b) dating c) in a relationship d) cohabiting e) married f) promiscuous") Miss G had ticked c), although I noticed that, mysteriously, she had left the box relating to quality for that relationship blank. I felt a brief stab of curiosity about what sort of man had managed to gain Miss G's affection. Doubtless some floppy-haired, poetry-spouting fop.

From the section on "sexual confidence" I learned that a man's eyes were more attractive than his buttocks; that she had been unfaithful once (was that, I couldn't help but wonder, the episode that had been both "excellent" and "unpleasant"?); that she thought her thighs unattractive (from my recollection of her, not actually the case); that she "slightly agreed" that "the best part of sex is the cuddling afterwards"; that she pre-ferred coition to be relaxed, playful, romantic, with the lights on, clean, regular and conversational (as opposed to energetic, serious, in the dark, messy, spontaneous and noisy); that she usually slept in a T-shirt, and preferred mornings.

According to her Myers-Briggs, she was an INTJ, or Idealistic Intro-vert, who preferred Thinking to Feelings, Judgements to Perceptions and Intuition to Sensation. According to her Derogatis, her ideal frequency of intercourse would be once every three months. She agreed with the state-ment that "human genitals are not generally attractive", and disagreed with "sex rarely goes on long enough", thus placing herself towards the conservative end of the sexual spectrum. According to her Minnesota Multiphasic Personality Inventory, she was neither sociopathic, psycho-pathic, dissociative, bipolar, depressive, anxious or obsessive. Her Female Sexual Function Index never really got off the ground after a poor start with question one ("Over the last four weeks, how often did you feel sex-ual desire or interest?" Answer: "Never"), thus making follow-ups such as question three largely irrelevant ("Over the past four weeks, how would you rate your level of arousal during sexual activity or intercourse?") although it certainly made her answer to question sixteen rather intrigu-ing ("Over the past four weeks, how satisfied have you been with your overall sexual life?" Answer: "Very satisfied").

I sighed. Interesting as all this was, it was of no help in solving the problem.

I flicked through the transcript of her interviews with Susan. There seemed to be large gaps – presumably Susan had not yet finished typing up her notes. Towards the end, though, a section caught my eye.

Susan: I want to talk to you now about fantasy.

Miss G: Fantasy! [*Sits forward*] Now there's a subject I *am* interested in.

Susan: Ah! I sense we're getting somewhere at last. Tell me your favourite fantasy.

Miss G: My favourite fantasy?

Susan: Yes…what sort of scenario is it, what are you doing, who's there with you.

Miss G: There are so many…

Susan: I'm getting a sense that this is important to you, am I right?

Miss G: Definitely.

Susan: Well, let's just pick a recent one. Something hot, please.

Miss G: OK. I should warn you, though, it's kind of complicated.

Susan: No problem.

Miss G: OK. I'm in the Gorge of Darkwind. It's pitch black, and there are poisonous miasmas all around me, swirling, burning everything they touch. I'm at the head of a band of fearless warriors –

Susan: What are they wearing?

Miss G: What? Oh, leather stuff, I guess. And one of them has the helmet of Azeroth. That's Nor, the leader of my troop of battle-hardened swordsmen. As I stand there, blasted by the fiery Azerothian winds, he moves to my side. "Lady Maud," he says respectfully, "I think we should turn east." I look east, and my heart almost fails – for to the east lie the lands of ancient lost lore, where the spirits of the tormented wander freely, preying on unwary travellers!

Susan: Go on.

Miss G: So then we move east.

Susan: And at what point does it become sexual?

Miss G: Sexual?

Susan: Yes. This is all very fascinating, Annie, but I'm wondering if we could jump to the point where you and Nor have sex.

Miss G: Me and Nor have sex! You must be joking!

Susan: What's so funny? This is your fantasy, not mine.

Miss G: But in real life Nor is a spotty historian called Willem. With a goatee beard.

[*Pause on tape*]

Susan: What do you mean, real life?

Miss G: I mean, outside the fantasy. Nor is only his character – and believe me, it's taken a lot of Experience Points for him to get this far.

Susan:	I think we may be talking at cross-purposes here, Annie. What sort of fantasy is this?
Miss G:	A level-three Swamps and Sorcerers scenario. It's the one the college S & S Society is playing at the moment – we meet every Friday in term time. I'm the secretary.
Susan:	Ah.
Miss G:	Do you want to come along? We always need more Orcs.
Susan:	No. Could you describe a sexual fantasy, please?

[*Lengthy pause on tape*]

Miss G:	I don't really have any.
Susan:	You must have fantasies. Everyone has fantasies.
Miss G:	No, sorry.
Susan:	[*sighs*] Why do you want to take part in this study, Annie?
Miss G:	It sounds interesting, I suppose.
Susan:	But you do want to become sexually functional?
Miss G:	Oh. Yes. Of course. That too.
Susan:	Well, you'd better start keeping a diary of your sexual feelings. That's definitely an area we'll need to work on.

I could not help smiling; partly at Susan's annoyance when Miss G refused to divulge her fantasies, but also at the image of someone as poised as Miss G playing something, well, as *uncool* as Swamps and Sorcerers.

The last thing in the file was a summary from Susan:

Miss G is a slightly built young woman who presents as somewhat dreamy in manner. She contacted us via one of our lab assistants, who apparently told her about the project at a party. There is absolutely no doubt that she has a sexual function disorder – indeed, by most diagnostic criteria she could be said to have several different disorders. However, when asked the standard question "What are you hoping to get out of your participation in this study?" Miss G gave the impression she wasn't really sure. Expectation management was therefore less of an issue than usual, although of course I impressed on her the standard caveats. At the end of this conversation Miss G professed herself still keen. Conclusion: recommend acceptance.

I put the papers down, unsatisfied. Clearly, Miss G was emotionally inconsistent and sexually somewhat confused. She differed from the vast majority of the population only in that she was getting – and wanting – less sex. It hardly explained what had happened in the lab.[2]

And then I had a sudden moment of clarity. I saw that everything I had read – the questionnaires, the statistics, the interview – these were not the real Miss G. They were simply a trail of data left behind her in the physical world. In the same way as a painting is not the person it portrays, everything in that file was only a kind of illusion, a guess at the real her. The facts, in fact, were not the answer; the data was a dead end; the empirical approach no approach at all. To solve the problem of her mysterious responses I would have to go well beyond the reach of conventional science.

In short, I was going to have to find some way of getting to know her. But how?

13.3

And then I'm reading *Enzymes and Influences* and I suddenly have this complete and utter moment of epiphany.

---

[2] The drawbacks of face-to-face interviews as a basis for assessing sexual history in the case of female subjects are well established. In one study, men and women were asked about their sexual behaviour under several different testing conditions, including a questionnaire in which the participants believed, falsely, that they were anonymous: the results were then compared to those given in a face-to-face interview, with markedly different results. "Women are sensitive to social expectations for their sexual behaviour and may be less than totally honest when asked about their behaviour in some survey conditions," said a co-author of the study, published in *The Journal of Sex Research*.

It's not that I'm with the Wrong Man. I'm just doing the Wrong Subject.

UrlGirl67 ☺

"When the only tool you have is a hammer,
you tend to treat every problem as if it's a nail"

Massive row with Simon. I tell him I'm going to give up English Literature to become a scientist. Simon – who is many things but no fool – immediately wants to know "who put *that* ridiculous idea in your head."

"That is so typical of you," I retort. "You assume that any thought in my head must have been put there by someone else."

His eyes narrow. "It's the pointy-head, isn't it? Fisher. The one who lent you that book."

"Of course it isn't," I say, unconvincingly.

At which Simon accuses me of collecting clever men like other women collect stamps.

I say that there are actually very few female philatelists, the urge to collect and classify being a male attribute linked to the hunter-gatherer instinct. (cf *Enzymes and Influences*, page 112.)

He asserts that I'm now trying to change the subject.

I suggest that it's him who's changing the subject, not me, and that all I was doing is correcting his lazy metaphor.

He contends that it was an analogy, not a metaphor, and notes that I have still not denied being attracted to Fisher.

I point out that a) he didn't actually ask me if I was attracted to Dr Fisher b) it's impossible to prove a negative c) the whole idea is completely ludicrous d) not everything comes down to sex, for Christ's sake and e) even if I did fancy Steven Fisher, which I don't, my feelings would have nothing to do with wanting to change to science. In fact, if I *were* attracted to him – which is, as I said, a ridiculous notion – it would make a change to science less likely, not more, given the theoretical restrictions on shagging your supervisor.

Simon shouts that I am now trying to blackmail him.

I respond that this is ridiculous. I have made no reference to blackmail, only to the fact that sleeping with one's students is generally frowned on as unethical and exploitative.

Simon begins to cry.

He tells me that I'm the best thing that has ever happened to him, that he loves me, that I'm his golden beacon of innocence and youth, and that if he sometimes gets angry, it's only because of his frustration at not being able to satisfy me sexually.

(Satisfy me – what an odd phrase. It makes me sound like a raging nymphomaniac, when the truth is nearer the opposite. I'm perfectly satisfied *not* being satisfied, thank you.)

But you can't go on being cross with a man who's crying, can you? So I say I love him too. And then of course he wants me to go to bed with him.

I even fake it, just a little.

What a mess.

UrlGirl67 ☺

"When the only tool you have is a hammer,
you tend to treat every problem as if it's a nail"

Was Simon right? *Do* I collect clever men?

It's true I've always been attracted to intelligence. Men who know things – smart men – make me want to get to know them. Partly because I want to know what they know, partly because I feel they'd be good at getting to know me. (Not that it worked in Simon's case.)

On the other hand, my perfect man is still Chewbacca.

Five Things That Make Chewie Sexy

5. Hairy. Well, obviously. But it's such nice hair.

4. Loyal. Han Solo once saved his life, so according to the Wookie

code of honour he has to spend the rest of his life making sure Han never comes to any harm.

3. Superbright. Wookies don't speak much, not having the facial structure for it, but they have a genius for all things mechanical. Chewie can always rebuild C-3PO from scrap, which is a pretty neat thing to be able to do for your friends.

2. Big. Strong. Dependable.

1. His name is based on the Russian word for "dog", and his face on a dog George Lucas had as a boy, who died in tragic circumstances. Bless!

UrlGirl67 ☺

"When the only tool you have is a hammer,
you tend to treat every problem as if it's a nail"

Something else about this whole KXC79 malarkey. I keep getting this sudden, vivid, uh, *thing*. What I can only call a fantasy.

Us, together. Me and Steven Fisher.

And what's disturbing about this is that it's the real deal – a real sexual fantasy, I mean, the sort I never have. In full pornographic detail, right down to the bad lighting and the cheesy music. And the naked stud – the surprisingly hard-bodied geeky scientist stud – who's holding my ankles up by my shoulders while he bangs me like a –

HEY, STOP THAT.

I think I've had enough of being sexually normal. It just seems to make everything much, much more complicated.

So later, still feeling miserable, I swap the KXC79 patch for one of the nicotine patches Simon bought when he was trying to quit smoking. No one will ever know – they look just the same. Maybe that will reduce the effects of the pills.

In the meantime, better try to think of some other way of resolving this whole science/literature dilemma.

I think I mentioned that I am obliged to do a certain amount of teaching of undergraduates. I say "obliged", but in fact the success of my research means that, if I wished to, I could now give up teaching altogether and concentrate entirely on lab work. Given the pressures of modern-day pharmaceutical research, it would probably make sense to do so. But somehow I always find myself resisting such a move. Partly it is because I believe that the primary function of a university should be to teach; but also because I remember all too well what it was like for me, as a fresh-faced undergraduate just up from grammar school, to see and hear in person the finest scientific minds of a generation; men at the cutting edge of research themselves, who week after week passed on not only their knowledge, but their *passion*: I regard it almost as a duty to try, in my own small way, to do the same.

Nevertheless, it has to be said that the passion is not always recip-rocated. More often than not, my attempts at imparting a sense of the glories of the natural world are met with a row of spotty heads bent over ringbinders as thirty diligent but dull-minded chemists concentrate on getting down enough notes to pass their exams. That week, though, one attendee stood out from the rest. To my surprise, Miss G was sitting on the end of the fourth row. Seeing me notice her, she smiled in greeting.[1]

---

[1] Smiles are usually grouped into two categories, Duchenne and Pan American. The Duchenne smile, named after researcher Guillaume Duchenne, involves movement of the major zygomaticus muscle around the mouth and the orbicularis oculi around the eyes. It is believed this smile can only be pro-duced as a result of genuine emotion, making it involuntary. By contrast, the Pan American smile involves voluntary use of the zygomaticus muscle and can thus be used to show politeness or conceal emotion. Miss G's smile, though brief, was most definitely a Duchenne, and lit up her whole face.

My subject that afternoon was how Otto Loewi, the father of modern biochemistry, discovered neurotransmitters in 1921. Remarkably, the experiment came to him in a dream. He woke up, wrote it down, and immediately went back to sleep. Next morning he looked at what he had written, aware that it was something momentous – only to discover that his writing was completely illegible, almost as if it were in some unknown language.

"Loewi spent the day in a state of extreme frustration," I told them. "To his amazement, though, the next night he had exactly the same dream again. This time he took no chances. Rushing to his lab in his pyjamas, he immediately set up the experiment he had dreamt about. Taking a beating frog's heart, with its vagus nerve still attached – luckily he happened to have some beating frogs' hearts to hand, or history might have been very different – he suspended it in a jar of saline solution, into which he introduced a second beating heart." I sketched the experiment on the board. "When the first heart was made to slow down, he observed that, after an interval, the second *followed suit*, thus proving beyond all doubt the existence of a chemical messenger between the two." (*Figure 13*)

Miss G listened to all this with an expression of intense concentration, occasionally jotting down a note. (What had Susan called her in her report – dreamy? There was certainly nothing dreamy about her that afternoon. In fact, she was one of the few people in the audience giving me their full attention, and one of only two to chuckle at my joke about Loewi having some beating

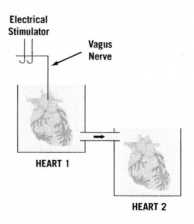

Figure 13: This experiment came to Loewi in a dream.

frogs' hearts to hand – and the other was Helen Chang, who laughs at everything.)

When I had finished my introduction I organised the students into small groups to replicate the experiment. This soon led to the usual undergraduate chaos – escaping frogs leaping all over the place, some trailing their half-removed hearts; iron-deficient and hung-over students fainting when they put the knife in, and so on. I went over to see how Miss G was getting on. I was pleased to note that she displayed no trace of squeamishness as she carefully prised an amphibious heart from its owner.

"I hope you don't mind," she said, looking up. "You mentioned the other day that you were covering this topic."

It is in fact a point of principle at our university that any lecture is open to any student, so she had a perfect right to be there. I just expressed surprise that she had time.

"I've given up going to my English seminars. They're so unbelievably dull. Nothing but the lecturer's stupid opinions."

"You should have been a scientist," I said without thinking. "We only deal in hard facts."

There was a brief pause, during which it seemed to me that Miss G was blushing slightly.

"Do you really think I could be?"

"What?"

"A scientist."

"You mean – switch subjects?" I said, surprised.

"Yes." Miss G bent her head back over her frog. "It's because of you."

"Me!"

"You and Susan. The way you talk about things. You even make sex interesting."

The student next to her paused, his scalpel in mid air.

"Yes," I said. "Well, sex *is* interesting. What does your supervisor say?"

"He *definitely* thinks sex is interesting," she said with just a hint of bitterness.

"I meant about switching."

Miss G speared the frog viciously with her scalpel. "I haven't talked to him yet."

"You should really discuss it with him before you do anything else," I said. "Giving up a DPhil isn't something to be undertaken lightly."

15.2

After the lecture was over Miss G and I found that we were the last two people in the lecture hall, so after she had helped me tidy up the bits of dead frog we left the faculty building together, talking about Loewi and the whole problem of neurotransmitters and their identification, and moving on from that to the odd/even rule of *Star Trek* movies.[2]

Without my even noticing it, we had reached the corner of Broad Street, opposite the Bodleian Library. It was one of those beautiful Oxford spring evenings, the honey-red sun slipping down behind Trinity, taking the warmth of the day with it. Outside the King's Arms, where our paths would take us in different directions, we stopped, still talking. Miss G shivered.

"I'm sorry. I'm going on as usual," I said.

"No, it's fascinating. I'm just a bit –"

"Would you like to – ?"

"Why not?"

[2] It is widely believed amongst fans that the even-numbered films in the *Star Trek* series are better than the odd-numbered ones. Lest this be dismissed as a subjective or self-fulfilling perception, a group of statisticians have analysed the films' respective scores on the Internet Movie Database and subjected the data to a Mann-Whitney test – that is, a non-parametric statistical hypothesis for assessing whether samples of observations have significantly valid differences. This indicates a 99% confidence in the statement that, for example, *First Contact* is better than *Search for Spock*.

We sat in a quiet corner, two pints of beer in front of us.

"Oh, it was just one of those random things," I explained. "My real interest was hiccups."

"Why hiccups?"

"Well, they're fascinating too, in their way. And relatively unstudied. As a scientist, that's what you're always on the lookout for – areas of interesting ignorance. 'Do Hamsters Get Hiccups?' – that was the title of one of my early papers. It turned out they didn't. I need hardly tell you the implications of *that*."

"That some animals don't get hiccups?"

"Exactly. And therefore – the question we must always ask – what are hiccups *for*? People used to assume it was something to do with the swallowing reflex – hence all the old wives' tales about drinking a glass of water upside down. But then I observed that bonobo apes had a particular way of stopping their hiccups –"

"Which was?"

"Having sex."

"Really? And that goes for humans too? If you have hiccups, sex can stop them?"

I nodded.[3] "The bonobo had worked it out, and we hadn't. That's why

---

[3] In order to avoid boring Miss G, my nod rather oversimplified the current state of research on sex and hiccups. See, for example, the pioneering paper by husband-and-wife researchers Roni and Anne Peleg: Sexual intercourse as a potential treatment for intractable hiccups, *Can. Fam. Physician* 2000: "On the fourth day of continuous hiccupping, the patient had sexual intercourse with his wife. The hiccups continued throughout the sexual interlude up until the moment of ejaculation when they suddenly and completely ceased." They conclude, "It is unclear whether orgasm in women leads to a similar resolution, an issue which could be investigated further." Indeed. Several commentators have noted that singultus (the medical term for severe hiccupping) is more frequent in men than women: some women report that they have never had a hiccup, others that they have never had an orgasm. Are they the same women? Is there an overlap? So much remains to be done.

it's so important to keep studying species like theirs: they know so much more than we do. Anyway, I was talking it over with Richard – I'd happened to bump into him on the stairs – when he said, 'There's your next project, Steven. Why don't you see if humans can get some of what those apes are getting?' And of course it turned out to be an area that had access to vast amounts of funding." I glanced at her. "How about you? Why did you end up doing English?"

She shrugged. "I'd always preferred science, actually. But Miss Liddell had this notion that blowing things up and making unpleasant smells was strictly for the boys. Us girls were steered towards the more artistic subjects. Like drama. God, how I loathed drama!" she said with feeling. "What was the point of giving a performance when you had to come back and give it all over again? Literature too – I can see the point of reading a book. But why sit around and *talk* about it?"

"But you must have been good at those subjects."

She nodded. "Straight As. Well, it was hardly difficult."

That explained something which had been puzzling me. The fact was, Miss G was so unusually clever that she had even been able to excel in subjects she didn't particularly like.

"And now you want to try to do science full time?"

She nodded. "If you don't think it's completely unfeasible."

"I'm afraid I do. Think it's unfeasible, I mean. Utterly unfeasible."

"Really?" she said, clearly taken aback by my answer.

"Science isn't a subject, Miss G. It's a *discipline* – a way of thinking. You can't just pick it up and study it like a new period of literature or a course in flower arranging. Without a solid grounding in the basics, you'd find yourself falling into error on a daily basis. I'm sorry to be the bearer of bad news, but it would be grossly irresponsible of me to suggest anything different."

"Oh," she said in a rather small voice. "I see."

Her attention was fixed on the table between us, where she began turning a blob of spilt beer into an irregular dodecahedron with her finger. Her long hair fringed her face, falling almost to the table, only slightly lighter in colour than the latter's polished surface. I felt a surge of tenderness, mingled with what I can only describe as a ferocious and involuntary vasodilation. In short, I was having an RAE. Luckily the moment passed without Miss G noticing.

I coughed. "But that's not to say that you can't continue to take a keen interest. As an amateur, I mean. How are you getting on with *Enzymes*?"

"Oh – I've reached the last chapter. It's very interesting, actually," she said with a heavy sigh. "Did you know there's a mud snail called *Potamopyrgus antipodarum* which switches between sexual and asexual reproduction to ward off parasite attacks? So Professor Collins hypothesises that all of sexual reproduction may have evolved from nothing more than a parasite infestation."

"That would make sense," I said thoughtfully. "Reproduction lets us shuffle our genes more rapidly."

"And there's more. He argues that if sex evolved in response to a parasite, it would quite naturally have taken on parasite-like properties itself."

"But that's brilliant!" Once again the sheer audacity of Richard's insights took my breath away. "It means that rather than human beings using sex to reproduce –"

"*Sex* is a parasite which uses *humans* to reproduce. Exactly. And that makes you look at the whole problem of sexual dysfunction a different way, doesn't it? For example, instead of developing a treatment to make women with low libido *more* interested in sex, you could solve the problem from the other end – you could start developing a treatment to make everyone else less interested. In fact, it would be much more logical."

"That's a very interesting suggestion, Annie," I said. "That could potentially be a doctoral thesis, right there. It might even open up a whole new area for research – "

"I know." She sighed again. "Unfortunately, for the moment I seem to be stuck with Victorian semicolons."

"Perhaps I spoke too hastily. If you had a mentor – someone who could teach you the basics, but also steer you in the right direction with reading lists and so on – perhaps it might just be possible to switch subjects after all."

"Yes," she said. "A mentor. That is *exactly* what I need."

As she looked at me, nodding, I wondered how I could ever have described her features as unremarkable.

"A good postgraduate or junior research fellow could probably teach you all you need to know in a couple of terms," I said.

She nodded again, even more enthusiastically. There was a long pause. She seemed to be waiting for me to say something else.

"I'd offer to do it myself," I added. "If only I weren't so busy. With the FSD study, I mean."

"Oh. Yes, I can imagine." Her face was once again hidden by her hair as she added some antennae to her dodecahedron.

"We've got a big conference coming up. There's no way I'd have time to teach chemistry to a beginner."

"Of course." She sounded a little wistful. "Perhaps I'd better just stick to being on your study, then. That is, if I'm still useful."

"You're extremely useful," I said. "In fact you're more than useful: you're really quite interesting. There are several aspects of your sexual data I'd certainly like to investigate further."

15.4

Not long after that, Miss G had to go. As she walked away, though, on an impulse I called her name.

"Miss G? Annie?"

She turned.

"There was something I wanted to ask you, actually. Something quite important."

Once again a Duchenne smile lit up her face.

"Last time, in the lab," I continued. "Did you have an orgasm?"

Her smile faded, and she shook her head. It was not clear to me, however, whether she was replying to my question in the negative or simply reacting to the fact that I had asked it at all.

"Men," she said disbelievingly. "You're all the bloody same, aren't you? All you care about is whether you can make me come."

As she pulled open the door – with what seemed to me to be unnecessary force – she paused again. "To answer your question, Dr Fisher, I've had more enjoyable afternoons at the dentist having a root canal drilled."

Which was, I'm sure you'll agree, a strange response to a perfectly reasonable enquiry on my part.

Although, of course, it is just possible that Miss G has an unusually attractive dentist.

So, still undecided about whether or not I am actually attracted to Steven Fisher, or if I should be trying to change to science, or both, I went along to one of his lectures to see if I understood it. And I did, mostly. Actually, it was pretty amazing. Did you know that two hearts can send chemical messages to each other, so that whatever one heart does, the other heart does too? OK, put like that it starts to sound like a metaphor from some stupid Victorian novel. But at the time it was just a fascinating bit of science. (And it's so nice, incidentally, to talk to people for whom things really are just what they appear to be and not some complicated symbol for something else entirely). Then afterwards we walked out of the seminar building together, talking. Talking about – everything. Our favourite films, and how he got into orgasms in the first place, and what he really wants to do – which is find a cure for hiccups – and –

And it's a beautiful Oxford sunset, the last rays of the sun hitting the honey-coloured stone of the colleges so that they almost seem to glow from the inside. He looks up and says, "Ah, look at that remarkable refraction. It's because the earth's atmosphere is filtering out the longer wavelengths of light, of course."

And in that moment, I realise that, whatever my feelings are for Steven Fisher, they are a) definitely not just physical and b) not just to do with KXC79.

Damn.

Then we're in the pub. Where I do a little fishing to try and find out what he thinks about *me*.

At which point he makes it pretty evident that a) I don't have what it takes to be a scientist and b) to him I'm just an interesting source of sexual data.

So that's that. Not that I was seriously thinking about any other possibility, you understand, but it's good to have things absolutely clear. So that we both know exactly where we are.

All the same, I feel remarkably depressed.

UrlGirl67 ☺
"When the only tool you have is a hammer,
you tend to treat every problem as if it's a nail"

On the following Tuesday Miss G came in for her fourth session. On this occasion my colleague Dr Minstock administered the series of standardised stimulation programmes known as the Duchowski sequence, involving visual, neurostimulatory and transcutaneous cues presented in a steadily escalating progression.

Miss G again reported that she felt no arousal or sexual response of any kind. In this session, however, the instruments seemed to confirm, rather than contradict, her statement. Even the GSA, to my surprise, showed absolutely nothing – what we call a flatliner.

Miss G seemed to me to be unusually quiet during this visit. She made few remarks, even in response to a direct question on my part about the final section of *Enzymes and Influences*. I can only recall one unprompted comment she volunteered that day, in fact: when the tests were finished and she was departing, she muttered something under her breath that sounded like: "There. Happy now?"

17.2

Later, upon examining the data more closely, I noticed that after seven minutes a series of jiggles appeared in the response line (*Figure 14*). "Look – there is *something* here," I said to my colleague.

Susan shook her head. "Ghosting from the stimulators. I had everything right up to the max."

"And we're sure she felt nothing?"

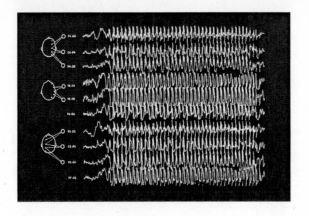

Figure 14: Secondary vibration from the stimulators.

"Of course she *felt* it – it would have been like standing next to someone digging up the road with a jackhammer. It just didn't *do* anything for her. Face it, Steve – it's a big fat zilch."

I brought up the other data. Temperature – nothing. Galvanicity – Miss G had broken a sweat, but not in the steadily escalating pattern that indicates arousal. On every measurement, she had shown minimal response.

"Maybe you need to look at the formulation again," Susan suggested.

"Maybe," I said doubtfully.

To recap: in her first session, Miss G had received the treatment and it hadn't worked. In her second and third, she had received the treatment and denied that it worked, even though the machines clearly showed that it had. In the fourth, she had received the same treatment, said it hadn't worked, and it hadn't.

This was getting more, not less, confusing.

Once again I emailed Richard Collins explaining my predicament, and once again I received no reply. Checking his website, I saw that he was currently engaged in a five-continent PR tour to promote *Enzymes and Influences*. So, somewhat reluctantly, I turned to Wulf instead.

"Wulf," I said as we left the faculty building together that evening, "that girl who said she wasn't having orgasms is now not having orgasms."

He considered. "Then you have, surely, no problem."

"But I still don't know why she was saying she wasn't having orgasms when she was," I pointed out. "And I certainly don't know why she isn't having them now. As for not having a problem, at the very least her current result means KXC79 isn't doing what it's meant to do."

"On one level, that simply indicates the existence of a profound submolecular chaos –"

"Unfortunately," I retorted, somewhat tersely, "I have to give a paper at a major international conference in just over five weeks' time. At which I do not want there to be a single submolecule of doubt that KXC79 does exactly what we are claiming it does."

"Ah."

"Ah indeed."

"In the case of Rhona's orgasms, I was able to prove their existence by means of a simple experiment," he said thoughtfully.

"What!"

He nodded. "I was worried by what you said – you know, about the possibility she was faking. So I borrowed a few basic testing devices from the lab and checked."

"But that's unethical!"

He looked a little shamefaced. "Perhaps. But I needed to know."

"How did you carry out the measurements without her realising?" I asked, interested despite myself.

"Air temperature, electrical charge, pheromone density. I doubt it's as accurate as lab readings, but it was good enough for my purposes."

"And what was the result? Did you get the answer you wanted?"

He looked even more crestfallen. "Not exactly. It seems sometimes she is lying, and sometimes she is telling the truth."

"Well, that's not too bad. Think of Schrödinger's Cat. On average, Rhona's moderately aroused by you."

"Yes," he said doubtfully. "On a submolecular level, Rhona's pussy does tend to confirm Schrödinger's Cat."

We were silent for a while, each contemplating our differing problems.

"So what you're suggesting," I said at last, "is that I need not only to establish the facts about Annie, but also to carry out some experiments to see if they hold true under different testing conditions."

"'Theory guides, but experiment decides,'" he said, quoting one of Professor Collins' favourite sayings. "Remove the guesswork, Steven, and what's left is science."

17.4

The key to research is to keep an open mind. Not many people know, for example, that Viagra was originally devised as a treatment for angina – it was only because an alert researcher followed up reports of some unexpected side effects that its potential as a treatment for male sexual dysfunction was spotted. Sometimes, what appears to be a problem turns out to be a solution in disguise.

However, this sort of discovery can only happen if you are accurately testing what your treatment is doing. This usually requires two separate groups, one of which unknowingly receives a placebo, a dummy pill, instead of the real treatment. On a more basic level, you can use the same test subject but swap the treatment periodically for a placebo, to see what difference that makes: without telling the test subject, obviously. Fortunately, I already had some dummy pills made up – the ones I had locked in Julian Noble's cupboard. I went and took out half a dozen, marking the pill bottle with a small X so that I could tell them from the regular pills.

As I was returning to my desk I happened to glance at the control room and noticed that the microphone light was flashing, just as it did in response to someone talking during a test session. I went to switch it off – and as I did so, heard tiny voices coming from the headphones that were lying on the desk. Curious as to why anybody should be in the testing room at that time, I raised them to my ears.

I didn't recognise the person speaking for a moment – in contrast to the soft, calm tones Heather usually employed, now she sounded tense, even angry.

I heard her say: "…because if this goes on, I'll have no choice but to make an accusation of sexual harassment against you."

After a moment Susan's voice said pleadingly, "Please – I'd do anything, you know that. Anything for you. Just don't tell me that there's no chance –"

I sighed, and switched the microphone off. There was a time, before Sexual Endocrinology, when I had wondered whether Heather and I might one day, perhaps, be more than just co-workers. That moment had passed – and now, listening to Susan's undignified, desperate pleading, I couldn't but help feel relieved that I had avoided the emotional and ethical complications such a development would inevitably have led to. It was the same with Wulf's problems with Rhona. It was always better in the long run, I reflected, to keep personal feelings out of the workplace.

Simon's away at some conference in Philadelphia. Thank God. We could both do with a break from each other.

I go into college for Swamps and Sorcerers night. Don't have to think about Simon or Steven all evening. But I do. In fact, after we've rid the Malevolent Marsh of hydrochloric imps I go for a drink with Beth, who's the Swampmaster, and talk about it endlessly.

"Look," she says when I eventually grind to a halt. "What you're basically saying is that you've finally realised Simon's a bit of a creep, right?"

I nod doubtfully.

"And as part of all that you've developed a slightly unlikely crush on this scientist person."

I nod again.

"The thing is, none of that's remotely surprising. It's like fancying your shrink – a classic case of transference. All it means is that you're suffering from low self-esteem because of your defective sexuality."

"Ye-es," I say. Beth's subject, as you may have gathered, is psychology. And while I can't fault her logic, something about this interpretation of events doesn't quite ring true to me.

"So it's pretty obvious what you've got to do," she concludes. "Finish the treatment, dump Simon, and start dating."

"Dating!" I groan.

"No pain, no gain. You could always use an online dating site."

I sigh. The truth is, the thought of dating just makes me feel weary. Why bother to go through all that, just to end up with someone you don't like any better than the person you dumped? Better to stick with the status quo.

"Thanks, Beth," I say. "But Simon and I are fine. It's just a rough patch. Really."

She shrugs. "If you say so."

Back at the house there's a message from Simon asking me to call him on the hotel switchboard. When I can't get through, I try his mobile – and hear it ringing down the back of the sofa. As I'm fishing it out, my own phone rings again. It's him, calling from his room.

"You left your mobile," I tell him.

"I know," he says. "Just switch it off, will you?"

"OK." I pick it up. "Oh my, you're mister popular. Nine unread messages. Want me to read them to you?"

"No," he says quickly. "Just switch the damn thing off. It'll be great not to have it beeping away all the time."

Too late.

Ever Simon's eager little helper, I've opened the first message. Cindy from nostrings.com. Downstairs in the bar, just like she said she'd be. Waiting.

"Annie?" Simon says. "Annie? Have you turned it off?"

I disconnect him. Then I scroll down the list of messages. Deborah from FunInPhilly.com, looking forward to their meeting. Delilah from XXX Escorts. And a couple more which seem to reinforce the idea that Simon's busy making up for lost time.

The fucking, fucking *bastard*.

UrlGirl67 ☺

"When the only tool you have is a hammer,
you tend to treat every problem as if it's a nail"

I call him back to tell him he's a cheating slimeball and a pathetic excuse for a human being. I tell him he's a spineless, amoral, pathological liar. By now I've been to his inbox and read his emails too – though I notice that it's only the ones promising "dirty flirty adventures" and "commitment-free naughtiness" he's bothered to reply to.

He listens to it all spilling out of me and it seems to me that he just sighs. Like this has been coming for a long time.

Then I get all my things together and move them out of his house.

Best to do it right away, you see. Before I start crying.

UrlGirl67 ☺
"When the only tool you have is a hammer,
you tend to treat every problem as if it's a nail"

The following Tuesday, I was at the lab at the appointed time, waiting for Miss G. In a paper cup I had some of the dummy pills. However, on this occasion an important variable was missing: Miss G herself.

Twenty minutes went by. "Looks like she isn't coming," Susan said, glancing at the clock.

After half an hour I had to admit Susan might be right. "Give it ten more minutes, just in case."

When ten minutes were up, Susan disconnected the neurostimulators and the session was terminated.

20.2

The days went by. Still there was no communication from Miss G.

On Thursday morning, the time for her test session came and went with no sign of her.

It wasn't the first time such a thing had happened, of course. In the nosebleed phase of our research, even the Ukrainian prostitutes only seemed to turn up when it was raining. But Miss G was different, I was sure of it. Something had to be very wrong.

To: urlgirl67@hotmail.com
From: Fisher.s@nb.ac.uk

Dear Miss G,

I have retrieved your email address from the back page of *Over the Knee* (Locke, Fiona, 2008), where you were kind enough to write it, along with your postal address.

I could not help but notice that you have not been present for your last two appointments. That is all very well, but you still have my copy of *Enzymes and Influences: How Biochemistry Built Our Brains*, by R.A Collins (Palaton Press, 2008). I shall be in your vicinity this afternoon, so I will drop by and pick it up.

Kind regards,
Steven Fisher

"Oh, it's you," she said tersely as she opened the front door.

She looked tired. Her hair, which was unwashed, was pulled back and fastened with an elastic band, and she was wearing a scruffy old tracksuit. Even her skin seemed more pallid than usual. Although – to my great relief – I could see no signs of acne, there was a small pimple high up on her forehead.

"May I come in?" I asked.

"Well, I suppose you're here now," she said grudgingly, standing back.

It was a typical Oxford graduate house, off the Iffley Road. There were bicycles in the hallway and, on the stairs, piles of junk mail from academic journals addressed to long-departed residents. Her own flat, though, was a surprise. I'd been expecting – well, cosy Victoriana, I suppose: dainty teacups, teddy bears, clothes drying everywhere, the usual female clutter. But it was nothing like that. In the kitchen there was a life-sized cardboard figure of Chewbacca, the hairy hominid from the *Star Wars* films. He was wearing a necklace of computer cables. More cables were festooned around the furniture, and there were bits of what looked like computer hard drive on the kitchen table. Even more incongruously, next to the fridge was a flip-pad on an easel. The top page was covered in what appeared to be wiring diagrams.

"Sorry about the mess," she said abruptly. "I'm networking my peripherals." She hung another LAN lead around Chewbacca's neck.

"Looks like a big job," I commented.

"It's keeping me busy." There was a brief pause. "I'm sorry I haven't been in touch, Dr Fisher. But you're here now, so I can tell you to your face. I won't be coming back to your study."

"Was it something we did?"

"Let's just say it's no longer relevant." Suddenly her eyes were brimming with tears. "It's the way I was made. It's like he said. I'm a – a defective frigid *failure*."

A tear spilled over her lower eyelid and made its way down the soft skin of her cheek, as slowly and deliberately as a snail. With a gulp she turned away from me. A desperate choking sob escaped her throat.

She put her hand over her eyes, as if she couldn't bear to have me see her crying – like a child who thinks that because it can't see, it can't in turn be seen – and that gesture, so futile and yet so vulnerable, touched me almost as much as the tears themselves. I took a step towards her. How I longed to take her in my arms and hold her, to encase her in the protective strength of my embrace until those sobs were gone!

But I didn't.

Instead I said, "There have been some interesting studies recently about crying – or lacrymation, to give it its proper name. Tears, it has been shown, contain the chemicals lysozyme, lipocalin and lactoferrin, as well as concentrations of the hormones produced by the body when stressed. So crying really does make you feel better. You are literally flushing the emotions out of your system."

She took a deep, shuddering breath, but otherwise made no sound.

"And yet humans are among a very small group of animals which cry," I continued. "Why? There may be a clue in the fact that saltwater crocodiles lacrymate, while freshwater ones do not. Crying may be a relic of a distant episode in our evolutionary history, when we lived in the sea like dolphins."

Both her cheeks were now lacquered with moisture. I took another step towards her, helpless to comfort her, my hands twitching awkwardly by my sides. "Whales, elephants and even pigs do it," I gabbled, "but chimpanzees and apes do not. When Bob Dylan wrote, "It takes a lot to laugh, it takes a train to cry," he was in fact revealing his ignorance, not only of locomotive engineering, but of basic biochemistry."

"Please shut up," she said in a strangled voice. And then, almost as if she were doing it without thinking – almost as if she were ignorant of what a momentous step it was – she had buried her face in my chest, and the dampness of her cheeks was on my neck. As if of their own accord my arms wrapped themselves around her, and the top of her head nestled against my chin.

I hardly dared to breathe. Images flipped through my mind. I was falling through space and time. I was in the shallow waters of a green lagoon, warmed by the tropical sun. But somehow I was, not just under water, but *of* the water; an aquatic porpoise-like creature, like nothing I had ever seen before. And there, nosing towards me in the warm sea, was another of the same species. As our sleek bodies touched, everything exploded into pieces, and then…then…

It seemed to me that her tears had subsided, a little.

"Miss G," I said to the top of her head. "I came here today to ask a very important favour."

"What?" she said, without lifting her head.

"You are of course at liberty to withdraw from the study at any time. But the truth is…" I hesitated. "The truth is that if you pull out now, I will have to abandon the whole project. You represent the final hurdle – the last box I have to tick before I publish. With you, I have a treatment. Without you, I don't."

She raised her head to look at me wonderingly, her bluey-grey-green eyes still big with tears.

"I can't tell you how important this is to me. Miss G, I am placing myself in your hands."

She took a step back. Tearing off a piece of kitchen roll, she blew her nose.

"Please, hear me out," I went on desperately. "I also believe that whatever is wrong with you – whatever problems you have been having – *I can solve them*. You can make the KXC79 project work, and KXC79 can make *you* work. All I ask is that you think about it – and that if you withdraw, you do so knowing that science may be the poorer for it."

"But what you don't seem to have grasped," she said flatly, "is that my boyfriend and I have split up. And since I was only doing this to please him in the first place, there's precious little point in going on. Personally I don't care if I'm cured or not. In fact, I think I'm happier as I am." She threw the paper towel in the bin. "And now I'd like you to go away, please."

The following days are pretty miserable ones. It's like a bad dream (even the bit – can it really have happened? – when Dr Fisher comes round and tells me that I can't come off his study or he won't be able to write me up for publication).

And then, gradually, I start to realise something.

I'm not actually as upset as I ought to be.

It's like when you cut yourself – sometimes, it just doesn't hurt as much as you think it's going to. I'd been dreading the break-up with Simon for so long that now it's actually happened it really isn't as bad as I'd feared.

And I think Simon, too – once the inevitable drunken phone calls and the tears and the rambling grovelling emails are out of the way – is only going through the motions. If anything, he seems just as relieved as I am that it's finally over.

I even start to think about what I might do with myself next. Fresh start, new chapter, all that stuff. Because this is more than a break-up, isn't it? This is an *opportunity*.

And I find myself thinking about Steven Fisher again.

Not in that way, you understand. Because one thing I'm very clear about is that I don't intend to get into another mess like the one I did with Simon, sleeping with my supervisor.

Ah, I hear you say. But didn't Dr Fisher make it quite clear he wasn't interested in being your supervisor?

True.

But I've had this germ of an idea. Which, the more I think about it, seems less and less like a germ and more and more like a way to take control again. A way to change my life.

And this time I won't be taking no for an answer.

UrlGirl67 ☺

"When the only tool you have is a hammer,
you tend to treat every problem as if it's a nail"

To: Fisher.s@nb.ac.uk
From: urlgirl67@hotmail.com
Subject: **Study**

Dear Dr Fisher,

Can you meet me in the Museum of Natural History at four o'clock? There's something we need to discuss.

Annie Gluck

She was waiting for me under the skeleton of *Tyrannosaurus rex*. She seemed different, somehow. More purposeful. More *determined*.

"Miss G," I said, "what is it? Why are we meeting here?"

"This is where it happened, isn't it?" She gazed around her. "The debate that launched the theory of evolution. Right here, in this room."

"Indeed." I have imagined that scene so many times – the dinosaurs and the stuffed birds watching over the heads of the audience; the great crowd of men with their black frock coats and Victorian mutton-chop whiskers held spellbound by the two principals as they argued back and forth, speaking the words that would revolutionise the way men thought about science, about God, about life itself. Sometimes, in my most private moments, I have dared to dream that the launch of KXC79 might also be an occasion of such historic significance. "But I fail to see –"

"To finish your paper, you need me on your study," she said matter-of-factly.

I nodded.

"Then I'll do it," she continued. "I'll help you. But I have a condition. And it's not negotiable."

"Name it," I said, vastly relieved.

"I want a job in your lab. As one of your interns. I want to help you write the KXC79 paper."

I stared at her, open-mouthed.

"I've been writing Simon's for years," she went on calmly. "I can do the citations, look up references, format the footnotes…[1] And I'm a far better stylist than you are – the syntax in that last paper you published was almost ungraspable."

"But…why?"

"If KXC79 is going to be as big as you say it is, once my name's on that paper I'll be able to walk into any university in the country and get a place on a science degree course. I'm changing disciplines. I've decided."

"Miss G," I said, as politely as I could, "this is all very well, and naturally I wish you good luck in your endeavour to become a scientist, but what you seem to have overlooked is that the assistants who work for me are accomplished biochemists in their own right. You, as I understand it, are not."

"Of course," she went on as if I hadn't spoken, "you'll have to teach me a certain amount of basic science as well. It shouldn't be too onerous. After all, I've got an IQ of a hundred and sixty-two. Even if I *have* been wasting it on Victorian poetry for the last five years."

"I'll think about it," I said, slightly annoyed.

"No, you won't. No teaching, no tests. If you don't agree, KXC79 is history. Like that iguanodon over there." She looked at me levelly. "Well? What's it to be?"

It was becoming apparent to me that Miss G had planned this meeting thoroughly – and that, moreover, she was not going to be swayed from her intention. If I wanted her back on the study, I would have to give her a job.

Fatally, I hesitated. "I suppose it's not completely unprecedented. Take

---

[1] Formatting footnotes, as Miss G observed, is a tedious business. Every time you add or subtract a paragraph or two, anywhere in the paper, all the footnotes shift position, and it can be the very devil trying to get the footnote back onto the same page as the sentence it relates to. For example, this footnote I am typing now has been on six different pages during the process of tonight's redrafting. I am not trying to justify the fact that I succumbed to Miss G's extraordinary proposal, but having someone take care of all the typographical details does save a lot of time. As I write this, now, I could sorely do with Miss G's assistance. In fact, I could sorely do with her presence in many, many ways.

Virginia Johnson – she started off as William Masters' secretary, but eventually she became a respected researcher in her own right."[2]

"So that's a yes?"

"Oh – very well, then. For the time being."

"There's one other thing."

"What's that?"

"This is going to be complicated enough without any personal feelings getting in the way. From now on, this is all about the science. And nothing but the science."

"Of course," I said, slightly mystified that she saw the necessity to make this stipulation.

"Then we have a deal," she said. "You'd better give me a reading list. I've obviously got a lot to catch up on."

I had been outmanoeuvred – and by an arts graduate, of all people. But – somewhat to my surprise – I found that I did not mind at all.

Quite apart from anything else, I reasoned, it would give me an opportunity to study her at much closer quarters. If I couldn't solve the puzzle under these conditions, it probably couldn't be solved at all.

[2] Sex researchers Masters and Johnson married in 1969 and divorced in 1999, citing pressure of work as a factor in their marital break-up. Incidentally, Americans still refer to penises as "Johnsons" – immortality of a sort. I am not, however, aware of any women who call their pudenda "Masters".

The others were somewhat surprised to learn that someone with none of the usual qualifications would be joining us as an assistant. But when I explained the unusual circumstances they soon rallied round.

"It's not like we're busy," Rhona pointed out.

"It'll be such fun going through Energetics again," Heather added. "There's so much about enthalpic reactions I've almost completely forgotten."

Rhona lent Miss G a lab coat and some goggles. A timetable was drawn up – biology, differentials, organic chemistry, kinetics, compounds, analytical chemistry; all interspersed with daily sessions to measure Miss G's sexual responsiveness. Now that she was on the staff, I saw no reason not to subject her to an even more rigorous regime of tests than previously.

"And we're going to be having regular breaks for pelvic floor exercises," Susan warned, to a chorus of groans from the others. "In fact, we'll get rid of these chairs altogether – if we replace them with exercise balls, we can all flex our PC muscles while we're studying."

"What about you, Dr Fisher?" Rhona called.

"Am I going to replace my chair with an exercise ball?"

"No – what will you teach Annie?"

"What's left?"

Rhona looked down the timetable. "We don't have anyone taking care of chemical bonding yet."

I bowed. "In that case, bonding it is. I shall brush up on my noble gases forthwith."

When I think back to those days – that brief, intense period during which we taught Miss G the rudiments of the scientific method – I find that my own scientific method deserts me, and I am no longer capable of thinking rationally. For all that they were days of anxiety, pressure and frustration, they were also some of the most rewarding days of my life.

There is an old saying that the teacher learns as much as the pupil. When you have a pupil as bright and enquiring as Miss G, it is certainly the case. As I explained things to her, I often found that I myself was looking at them with fresh eyes – browny-grey-blue eyes: certain long-held assumptions suddenly seemed questionable or curious, and more than one topic was mentally earmarked for further investigation at a later date. There was no time for that now, of course: there was no time for anything except the project. But despite our workload, I sometimes found myself day-dreaming, my attention wandering as I remembered some especially delightful insight she had made in our last tutorial session, or her look of wonder as yet another facet of the natural world became comprehensible to her.

I even bought flowers for the lab – great armfuls of daffodils, irises and tulips, the fresh, vibrant colours of spring. If the others thought this was odd or out of character, they made no comment – we were all caught up in it, in the excitement of working together on the approaching launch.

And yet, all the time, we were sleepwalking to disaster. And that, too, is part of the bitter-sweet taste of my memories of those days: the knowledge that, for all our expertise, we were completely ignorant of the dark times that lay ahead.

But all that, of course, was much later: I must be careful not get ahead of myself.

"Basically, you've got chemical reactions which take place in one direction – that is, they're irreversible," I heard Rhona's voice say. "Then you've got others where the products combine and reform the reactants. Those will eventually reach a state of equilibrium in which –"

"– both reactants and products are present?"

"Excellent! I think you've got this."

I glanced through the open door of Rhona's cubicle. The two women were sitting on those ridiculous silver exercise balls. On the desk was an open coursebook. Two sets of brown hair fringed its pages.

"So," Rhona said. "Ready for homogenous reactions?"

"Bring 'em on."

I must have made a sound, because one set of hair turned. Miss G looked up and flashed me a radiant smile before turning back to the book.

"Let's start with Haber-Bosch," Rhona said. "Now, this is a process particularly used in industrial laboratories…"

Does it seem so very strange to say that this was a perfect moment, one that I will treasure all my life?

24.4

"Goodnight, Dr Fisher."

"Goodnight, Heather."

"'Night, Dr F."

"Goodnight, Rhona. Wulf, I'll call you."

Wulf waved as the two of them left.

"I'll see you tomorrow, Steven," Susan said, putting on her coat.

"Yes. And Susan…thank you for all your help."

"No problem. Annie and I covered a lot of ground today, actually. She's a smart girl."

"She's certainly that. What's she doing now?"

"I've left her a reading pile. I think she has homework from Rhona, too."

"OK. I'll see how she's getting on."

I have always enjoyed the stillness of a deserted laboratory. Sometimes it feels to me as if this is the one place in the world where I am completely and utterly at home – like a fish in water, or a meercat in sand: this is my element; almost as if I had been designed for it. I often stay late after the others have gone, just to enjoy the sense of peaceful, purposeful solitude.

But tonight, there was no solitude. Despite the silence, Miss G was there, in Rhona's little cubbyhole, working her way through her reading list.

And somehow it felt even more peaceful – even more right – than it did when I was alone.

I walked over to Rhona's door. Miss G was there, but she wasn't working. Her head was resting on a pile of open books amidst a swirl of conker-glossy hair, her eyes closed.

I picked up her ringbinder.

"What?" she said, starting upright.

"These are pretty good," I said, flicking through her notes. "You've mixed up sodium chloride and sodium carbonate. But that's an easy mistake to make."

She groaned. "My head's spinning." She glanced at the clock. "Is it time for sex again?" She blinked. "Damn – that didn't come out how I meant it."

"Don't worry, I know what you meant. Go home and get some sleep."

"Nope." She yawned. "Gotta finish reacting calculations. I'm on a schedule."

"You're pretty determined to do this, aren't you?" I said quietly. "An

A-level syllabus in a week, a degree in a fortnight, your first graduate paper in less than a month…"

She nodded. "Think anyone's managed anything like it before?"

"Actually, I know they have. Eleven years ago. A schoolboy – the youngest person ever to get a science degree at Oxford."

She looked at me, suddenly thoughtful, completely alert. I could see her brain – that giant brain of hers – working away.

"So, Dr Fisher," she said at last, "any chance I can beat your record?"

"No. But you'll be the first person who's come close."

As I walked away I called, "Turn the lights off when you leave, won't you?"

24.5

Checking my inbox later that night, I found that I had been sent a Wink by a female scientist at Birmingham University. She worked in a similar field to mine – her specific area of research was the phosphorylation of fructose-6 on the glycolitic pathway – and she wrote a sweet note explaining that she'd realised she was spending too much time in the lab and not enough meeting new people. Hence she had joined the same dating site I had.

> So – basically – if you fancy meeting up for a drink, or even just going to one of the Royal Society lectures together, let me know.

> Best, Ruth Cowper.

> PS I'm attaching a photo.

It had been so long since I'd registered on the site that I'd almost forgotten about it. Ruth Cowper looked nice – beautiful, even. I knew I should reply in the affirmative. After all, why else had I joined the site, if not to meet people like her? But the truth was that I had no desire whatsoever to make a date with her. I sent a reply, hopefully polite, pleading pressure of work.

I've been way too busy to write this blog for – what, must be almost two weeks now. Too busy and – if I'm honest – too happy, too.

Science is fantastic – everything I expected and more. It's hard work – I'm trying to cover about four years' worth of syllabus in a couple of months – but I actually like a challenge as crazy as that. And it's such a relief to finally be free of that other lot – Simon, Lord Alfred Tennyson, Victorian semicolons and the Mythical Feminine (I swear I will never use a semicolon again. Except maybe as an emoticon ;-)

The lab's an interesting place – the dynamics between the five of them are interesting, I mean. There's Wulf and Rhona, trying desperately to pretend that it's just a casual thing and they don't completely adore each other. There's Susan, who now that I'm getting to know her better seems a bit sad, somehow. It's odd that someone can know so much about sex and G spots and relationships and yet be so clearly unfulfilled.

Rhona told me Susan's basically into women, which may be why things are more complicated for her.

And then there's Heather. Goodness, she's beautiful. She has these amazing cheekbones, and her eyes are so perfect, it's like she's wearing a mask. When you first meet her she seems a bit reserved, but actually there's something going on there – some slightly mischievous core that pops out at the most surprising times, rather like a glimpse of a red bra under a white lab coat.

Take yesterday. We were both in the kitchen at the same time, making coffee – and she casually asked me if I could get hold of some KXC79 for her!

I just boggled at her. "You mean – pinch some?"

She shrugged. Little glint of naughtiness in her eyes. "I mean, maybe take a few extra, and slip them my way when no one's looking. I can't believe I've spent the last twelve months helping to develop a pill that's going to give women mindblowing orgasms and I still haven't got to try some for myself."

"Can't you just ask Steven?"

She sighed. "Dr Fisher, although a sweet and lovely man, is strangely reluctant to grasp the fact that, once his invention becomes licensed, millions of women who aren't sexually dysfunctional in the least are going to be popping KXC79 just for the fun of it." A sideways look. "Those who aren't already, that is."

Does she know something? I don't see how she can. I haven't told a soul – except for this blog, of course, and I'd swear my password (which is in Middle English, with a couple of umlauts and a caesura thrown in for good measure) is so strong it can't be cracked by anyone.

She laughed, as if my hesitation had just confirmed something. "I thought you were having way too much fun in there, whatever you were telling Steven. Don't worry. I won't tell anyone."

I said hesitantly, "But I couldn't get you any pills even if I wanted to. He keeps them locked up. In Professor Noble's cupboard, I think he said."

For a moment she looked at me thoughtfully. "Professor Noble, eh?" she said. "Well, that is a coincidence."

"What is?"

But she didn't answer, and pretty soon the conversation moved back to the latest goss about Wulf and Rhona.

And then of course there's Steven. Who, it turns out, is just the most AMAZING teacher. Well, OK, he's way too bright for his own good, and he still occasionally smirks at me if I say something particularly second-rate – but at other times, he just gets fantastically, brilliantly carried away on incredible flights of thought, ideas whizzing out of his mind in all directions. He spends hours – hours! surely he ought to be too busy on his paper? – talking to me about his heroes: people like Isaac Newton and

128

Galileo Galilei and Nikola Tesla and Niels Bohr, and of course James Watson and Francis Crick. And you can tell that these people – far more than anyone living – are, in a weird way, his friends, or at any rate his peers: the people he measures himself against.

(There's Richard Collins, too, of course, but I think that's somehow different – that's more because it was Richard who first opened Steven's eyes to the possibilities of biochemistry. I somehow doubt that Richard Collins, genius though Steven thinks he is, is actually in quite the same league as Galileo.)

I'm feeling a bit guilty that I still haven't told Steven about what actually happens during the tests. Clearly I'm going to have to find some way of letting him know I'm not dysfunctional after all...while at the same time making sure he doesn't simply boot me out of the lab with a great big tick next to my name.

And I haven't forgotten my resolution not to let my feelings get involved in all this, either. But my goodness, it's an effort sometimes. Sometimes it's almost a relief when I have to break off from a tutorial to do a test. Even if my teeth are getting ground down from trying to keep quiet.

For all that Miss G was undergoing more testing than previously, we didn't actually seem to be making much headway – her results were providing much the same perplexing data as they had done before. (On the positive side, she reported that she was not feeling in the least bit drowsy during these sessions, although I had noticed that on several occasions – notably after a late night writing no fewer than four essays on ionic compounds – her eyes had been closed during the latter part of the tests.) So, while the others were teaching her, I began researching her unusual combination of symptoms on the internet.

Few people now remember that the internet was actually invented by scientists looking for a way to share information.[1] The legacy of this academic parentage still quietly survives, almost unnoticed amidst the pornography and the chat forums. Take scientific studies, for example: once stored in a dozen far-flung libraries, now they get archived online as soon as they're published. Scientists can access all of human knowledge within moments.[2]

---

[1] The first "live" image to be transmitted on the world wide web – a term that was originally intended to be ironic – was of a coffee pot at Cambridge University. According to Quentin Stafford-Fraser, "Being impoverished academics, we only had one coffee filter machine between us… Some members of the 'coffee club' lived in other parts of the building and had to navigate several flights of stairs to get to the coffeepot, a trip which often proved fruitless if the Trojan Room's all-night hackers had got there first." You can see the coffee pot's homepage at http://www.cl.cam.ac.uk/coffee/coffee.html

[2] For example, I have just used the internet to double-check that the etymology of "Johnson", meaning penis, really does come from Virginia Johnson, sex researcher. To my surprise, this derivation is by no means universally accepted. Amongst Australians, it is widely believed that it derives from "Dick Johnson", a well-known – and apparently somewhat priapic – racing

I typed in "orgasms" and "can't feel them" and then added "peer-reviewed".

There was some very interesting literature. In fact, the more I read, the more intrigued I became. It seemed that Miss G's presence on the study, despite all the problems it had precipitated, might actually have saved us from making a fundamental error in the formulation of KXC79.

"What's up?"

It was Annie herself, coming over to see what I was doing. She was sipping from a bottle of water, her face still flushed from Susan's Kegels.

"Nothing much. How are you?"

"Somewhat overwhelmed. I've just done three terms' worth of A-level modules in one morning. *And* flexed my pubococcygeus muscles at the same time."

"If this gets too much…" I warned.

"No, I'm enjoying it. But it'll be good to take a break."

"Oh – of course." It was almost noon: time for her next test session. "I'll be right with you. I just need to print these out."

"Dr Fisher?"

"Steven, please. We're colleagues now."

"Steven… Before we do today's tests…there's something I probably ought to mention."

"Yes?" The printer gave a sudden mechanical death-rattle. "Oh – damn. No paper."

She was looking a little embarrassed. "Some of those earlier results of mine… I'm just wondering if they might be open to misinterpretation."

driver. Some Americans believe it refers to a town called Dick Johnson in Indiana; others, that it refers to R.G Johnson, a baseball bat manufacturer, who burned his name into the side of his bats. Here in the UK, it is thought by some to be a corruption of "John Thomas", first used to describe the male organ in 1887, while the OED ascribes the neologism to a Canadian explorer called W.B Cheadle, who related in his *Jrnl. Trip across Canada* in 1863 how his "neck, face and jnsn" were all frozen by the inclement weather. Another suggestion is that it refers to President Lyndon Johnson, who apparently had a penchant for displaying his organ in public. There seems to be no way, now, of proving which hypothesis is correct.

"I agree. That's what I've been researching, actually. What is it *now*?" The printer was flashing an error light at me.

"American source material, perhaps? You may need to set it to US Letter instead of A4," she suggested helpfully.

"Thank you. Where were we? Oh, yes – take a look at this. 'Muffled Orgasm Syndrome: a condition in which the sufferer experiences orgasm without gaining sensation or satisfaction from it.'[3] You see, Annie, what's been puzzling me is that, according to all our readouts, you *appeared* to be orgasmic."

"Oh," she said slowly. "So the readouts told you that?"

I nodded. "At first I thought it must be some problem with the formulation. But actually it's good news."

"It is? Why?"

"Because KXC79 is all to do with the neural pathways between the brain and the sexual organs," I explained. "If *any* treatment is going to work on muffled orgasms, it's this one. Basically, it's a whole boxful of nails in the coffin of rival, testosterone-based approaches."

"So my results…they've actually been useful?"

"Very much so. If I'm right, we're going to unmuffle your orgasms and prove KXC79's validity across an entirely new subset of sexual disorders. The science is somewhat comple…complicated, but in layman's terms, we're going to vastly increase your dose. That should deal with the muffled orgasm, and restore normal function."

"And what would that mean," she said hesitantly, "for someone who already *had* normal function? Hypothetically, of course?"

"Well, you'd never give KXC79 to someone like that, obviously. But hypothetically, I think it's fair to assume you'd be scraping them off the

[3] "There were extended discussions among panellists about the introduction of a new diagnostic category of sexual satisfaction disorder. It was proposed that this diagnosis be applied when a woman is unable to achieve subjective sexual satisfaction, despite adequate desire, arousal and orgasm. It was noted by several panellists that this diagnosis applied to a significant number of women who sought help for sexual dysfunction… Further research on this topic is strongly encouraged." Basson et al, *Journal of Urology*, 163, 3, 888-893.

ceiling. If not the ceiling of the room above."

"I see," she said, in a rather small voice.

"I wonder if we should start with an 'attack' dose – quadruple it, say," I mused. "We might even blast open a whole new pathway to the genitalia." I suddenly remembered how this conversation had begun. "Didn't you have a question? Or did I answer that?"

"You answered it."

"Good. Shall we get to work?"

26.2

In her twelfth session Miss G performed a standard set of tests, with my colleague Dr Minstock running through a basic three-stage stimulation programme.

At four minutes forty seconds, Miss G began to shake. The shaking was recorded by the monitor as being at a steady 14hz. By five minutes this had increased to 18hz, and was of a markedly pronounced amplitude. Skin galvanicity of ±9.5u indicated that Miss G was now perspiring freely across her chest and neck.

At six minutes two seconds, as the alternating mild-and-forceful stimulation phase commenced, Miss G uttered what Dr Minstock described – accurately in my opinion – as "a strangled groan through gritted teeth".

At six minutes thirty-five, the first of twenty-eight internal muscular contractions began. These were at exactly 0.8 second intervals.

When the contractions ceased, Dr Minstock ended the stimulation programme. Her voice is audible on the tape at eight minutes five seconds, asking: "Anything that time, Annie?"

Miss G does not answer.

At eight minutes twelve seconds Dr Minstock repeats the question.

At eight minutes eighteen seconds – ie a full six seconds later – Miss

G replies, "I definitely. Something. That time. Yes. Little bit."

On the recording, you hear what appears to be the sound of Miss G panting. Then you hear Dr Minstock's voice again.

"Good! We seem to be making progress. I bet those Kegels are helping, too."

Kes Riley called.

"How's the ice maiden? Ohhgasm melted her knickers off yet?" he wanted to know.

"'Ohhgasm?' What happened to 'Desiree'?"

"Oh – turns out Desiree's the name of a potato. Ohhgasm's going down a storm in the focus groups. But do we have a product to go with it?"

"We're making good progress, Kes."

"'Good progress?' You mean you're stuck?"

"I mean we aren't quite there yet."

There was a sharp intake of breath at the other end of the phone. "Two and a half weeks, Steven. Two and a half weeks before you're standing on that stage at SexDys. Or not. It's in your hands."

He was right, of course. However pleasant it was to teach Miss G the rudiments of science, I had to focus on what was really important here: her sexual dysfunction. We were running out of time.

The next morning, a very large box marked "Fragile – Scientific Equipment" was delivered to the lab.

"What is it?" Heather asked, as the team of engineers who had travelled with it from Cologne began to unpack it.

"It's a brain mapper," I said. Rhona whistled.

"A what?" Susan asked.

"A brain mapper," Heather explained, "is a very powerful scanner that allows you to see neural network of a living brain in real time. All the billions of connections show up as a kind of three-dimensional electronic hairnet. They cost a fortune."

I nodded. "And we've got this one for as long as we want it, courtesy of Trock."

"What's it actually for?" Susan wanted to know.

"Well, we've established that it isn't Annie's body that's stopping her from experiencing orgasms. If it's muffled orgasm syndrome, it must be something to do with her brain. I'm hoping that if we can see exactly where the neural blockage is, we can fix it."

Next to me, Miss G was looking somewhat anxious.

"Don't worry," I said, patting her on the shoulder. "It's basically just a glorified photocopier. There's nothing to be worried about."

27.3

The results of the next set of tests were fascinating. We turned on the mapper and Miss G's brain – her beautiful, vast, Rolls-Royce of a brain – was revealed in all its glory (*Figure 15*). On the 3D monitors, it pulsed

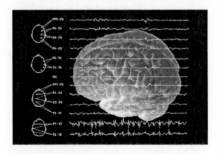

Figure 15: Miss G's brain. Note the unusually well-developed frontal lobes.

and glowed like a jellyfish in the deepest, darkest oceans. When stimulation was applied, you could actually see her sensory cortex becoming incandescent, like the coil of a lightbulb. When stimulation was alternated in intensity between mild and forceful, her motor areas flashed as if in response. And when her body was gripped by a cascade of muscular spasms, each one exactly 0.8 seconds apart, hundreds of brilliant connections flickered back and forth across the parietal lobes – a textbook firestorm that started as a warm glow in her thalamus, flared into her cingulate cortex, insula and amygdala, and finally exploded into the hypothalamus and caudate.

Yet she still reported that for her, the sensation was almost non-existent.

I sighed. There was no obvious blockage anywhere. I was still no closer to solving the puzzle.

27.4

I was at an impasse. I had at my disposal some of the most technically sophisticated diagnostic equipment known to man on the one hand, and a willing, full-time test subject on the other. It should have been the perfect opportunity to resolve the only hurdle that stood between KXC79 and its launch. Yet I was, as Kes had so aptly put it, stuck.

27.5

I needed to think. It was impossible in the lab – apart from anything else, Rhona and Susan were now retesting the Ukrainian prostitutes, who seemed quite unable to undergo any kind of sexual activity without launching into an operatic flurry of moans, yells, sobs and shrieks.

I made my way down to the basement. When Lucy saw me she bared her teeth and pointedly turned her back.

"I know, I know," I said apologetically. "Far too long. But something came up. Fancy an outing? I could do with a walk."

She danced to the bars of her cage, shaking them enthusiastically with all four hands, shrieking her agreement.

I took her to the University Parks, situated just a few minutes away. Even before we got there, Lucy was enthusiastically signing "tree" and "play", but she had to contain her impatience until we had crossed the open areas of grass. Then she was off like a bullet from a gun, straight into the trees lining the river Cherwell.

A park attendant strolled over to watch as she effortlessly hoisted herself arm over arm into the branches, before flinging herself with casual grace into the next tree. Then, catching sight of a labrador and its owner out for a stroll, she stood on a branch and started to display.

"Why's your chimp doing that?" the attendant asked curiously.

"She's not a chimp. She's a bonobo. And the reason she's doing that is –" I stopped. Better not to say that Lucy was rubbing her genitals in order to signal to any other bonobo in the vicinity that she was ready to trade sex for whoever would take care of that damned labrador. "…is because she's not very keen on dogs."

He grunted. "Don't blame her. Anyway, that one should be on a lead." And he strolled off again, to intercept the owner.

When the dog had gone Lucy and I continued on our way. It was a perfect spring afternoon, cold and clear, the ground beneath the trees covered with a mass of daffodils and crocuses that stretched, like an endless Milky Way, around the trunks; the ideal place to contemplate the enigma that was Miss G.

In front of me, two young people – students, from the look of them – were strolling hand in hand. They paused for a moment, then turned to kiss each other, oblivious to everything around them, and indeed the presence of Lucy and myself. Something snagged at my mind – something too fleeting and ethereal to be called an idea: a feeling almost, a half-realised intimation, no sooner glimpsed than gone.[1] What had it been? Something about that pair of lovers, the way they laughed as they looked into each others' eyes…

Suddenly, Lucy gave a cry and hurled herself up a large cedar. She'd seen something, but her eyesight was far sharper than mine and I couldn't at first make out what it was. Then she enthusiastically displayed herself to what I now saw was a small, duffle-coated figure, also clambering into the branches.

"Mum!" a terrified voice shouted. "Mum! Help!"

It is hard to say who was the more frightened, Lucy or the child. Unfortunately, Lucy showed her fear by baring her teeth, then rubbing her genitals some more, neither of which is calculated to go down very well with a small child who at that moment is hanging by one arm from a tree twelve feet above the ground, or indeed the small child's alarmed mother, standing just below with her labrador. There was a yell, followed by the words "I'm falling!" as the child bounced from branch to branch before hitting the ground with a sickening thud.

27.6

Ten minutes later Lucy and I were out on the street. "Sorry," the park attendant said apologetically. "We could stretch a point before, but health and safety… From now on that chimp of yours will have to be classed as a dog."

---

[1] It is a curious fact that many discoveries of science have come about in a quiet moment of intuition, rather than by logical deduction. Newton was struck by a falling apple. Archimedes was soaking in a bath. Watt invented the two-chamber steam engine during a Sunday walk. Einstein said that the formula for relativity came to him long before the proof. Loewi, as related elsewhere, discovered neurotransmitters in a dream. And when they started to pursue the structure of DNA, Crick and Watson decided they would recognise the correct answer when they saw it because, as they said, in nature the truth is always beautiful.

"Of course she's not a dog," I said wearily. "She's not a chimp either, for that matter."

"Whatever. The point is, in future she'll have to stay on a lead."

"She can't possibly climb trees on a lead."

"Then you'll just have to take her somewhere else," he said, with the finality of one who believes his own logic to be irreproachable. "This isn't the African jungle, you know."

I did know. Of course, I had tried to explain what had happened – that Lucy had simply mistaken the small child, climbing with childish agility up the tree, for another bonobo, and that her genital display was simply her equivalent of a friendly hello. But in my heart I knew we had had a lucky escape.

I glanced at her as we walked back to the lab. She seemed subdued. I could guess why: it wasn't because of the park attendant's shouting, or the small child's tears, distressing though both of those had been.

It was because she'd thought, just for a moment, that she'd finally found another bonobo to have sex with.

"Never mind, Lucy," I said. "Not your fault. We'll find you a partner one day, I promise. It's not much fun being on your own, is it?"

Then the idea I had half-glimpsed earlier slipped back into my mind, more clearly this time. "Of course!" I said aloud. "Those students! Lovers! A courting couple! Lucy, I think I know where we've been going wrong!"

27.7

"My idea," I explained to Miss G later, "is *context*."

"Context?" she repeated.

"The lab is a sterile environment. Not literally. I mean, it's unexciting."

"I quite like it, actually," she said, looking around.

"Well, so do I, but that isn't the point. Women don't normally have

140

sex in science labs. Usually it's after they've been out on a date. When they've been courted. Seduced, even. Wooed. "

She frowned. "You're saying I need to be *wooed*?"

"It's a possibility. And if it's a possibility, it needs to be tested."

"And who's going to do this…wooing?"

"It should be a man, I think, so it had better be me rather than Susan. Unless you have any objection?"

"No. No, being wooed sounds… fascinating and rather pleasant. When?"

"Shall we say eight o'clock? I think the simulation would have more verisimilitude if we were alone."

I spent considerable time, with Wulf's help, preparing for this session. When Miss G arrived at eight o'clock the lights had been turned off, and the lab was illuminated only by the violet flames of half a dozen Bunsen burners.

"What's *this*?" she asked, looking around.

"Today's context," I told her, "is dinner."

I had laid a bench table for two in the centre of the lab, improvising from what was available. The bench was spread with graph paper instead of a tablecloth, and the wine and water glasses were test tubes held upright in a rack. The wine – a Puligny-Montrachet – was chilling in a portable freezer, and in place of a candle the centre of the table held a single Bunsen, its flame turned down low to make a smoky, drifting cuticle of yellow.

I pulled out a stool for her. "Do you do this for everyone on the study?" she asked as she sat down.

"Oh, no," I said, pouring her some wine. "You're a special case. But it's a perfectly valid hypothesis that social environment may affect sexual function, for example by relaxing you. All we're doing here is replicating the circumstances of a normal date – purely for scientific purposes."

"I see," she said – and it seemed to me that she did visibly relax as she slid her napkin from the myograph ring in which it was rolled. "So, is there a menu?"

I shook my head. "But here's the first course."

I put in front of her a plate on which were three small pink pills. Her face clouded momentarily as she washed them down with some wine.

"And now," I said, "for the food." I placed a small box on the table and opened it. Smoke immediately began to pour out – but this was heavy smoke. It cascaded onto the table, surrounding the base of the test tubes and the burner in a thick mist, and from there slipped to the floor in long, sinuous scarves.

"Liquid nitrogen," I explained. "Or, in common parlance, dry ice." I plunged two spoons into the mixture. "And this is ice cream."

"We're starting with *ice cream*?"

"Not just any ice cream. Freeze-dried carrot and violet ice cream."

She made a face. "Sounds revolting."

"May I suggest, Annie, that if you really want to be a scientist you should refrain from jumping to conclusions," I said mildly. I passed her the spoon and watched as she put it into her mouth. Her eyes grew very round.

"Forget the words," I continued. "Think about the *chemistry*. Carrots and violets both contain a flavour molecule called an ionone. Putting them together means each amplifies the taste of the other. How is it?"

"It's…it's the most amazing thing I've ever eaten," she said, astonished.

"Oh, I nearly forgot. Some music." I pointed a remote control at the CD player, and Stockhausen's *Kontakte* filled the air – shimmering, almost-there whispers of almost-music, like a computer dreaming in its sleep.

"Who made this?" she said, licking the spoon.

"Did I not mention? Molecular gastronomy happens to be one of my hobbies. Here." I handed her a plate. On it was a tiny jelly, on a bed of what looked like liquorice.

"What's this?"

"Salad. Chocolate jelly and caramelised cauliflower salad, to be precise."

She almost made another face – then caught herself and took a first, experimental mouthful. Moments later, her face lit up. "That's *fantastic*. Even better than the ice cream."

"Of course. Everything I serve you this evening will be fantastic,

Annie. I can say that with confidence because it's all based on valid principles of science." I stood up. "And now, if you'll excuse me, I have to prepare the steak."

"Steak? I was starting to imagine something more adventurous."

"Believe me," I said, "this is steak cooked under laboratory conditions. I don't think you'll have eaten anything like it before."

The steak, in fact, had been vacuum-packed and then cooked at a very low temperature for over two hours in a thermostatic basin, making the meat as soft as melting butter. All I had to do now was to take it out and brown it for a few seconds with a powerful Primus burner, thus producing the Maillard reactions which are such an important part of the taste of vintage champagne, caramelised onions, and roast beef. Meanwhile, an ultrasonic bath was mixing together eggs, vinegar, butter and lemon for a perfect Hollandaise sauce. There was mashed potato to provide a carbohydrate base, infused with a little yeast to complement the tubers' methional compounds. This was now being stirred to a perfect creaminess by a magnetic whisk set at exactly 15 rpm. Finally, the peas were being slow-cooked in a rotary evaporator to ensure that none of their flavour molecules were boiled off. Each pea had previously been injected by Wulf and myself with a single droplet of vaporised ham stock, using a needle so fine it was capable of fertilising a human egg.

None of this was particularly groundbreaking – as I explained to Annie while we ate, molecular scientists and a few enlightened chefs had been using these techniques for years. But for someone used to the haphazard cuisine of commercial restaurants, every mouthful was a revelation.

"So," she said at last, wiping her plate clean, the flickering lilac flames of the Bunsens reflecting prettily in her eyes. "I have to tell you, Dr Fisher, that your attempt to replicate a normal date has failed completely."

"Oh?"

"This is way, way better than any date I've ever been on." She blushed and added quickly, "Food-wise, I mean."

"Good." I took her empty plate, and replaced it with a parmesan and blood-orange sorbet made in the PacoJet and shaved into wafer-thin curls. "But if you think there's anything missing from the simulation – anything we could do to make it more realistic – will you let me know?"

"Well, if this were a normal date you'd probably be trying to get me drunk. Whereas…" She held up her empty test tube.

"Oh – my apologies. That's one condition we can easily replicate." I poured her some more Puligny-Montrachet.

"And if it were a normal date – that's fine, thanks – you'd probably be doing some cheesy flirting by now."

"I'll do my best," I said. "Although I should warn you, I'm rather better at cooking than I am at flirting."

"Maybe you just haven't met the right person to practise flirting with."

I glanced at her, surprised. "Ah!" I said, understanding. "I see what you did there. You were replicating the flirtatious banter of a real romantic encounter."

"Exactly."

"In the same spirit…if I were to enjoy exchanging sexually-charged chit-chat with anyone, Annie, it would certainly be with you."

"Thank you. Speaking of which," she said thoughtfully, "I've been thinking about that theory you were telling me about. You know…about kissing. That it might be a way of exchanging chemical messengers with someone?"

"That overly sentimental, unproven theory," I said, getting up to fetch the dessert – a single piece of freeze-dried banana wrapped in parsley on the one hand, and a single caramelised strawberry, halved and layered with coriander leaves, on the other: another example of matching and contrasting volatiles.

"Yes, but –" She gasped as she bit into the strawberry. "Oh my God that's good by the way – I was wondering how one knows what the messengers have decided."

"You'd have to trust your instincts, I suppose. Although, now I come to think of it, some kind of blood test could prevent an awful lot of unsatisfactory relationships. I'll get the last course."

I went to get the final dish – four tiny slivers of concentrated choco-late, variously flavoured with pink peppercorns, smoked eel, caraway seeds and merlot vinegar, each one combined without heat using a vacuum aspirator. As I turned back from the bench she was standing by the CD player, changing the music. Something soft and funky filled the air. One of Susan's.

She stepped out of the way to let me past. I did the same – and inad-vertently found myself moving in the same direction as her.

"Oops," she said with a smile.

We both moved the other way, at exactly the same moment: two dancers executing a pavane.

Our eyes met.

Just as in the bookshop, I had the curious sensation that the distance between our heads was shrinking. It was like the optical illusion you get when you look up at a skyscraper and it appears to be falling on you, even though it isn't.

"Because if it *were* a real date," she said a little breathlessly, "we would almost certainly be – that is –"

"Yes?"

"It would probably be much more realistic if we – " Her head was by now very close to mine.

"Naturally, it would only ever be…that is, strictly and exclusively… controlled experiment…laboratory conditions…" I said, taking a step towards her.

"Quite," she breathed.

I covered her lips gently with mine, feasting for the first time on the sweetness of her breath.

Ohhhh…

Something extraordinary was happening – something so strange I hesitate to write it here, lest you think my own perceptions were in some way distorted by the agreeable context of that evening's experiment. But science is nothing if it is not the truth, so I will set down my reaction to that kiss honestly, no matter what mockery it may expose me to.

146

As our lips met, I felt what I can only describe as a sense of temporal dislocation. The fabric of space-time seemed to loop around itself, encasing us in one endless, frozen moment. Something clicked. It felt like tumblers in a combination lock slotting into place. It felt like two computers whistling and beeping as they connected across a network. Like a million bytes of data, downloading and uploading in a flash –

I have no idea how long that kiss lasted. Possibly it was less than a minute. But – and once again I find myself at the limits of what scientific language can convey – it seemed as if in that brief moment our bodies had begun a conversation of their own, a conversation that they would now continue of their own accord, without any more agency on our part.

"And if this *were* a date," I said at last, pulling away, "would you be... might your companion be suggesting round about now...that you and he have sex?"

She nodded.

"I'd say no, of course," she added, a little reluctantly. "On a first date. I'd almost definitely say no."

"Then let's say it's a second date we're replicating."

"Well..."

"Or even better, a third."

"In that case..." Once again our lips met. Once again time seemed to solidify. Past, present and future were one and the same, an infinite Mobius continuum.

"Sex. Would. Definitely. Be. A. Possibility," she murmured.

"Good," I said. I released her. "We'd better start the tests."

"Tests?"

"Everything's set up next door – I know Susan isn't here but I think you're familiar enough with the equipment not to need –" I stopped. Miss G was staring at me.

"Steven," she said slowly, "I don't quite know how to say this. I just don't feel like – like doing those tests right now. For some reason I just feel completely asexual."

"Do you mean anerotic? Asexual would mean that you reproduce without a partner. Like a mud snail."

"Oh. Yes. Anerotic, then."

"Ah," I said, somewhat nonplussed by this turn of events. "Well, of course, that's perfectly all right."

"Thank you."

"Was it something I said?"

She shook her head.

"My kissing?"

"No."

"Some error in the date-replication scenario?"

"I don't think so."

"Well, another time, perhaps."

"Yes, another time."

We looked at each other.

"Goodnight then, Steven."

"Goodnight, Annie."

We kissed each other awkwardly on the cheek.

"Would you like me to walk you home?"

She shook her head. "Best not. But thank you anyway."

Then she was gone.

I was left with a feeling that, in some way I couldn't quite fathom, I had not handled the evening particularly well.

28.2

What could I conclude from the latest experiment?

First, that a romantic meal, no matter how well-cooked, was no guarantee of sexual arousal.

Second, that kissing her, whilst very pleasant, did not seem to make much difference either.

Third, that this particular context – wooing – did not appear to be the missing factor.

So far so good, although it was a shame she had declined to take part in the tests – while I could assume from what she had said that they would once again have been unsuccessful, it would have been useful to have the data to confirm it.

Then Steven gets me doing this whole date-replication thing. And that's nice in a completely different way. In fact, I get so caught up in our pseudo-dinner that I completely forget it's an experiment. And I've just got to the point where I'm practically melting into his arms when I realise it isn't him this is leading up to, it's his tests.

Suddenly everything – the whole perfect fantasy he's conjured up – just goes pop and vanishes. I find myself standing in a lab lit by Bunsen burners instead of candles, with some kind of horrible sex drug coursing through my body, and Steven looking at me like I'm a lab rat he's particularly fond of.

I do a runner. Which I feel bad about, but it's got to be better than the alternative. Quite apart from anything else, I'd have lit up his machines like a set of Christmas tree lights.

(Or would I? Even with KXC79, there's a point where neurostimulators are not enough... What I really want is to be kissed all over, tenderly, and to dance naked in the rain, and have forget-me-nots threaded through my pubic hair like Mellors does for Lady Chatterley, and then be laid down on a bed of soft moss and opened up slowly and sensually like a blossoming flower before...)

WHOA! NOT AGAIN!

Bloody, bloody KXC79. Better find some work to do.

The next morning I arrived at the Department still feeling somewhat perplexed. Nor was my temper improved when I discovered that the space where I usually parked my G-Wiz, next to Julian Noble's Renault Laguna, no longer existed. Instead, two boxes had been painted on the ground. One read RESERVED FOR DIRECTOR. The other read VISITORS ONLY. Of Julian's Laguna there was no sign.

Annoyed, I reversed onto the road and slipped the G-Wiz in between two motorbikes. As I strode towards the lab, however, I was amazed to see a brand new Porsche with the numberplate JUL1 roar into one of the new white-painted parking spaces. To my even greater astonishment, Julian Noble stepped out of it.

As he swung the door shut he paused for a moment to admire its gleaming bodywork.

30.2

"What on earth is going on?" I asked Susan as I went into the lab. "Julian Noble appears to be driving a Porsche."

"Didn't you read the press release?" She handed me a sheet of paper that was lying on the desk.

"'With immediate effect'," I read, "'the Department of Molecular Biology, Oxford University, will be renamed the Trock Institute of Submolecular Medicine. This recognises new sponsorship arrangements put in place to secure the long-term future of the Institute and to establish it as a leading supplier of effective, evidence-based research to the pharmaceutical industry. Professor Julian Noble, named as the Institute's first Director, confirmed that a number of projects are already being developed, including a genetically-modified earthworm that may have important applications in agriculture, and a possible treatment for Female Sexual Dysfunction.'" The press release was illustrated by a black-and-white portrait of Julian, beaming proudly at the camera.

"He's wearing a tie," I said.

"More than that." She pointed. "Unless I'm very much mistaken, that's a toupee."

"'Welcoming the announcement, Trock's International Director of Marketing Kes Riley said, 'This partnership between the world's number one pharmaceutical company and the world's number one centre of research excellence is good news for all involved.'"

"Is it?" Susan asked.

"Is it what?"

"Good news."

"Frankly, I don't think it means anything at all."

"But Julian gets a Porsche."

"I suppose so."

"I hope you don't mind my asking, Steve, but what are you getting out of this?"

"This?" I pointed to the press release. "Oh – I didn't even know it was happening. It's just marketing, Susan. They're trying to ramp up expectations ahead of the big announcement at SexDys, that's all. It's of no concern to us."

30.3

"I've been through the KXC79 paper," Miss G said briskly, handing me a sheaf of pages. "My suggestions are in blue."

"Thank you. But when on earth did you find the time?"

"Oh, I've been fitting it in at odd moments." She shrugged. "Here and there."

I looked through what she'd done. Even I could tell that it was much better. She had not only improved the style immeasurably, but had brought in references from past papers to make it clear that KXC79 was both based on, and a radical development of, a number of previous attempts by other scientists. It was a very good job, and indisputably the work of someone who had a clear grasp of the science involved.

I went and told her so.

"Anyone can polish a document," she said modestly. "And after all, you made me dinner."

"Nevertheless, I do appreciate it."

As I turned to go she said, "Steven, what will happen…that is, assuming I *do* become orgasmic. Will that be the end of my involvement with the project?"

"Well, it could be." I guessed that she was referring to the episode the night before, and her reluctance to take part in the tests. "Annie, of course we'll completely understand if you decide at some point you've had enough. My hope, though, is that you'll stay with the programme while we're refining the treatment. That way we'll be able to double-check each development against your responses, to make sure we're still on the right track – you'd be a kind of ongoing control. But we're leaping ahead of ourselves here – we still don't know for sure that KXC79 is going to work."

"I think it will," she said slowly.

"Oh? Why's that?"

"Each time I do the tests… Something's starting to happen. I'm sure of it. It might just take…a little while."

"Well, fingers crossed. But whether the tests are successful or not, you've proved your worth here. As far as I'm concerned, you're just as much a scientist as any of us."

I saw her shoulders lift as she took a deep breath. It seemed to me that she was struggling with some emotion so large it was preventing her from speech.

Then she nodded, and I nodded too, and we both got back to work.

30.4

OK. Crunch time.

Now that I've taken a look at Steven's paper, I'm starting to understand just how big this project is.

His new results aren't just encouraging. They're *amazing*. KXC79 appears to have a completely unbroken track record of solving FSD.

So, while one dodgy result (ie me) is hardly going to make that much difference, it hardly seems fair to pretend to be evidence of KXC79 not working when in fact exactly the reverse is true. Besides, now that I've helped to redraft the paper, I need it to be published just as much as Steven does if I'm to use it to get onto a degree course.

All the same, I can't help having mixed feelings about that... It's hard to believe that any undergraduate course is going to be as interesting as what I've learnt here at the lab.

But what a relief it will be to finally stop pretending! Not to mention how pleased this is going to make him.

30.5

She spent the morning polishing off A-level energetics. At twelve o'clock, it was time for her tests.

While Susan took her into the testing room I put on a CD – Enigma's *Principles*, if my memory serves me right. The swooping mixture of electro-melodies and Gregorian chant mingled with the beeps of booting-up computers as I prepared the GSA.

"Someone's happy today," Susan commented as she came back into the testing room.

"She certainly seems to be in a good mood."

"Who?"

"Annie."

Susan pressed some buttons, and the music was joined by the tenor-and-bass choral hum of multiple stimulation devices whirring into life. "Actually, I meant you."

"Me?"

"You were whistling."

"Was I?"

"And I notice Annie's bought herself some new knickers. It's a good sign, don't you think?"

"In what way?"

"Well, it might suggest she's becoming more sexual. Ready for me to start?"

I nodded. Susan fitted her headphones and turned on the mikes. "OK, Annie. You know the drill. Nice and relaxed, please."

"I'll try," Miss G's voice said.

"Good girl." Susan twisted a knob. "Here we go."

We waited.

"Dr Fisher?" Miss G's voice said in my ears.

"Yes?"

"When I read the KXC79 paper...there was just one thing I still didn't understand."

"What's that?"

"What was the breakthrough? In the paper you said you were walking by the river one evening when you had this insight. But what exactly was it?"

"Oh... Well, I was thinking about sexual function in bonobos, actually, when it occurred to me that really thinking is the key to it all. You see, up to that point no one had investigated the role of the cerebral cortex."

"Annie, I'm going to play some video clips on your monitor," Susan said sharply. "Try to concentrate on them." She typed a command into her laptop.

"Because, you see, most people had been looking at sex as a purely physiological phenomenon," I went on. "But if that's the case, *why is merely thinking about someone you find attractive enough to cause arousal?* Clearly there's a mechanism somewhere, deep in our brains, that converts thoughts into physical response…a kind of neurochemical network interface. It occurred to me to look for a way of hacking into that system."

"So KXC79 isn't really a drug at all?"

"Exactly. It's a chemical messenger – in essence, it's a *thought*, just as all thoughts are ultimately chemicals, flooding from synapse to synapse within the brain."

Beside me, Susan was furiously typing more commands on her keyboard.

"Did I tell you," I said, "that amongst females of other species, it's only the intelligent animals, the higher primates and dolphins, which have orgasms? The logic's inescapable, really: it's all in the mind." Was it my imagination, or had a low sound just escaped Miss G's lips? "Well, the rest was straightforward. After binding to cytoplasmic receptors in your brain cells, the receptor-hormone complex translocates to the cell nucleus. The result, obviously, is release of new proteins with the same information into the cytosol, where the physiologic response is triggered."

I distinctly heard her gasp. "But the peptide action…"

"Simply a correlation of brain function."

"I hate to interrupt," Susan interrupted, looking at her screen, "but I think the moment is right to go to five."

I waved her on. "Once you know that every thought in your mind is only a chemical equation, the question is: what thought, what chemical, shall we place there? Everything else is just molecular fine-tuning."

"Something's happening," Susan said, peering at a monitor.

"What?"

"Put it this way," Susan said, pressing buttons rapidly, "unless I'm very much mistaken, she's not going to be thinking about peptides for a while."

On the thermograph a warm flush suffused Miss G's chest, rising up her neck in a brilliant sunrise of yellows and oranges. She moaned. She has, as I have probably remarked already, a pleasant voice, dry and husky. But that moan was something more – it was like the sweetest, richest song that lips had ever uttered.

My colleague was undoubtedly right. Something was happening.

"Come on," Susan muttered. "Come on, Annie. Come on."

Miss G gasped.

"Yes!" Susan said.

"YAARGH," Miss G said.

"Houston to Shuttle: launch in zero minus ten," Susan said.

"BORIS YELTSIN," Miss G yelled. Quite why she was shouting the name of a former president of the USSR I do not know.

"Eight…seven…six…"

"Is this what I think it is?" Heather said, sticking her head round the door.

"It's certainly looking that way," Susan agreed.

"Rhona! Quick – Annie's having an orgasm," Heather called. After a moment Rhona too pushed into our tiny control booth.

"Four…three…two…"

"Whoa!" shouted Miss G. Her heartbeat was at the very top of the graph. Temperature was off the chart, and skin moisture was going crazy.

"Lift-off," Susan said.

For a long, agonising moment nothing more happened. Then, abruptly, the EMG erupted into an arpeggio of peaks – a volley of uncontrollable spasms, each successive contraction-and-release more splendid than the one before (*Figure 16*).

"Oh!" Miss G cried in a strangled voice. "Yes! No! Gorbachev! Putin! OH MY GOODNESS!"

We watched the spikes on the graph resound for what seemed liked an eternity, then gradually fade away. There was a long silence, broken only by the amplified sounds of Miss G's panting. Susan leaned forward to her microphone.

"Annie?"

"Uh?"

"How was that?"

"Fucking amazing," Miss G said in a strangled voice.

"We've done it," Susan said wonderingly. She turned to me. "Steven, we've done it."

"Thank you for your help, everyone," I said. "The results are quite unequivocal. Annie has just experienced an orgasm."

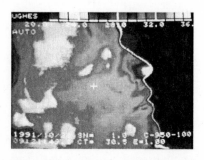

Figure 16 (a): Thermograph view of Miss G at T07.43.

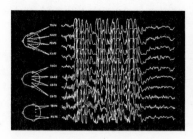

Figure 16 (b): Another view, T07.50–T08.21.

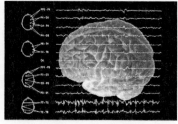

Figure 16 (c): Brain mapper output, T07.50–T08.27.

Figure 16 (d): Subjective impression of T08.18, chosen by Miss G. The American government codenamed this 61-kiloton XX39 atomic bomb "Climax".

Figure 16 (e): Francis Crick and James Watson with their DNA model. "It's beautiful…so beautiful," Watson was later heard to observe.

We scientists are not given to over-demonstrative shows of emotion. It is said, for example, that when Watson and Crick completed the first helical model of the structure of DNA and saw, as the last molecule slipped into place, that it was beautiful and it was right, Crick offered Watson his hand and the other man shook it. In our own lab, I am glad to say, there was nothing unseemly. We exchanged handshakes – that is to say, I offered Susan my hand, and she, completely missing the quiet symbolism of the gesture, ignored it and hugged me. Then everyone was laughing and hugging everyone else, and Susan started crying, and Rhona did a rather extraordinary little war dance in the middle of the lab, breaking off occasionally to high-five Wulf, and all the while Miss G lay there in the testing room, panting, the aftershocks bouncing along the floor of the EMG printout, like a dying cascade of echoes.

30.7

That lunchtime, to celebrate, they went off to play Swamps and Sorcerers with Annie's Fantasy Society.

"I'm going to be an Orc! I'm going to be an Orc!" Susan said blissfully.

"Are you coming, Dr Fisher?" Rhona called.

"I'd love to, but I can't – there's some work I've got to do, writing up these latest results."

"What about you, Heather?"

"Sorry – I'm meeting someone."

"Ooh – anyone exciting?" Susan asked.

"It's just lunch in a pub. I'll be back by two."

When the lab was empty I exhaled a long, quiet breath. Then I went back to Miss G's test results and ran through the data.

There was no doubt about it – she'd had an orgasm, and one of impressive amplitude at that.

I put my head in my hands. If I had been a different sort of man, I might have wept.

30.8

I sat there, thinking.

Why had Miss G's orgasm today been different – why had this been the first one she had actually *felt*?

You see, it wasn't the KXC79.

I knew it wasn't the KXC79 because she hadn't been given any.

On this occasion, the pills I had administered to Miss G fifteen minutes before the start of the tests had been dummies. I had given her a placebo.

30.9

I went through the tests again. Backwards, forwards…

Nothing made sense.

The only thing I could spot was a faint glow on the brain mapper output in a part of the brain I hadn't expected to be working at all – the anterior cingulate. According to the literature, that part isn't associated with sexual response at all. According to the latest studies, it's associated with conflict resolution, strategic planning, and deception.

30.10

Oh, and something else rather curious happened that lunchtime. Towards two-thirty I heard a roaring engine pull up below my window. I looked down, annoyed: it was Julian Noble, parking his ridiculous German sports car. As soon as he got out, he hurried round to open the other door for the young woman who was swinging her rather shapely legs out of the passenger seat.

Somewhat to my surprise, it was Heather Jackson.

30.11

"You know, we should probably make sure those results are replicable," Miss G said to me later that afternoon. "After all, one success might just be a fluke."

I nodded. "The same thing had occurred to me. You're already thinking like a scientist, Annie."

She flushed with pleasure.

That evening, before she left, we carried out an identical set of tests. Once again, without her knowledge, I gave her a placebo instead of the real KXC79.

Once again she reported that the treatment was 100% effective.

30.12

The following day, I switched the placebo back to KXC79.

The results were identical in every respect to the placebo sessions. Once again, the machines showed that Annie was experiencing climax:

once again, Annie reported that this was indeed the case.

And once again there was a faint, flickering luminescence in the depths of her anterior cingulate.

Eventually, of course, I had to break the news to the others. I hated to crush their elation, but there was no choice.

"We should repeat the tests —" Rhona said immediately.

"Yes — do them again. We'll take a mean score across all the results, subject it to a Mann-Whitney analysis —" That was Heather.

So we retested again. Three times.

On the first occasion Miss G reported that she did not have an orgasm. That was after I had just given her a triple dose of KXC79. The time after that, she reported that she did. Unfortunately, that one was a placebo.

"Damn," she said after the third and final test. "I just can't seem to get this right, can I?"

"It isn't your fault," I pointed out. "The failing, such as it is, clearly lies with the treatment."

She didn't reply.

There were a number of possibilities to consider:

1:   That Miss G's FSD was intermittent.
2:   That the "attack" doses of KXC79 she had been taking were actually having a negative effect — that they were, in fact, somehow compounding rather than curing her problem.

3:    That there was some kind of complex placebo effect at work.

4:    That there was some other explanation I had not so far thought of.

31.3

I was getting so desperate that I even asked Susan for advice.

"Well, the first thing to look at is obviously the formulation," she began.

"Susan," I said firmly. "The formulation isn't the issue here. Quite apart from anything else, she hasn't even been receiving KXC79 half the time. If I'm to change anything, first I need to understand *why* it isn't working."

She sniffed. "Perhaps the problem is that you're approaching this whole question like a typical man."

"What do you mean?"

"You're assuming that you can just turn Annie on like a…a computer or a lightbulb or something. Women aren't like that, Steven. You've got to get inside our heads."

"That's exactly what I was trying to do with the dinner-date scenario."

Susan hooted with laughter. "If women had sex with every man who took them out to dinner, there'd be a lot more men going round with smiles on their faces. Men *think* dinner is the way to get a woman into bed. And women let them think it, because they get dinner out of it. But actually it takes a whole lot more than that."

"So what does work for women?" I asked, interested despite myself.

"Imagination."

"Imagination?" I responded uneasily.

"*Ideas*. You know, erotic roleplay. Mind games. The most powerful sex

165

organ in the human body is the brain"[1] – a remark I had heard her make on a wearyingly large number of occasions before: still, I reasoned, that didn't mean there was absolutely nothing in it.

31.4

"What should I do, Wulf?"

"The only thing you can do – hypothesise some possible explanations, and devise an experiment to test each one. Don't try to pre-judge the results. Keep an open mind."

"Sometimes," I said moodily into my beer, "I think an open mind may actually be a disadvantage."

"Oh? How?"

"Perhaps there's some totally obvious conclusion that we're failing to see, because we're so intent on considering all the possibilities. You know, like that tomato effect you talked about."

Wulf nudged me. "This will cheer you up." He took something from his bag – or rather, two things: a small white box with an aerial attached, and a strange, bulbous, corkscrew-like object.

"What is it?"

"Can't you tell?" He pressed a switch on the box, and some lights along the base of the bulbous object flickered into life.

"No," I said, still mystified.

He pressed another button, and the top part of the thing began to rotate, like some kind of burrowing machine.

"It's a stimulator," he said proudly. "The Evans-Sederholm Sub-

[1] I should point out here that Susan was repeating a cliché, and not expressing a biochemical insight. Although it is true that KXC79 is effectively a neuro-cognitive peptide chain, Dr Minstock was never fully aware of its precise workings.

molecular Bio-Uncertainty Stimulator, to be precise. It's only a prototype, but it's fully functional."

Intrigued, I picked the thing up. It was soft to the touch, almost warm, and it was vibrating very quietly and smoothly at a low amplitude. As I held it, I felt the vibrations move up a gear, then another. I glanced at the white box, although so far as I could tell Wulf hadn't touched it. "What is that – some kind of remote control?"

He shook his head. "Biofeedback."

"Biofeedback!"

I loosened my grasp, and the vibrations settled to a steady but pulsing rhythm – almost, I thought, as if the thing had a heartbeat.

"I got the idea from talking to Rhona," he explained. "It responds to temperature, galvanicity, muscular activity, vasodilation – that LED there is the photoplethysmograph diode. Basically, the stalk contains a tiny Bluetooth transmitter that sends information to the box, where a simple piece of software processes it and sends back instructions." He pointed. "There are dedicated stimulators for each of the major erogenous zones – even the AFE. This ledge here at the base contains a stimulator and a logic gate –"

"Wulf," I said. "Wulf…"

"Wait – there's more," he said happily. "I wanted to find some way of incorporating my own work on chaos theory. There's a secondary software program which completely randomises the experience, depending on a whole range of complex variables – date, time, weather, frequency since last use –"

"Wulf," I said incredulously, "this vibrator has *moods*?"

He nodded. "But – and here's the kicker – they aren't immutable. For example, it reacts to the user's level of arousal. Depending on the other variables, it can then decide to make more of an effort, or not to bother – it can just switch itself off, if it wants to, without warning. If my theories are correct, it'll make for a much more realistic sexual experience. What do you think?"

I looked at the stimulator. It seemed to have gone to sleep – bored, doubtless, by our conversation. "I think you should probably destroy it. Now. Take it outside and drown it." As I spoke it buzzed and hummed briefly, like an angry chainsaw.

"Rhona thinks it's great."

"I bet she does. Wulf, don't you see – all you need is an artificial inseminator attachment and you and I are completely redundant."[2]

He laughed. "It's just a bit of fun." On the table, the stimulator shook briefly in response. For a brief moment, it almost looked as if it were chuckling too.

"Susan thinks I should be engaging Annie's imagination," I said. "What do you think?"

"Exactly. Get her in the mood, that's the answer. Want to borrow my prototype?"

"Thanks, but I don't think that's really what Susan had in mind."

31.5

Whatever I thought of Susan's suggestions or Wulf's invention, their reminder that I should stick to basic science in tackling the problem of Miss G was pertinent. After some further thought, I narrowed down the possibilities to what I considered to be the most likely one: the placebo effect.

Researchers have long been aware of this difficulty, and indeed, many studies have been confounded by its unpredictable effects. In a nutshell,

---

[2] My comments about Wulf's bio-uncertainty stimulator may be thought unnecessarily alarmist, given that surveys consistently point out that what women look for in a partner is a good sense of humour (72%), a kind smile (61%) or financial generosity (48%). However, one high street chain of sex shops now reports sales of over two million vibrators a year (Anne Summers Press & Marketing Pack 19/1/05). Assuming an average product lifespan of seven years, by 2015 there will be more vibrators in the UK than there are men. Presumably they are not all being bought for their ability to make women laugh.

it has been proven that if you give someone a pill and tell them it will have a certain result, in many cases it will have that result even when it is actually a dummy. This is because we are all of us deeply suggestible, irrational beings whose brains do not function as logically as we would like to think. For example, studies show that a placebo is far more effective than any real treatment for back pain, leading to calls amongst some scientists for dummy pills to be prescribed by doctors just like medicines.[3]

This could be what was happening to Miss G. It was not that the KXC79 wasn't working, but rather that, *having helped to rewrite my paper*, she had convinced herself so thoroughly of its effectiveness that any pill which she believed to be KXC79 would have the same result, irrespective of what it really contained. Of course, this result might well be erratic, given that it had no real basis in chemistry. It might also explain why the anterior cingulate was becoming luminescent during the tests – I was literally watching the brain fool itself into producing the placebo effect.

In future, therefore, if I was to rely on the evidence I gathered, I would have to gather it in a situation where Miss G did not think she had been given KXC79. Since the reverse placebo effect would also apply – ie she would be equally suspicious not to receive any treatment in the lab, and would simply tell her brain that she was no longer orgasmic – I would have to proceed under a different set of conditions altogether, particularly if I was to heed Susan's strictures to go beyond the obvious dinner-date scenario into the realms of erotic roleplay.

In short, I was going to have to take my experiment out of the laboratory and into the real world: or, as we scientists call it, "the field".

---

[3] Obviously, they couldn't actually be called "dummy pills" as that might limit their acceptability. Some name would have to be thought of which conveyed that this was a tested, effective treatment, such as "Placibrium". Something similar already happens in the labelling of food ingredients, where water can perfectly legally be called "acqua".

For further inspiration, I turned to the book Miss G herself had recommended: *Lady Chatterley's Lover* (Lawrence, D.H, 1928).

I have to confess that I am not a great reader of fiction – it seems to me unhelpful, when we spend so much time trying to eradicate the imaginary, the subjective and the downright made-up from what we do, to contaminate our minds with something that is, by the author's own admission, all of those things – and, as I ploughed through this particular work, I found myself becoming increasingly incensed. It was not so much the sex – although the way the author described it made it almost impossible to work out what was going on: what on earth were "glimpsey" thighs or "meaningful" breasts? Rather, it was the way the book's real hero, a brilliant wheelchair-bound academic who single-handedly sets about saving the local mining industry by introducing more progressive engineering practices, was completely overlooked by the author and his female creation Connie in favour of a surly, bad-tempered, over-sexed gamekeeper. As for their love-making, once again I could make neither head nor tail of Lawrence's physiology:

> And this time his being within her was all soft and iridescent, purely soft and iridescent, such as no consciousness could seize. Her whole self quivered unconscious and alive, like plasm.

"Plasm" – I knew that word, of course. But Lawrence appeared to have completely misunderstood its meaning. According to the Oxford Dictionary of Biological Terms, "plasm" – which should only be used as a suffix – refers to the proteins and other contents of a cell. Hence "protoplasm" (the cellular nutrients) or "cytoplasm" (the part surrounding the nucleus). Despite being a published author, D.H Lawrence had failed even to consult a textbook before using an unfamiliar word! I was certain it could not be these passages that Annie had found stimulating. And I hoped it was not the dialogue between the two lovers:

> 'Tha'rt not one o' them button-arsed lasses as should be lads, are ter! Tha's got a real soft sloping bottom on thee, as a man loves in 'is guts. It's a bottom as could hold the world up, it is!'

Frankly, I couldn't imagine Annie ever having a conversation about whether her bottom could hold up the world. However, if it was game-keeping she wanted, then gamekeeping I could provide. Like most Oxford colleges, mine owned vast swathes of the Cotswold countryside, and there were huge wooded estates not far from Oxford where Fellows who were so inclined could still blast innocent birds pointlessly out of the sky. A twenty-pound note slipped to the burly Foreman of Works, and I was in temporary possession of the key that unlocked the gates of Stowood Farm, five miles beyond the Oxford ring road.

32.2

I intercepted her by the stairs before lunch.

"I thought perhaps we wouldn't stay in the lab today. After all, it's a lovely afternoon. Let's take a bit of a break, shall we?"

"You mean, another date-scenario experiment?" she said eagerly.

"Sort of. I thought we'd go for a picnic." And despite her questions, I refused to tell her any more until we were driving out of the city centre.

"This car's so quiet."

"Climate change is a scientific fact, now – the evidence is incontrovertible. Driving an electric vehicle is the only logical choice." I pumped the accelerator as we struggled up the hill towards Headington. "Unfortunately it's not very powerful."

My low-emission G-Wiz is fine for two people, although it can be an unsettling experience being overtaken on downhill stretches by energetic cyclists. Several times as we made our way out of the city that day I had to pull over to let the queue of lorries which had built up behind us go past, which they did in deafening clouds of foul-smelling diesel. Once we were beyond the ring road, though, it was just us and the near-silence of the electric motor, as we inched jerkily up the hill towards the little village of Elsfield.

"Incidentally," I said, "if you reach into that bag at your feet, you'll find something I'd like you to wear."

She reached into my rucksack and pulled out the device I had rigged up especially for this afternoon's outing. It looked like an ordinary baseball cap, with the insignia of Oxford University embroidered on the front – I had got it from the University Merchandise shop on the High.[1] But its appearance was deceptive: it was actually an impressive work of miniaturisation, rigged up by Wulf and I, incorporating sensors from the brain mapper, as well as biofeedback technology from Wulf's stimulator (*Figure 17*). On the outside, positioned where the wearer could not see them, coloured LEDs – blue, amber, green and red – ran up the seam towards the crown. These were driven by a tiny processor which in turn channelled data from electrodes on the inside of the cap. Apart from a few wires sticking out here and there, the electronics were unobtrusive.

---

[1] Now I think about it, it is perhaps odd that they stock them, since baseball is a sport Oxonians rarely play.

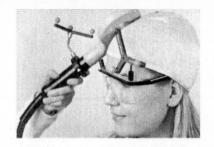

Figure 17: Specially-adapted baseball cap (left) incorporating battery-powered sensors from the laboratory brain mapper (right).

I had got the other lab assistants to road test it, and they reported that there was indeed a rough correlation between the lights and the wearer's physio-emotional state: blue meant no or negative response, amber meant receptive, and so on.

"You want me to put this on now?"

"Yes, please. You just need to turn the power on – here."

I showed her where the switch was. The lights flashed once to show that the device was operational.

As I drove I explained the ground rules of the experiment we were about to conduct.

"We're going to roleplay a scenario that I have reason to believe you may find enjoyable. I'll be with you, guiding you through it, but I want you to pretend I'm not here – I'm an observer, not part of the experiment."

"But how will that work, if you've got to tell me what to do?"

"Well – imagine I'm invisible, then. Think of me as a ghostly voice inside your head."

We had reached the farm. I parked in the farmyard, and consulted an Ordnance Survey map before leading her down a track into the woods. The bluebells were out, carpeting the trees on either side in a shimmering mist of bright blue.

"If I'm right," I said, "it'll be round here somewhere… Yes, over there."

In front of us, in the middle of a clearing, was a small hut with a corrugated iron roof. Next to it, an enclosure about forty feet long had been fashioned out of chicken wire.

I pushed open the door. Inside, it smelt of moist earth and beechnuts and old sacking. Along one wall were some wooden pens, above which glowed a row of infra-red heat lamps.

"After you," I said, standing back to let her past.

As she went inside I heard her give a cry of delight. Taking out the two copies of *Lady Chatterley* I had brought with me, I followed her.

32.4

"You read it!" she said. She was crouching down by one of the pens. In her cupped hands she held a tiny, peeping pheasant chick. "You read *Lady Chatterley*!" Even in the blood-red light I could see how pleased she was, not least because the LED on her baseball cap had flicked to amber.

"'Tha's got a real soft sloping bottom on thee, as a man loves in 'is guts,'" I said proudly. I stopped. Had I really said that? And if so, was it offensive? But Miss G seemed not to mind. In fact, the lights on her cap flickered rapidly, right up and down the scale, as she stroked the tiny bird.

I found the place in my text. "'She took the little drab thing between her hands,'" I read aloud, "'and there it stood, on its impossible little stalks of legs, its atom of balancing life trembling through almost weightless feet.'"

The chick peeped again, more anxiously, and Miss G returned it carefully to the pen. "This is the hut, isn't it?" she said, looking around. "The gamekeeper's hut in the woods where Connie and Mellors make love for the first time."

"It's very like it," I agreed. I handed her one of the copies. "Your script. Page 221, if I'm correct. Shall we take it from line seven?" Lifting my own copy, I read: "'Suddenly he was aware of the old flame shooting and leaping up in his loins, that he had hoped was quiescent for ever.'"

"'He came quickly towards her and crouched beside her,'" she continued seamlessly. She paused, and looked at me expectantly. Evidently, she was waiting for me to go and join her, just as the text described. I hesitated, conscious that this was hardly removing myself from the experiment. But then, I reasoned, it was only a roleplay. And there was something in the way she looked at me – so trusting, and so eager – that made it hard to refuse.

"'His heart melted suddenly, like a drop of fire, and he put out his hand…'" I matched this action, too, to the text.

"'He laid his hand on her shoulder… And softly, gently, it began to travel down the curve of her back –'"

"'Blindly, with a blind stroking motion, to the curve of her crouching loins.'" 'The curve of her crouching loins' – that, presumably, was Lawrence struggling to recall the word 'buttock'. Her buttocks were, in fact, remarkable – both soft and firm, full yet graspable – and it was with some reluctance that I broke off to turn the page. "'His hand softly, softly stroked the curve of her flank, in the blind instinctive caress…'"

"'The hand stroked her face softly, softly," she murmured. "'With infinite soothing and assurance, and at last there was the soft touch of a kiss on her cheek.'"

I touched my lips to her cheek. Sighing, she lay back, until she was stretched full length on the floor.

"'Then with a quiver of exquisite pleasure,'" she read, "'he touched the warm soft body, and touched her navel for a moment in a kiss.'"

Again I hesitated. Her navel *was* exposed, where her sweater had ridden up as she lay down – like a perfect tiny four-leaf clover, or the knotted mouth of a balloon. Placing my lips against it, I kissed it gently.

"'She lay quite still,'" I said, turning back to the book, "'in a sort of sleep, in a sort of dream.'"

"'She quivered as she felt his hand groping softly, yet with queer thwarted clumsiness, among her clothing –'"

"'She lay still, in a kind of sleep, always in a kind of sleep –'"

"'The activity, the orgasm, was his, all his; she could strive for herself no more –'"

"Hang on," I said, puzzled. I must have missed this point in my earlier reading. I flicked forward a couple of pages. "So she doesn't actually – "

"Not that time, no. But it doesn't matter!"

"It doesn't?"

"That happens later." Twisting impatiently so that she was kneeling astride me, she read: "'Oh, and far down inside her the deeps parted, and rolled asunder in long fair-travelling billows – '" She arched her back. "'Till suddenly – '"

"Suddenly?"

"'Suddenly, in a soft shuddering convulsion, the quick of all her plasm was touched,'" she gasped. "'And she was born: a woman.'"

"'Plasm?'" I said.

"That's the word he uses."

"Do you think he means protoplasm or cytoplasm?"

Miss G kissed me.

Or rather, she tried to. Presumably it is possible to kiss someone while wearing a baseball cap, but it must take considerable ingenuity.

"Are you all right?" she asked anxiously.

"Yes, I was just –" I rubbed the spot on my forehead where the hard brim of the cap had struck me.

"Here," she said, pulling the cap off.

We kissed again, properly this time. I kissed her slowly, hungrily, as Mellors and Lady Chatterley would have kissed. I put my hands around her head and held it against mine – so fragile in my rough male fingers, like a delicate porcelain bowl, a bowl from which I drank, deep and long.

And – once again – it happened: that bizarre sense of time coming to a standstill. It was like two sides of a complicated equation suddenly cancelling out, so that x really did = y. It was like ice cream sellers all over Oxford simultaneously bursting into song. It was like pheasant eggs hatching and bluebells blossoming. It was soft and iridescent and throaty and caressive. It was like current flowing through a brand-new circuit, and applause, and rain drumming on a corrugated roof –

Reluctantly, I released her. As I did so I realised that the noise I had heard *was* rain – a sudden downpour, almost deafening us.

"And that's the clearing, isn't it?" she breathed, looking towards the door. "Where they danced naked in the rain, their wet feet trampling the bluebells like two pagan gods, at one with nature and the tumultuous passions of the earth."

"I believe it is," I said anxiously. Much as I liked Miss G I was not sure that my plans for that afternoon had included dancing naked in the rain.

She got up and went to the door. Outside, raindrops the size of golf-balls were tearing great chunks of earth out of the ground. It had also gone rather chilly. She had put the cap back on: the lights, I noticed, were now flickering hesitantly between amber and blue.

Taking a deep breath, she ran out a few paces. Immediately, she was drenched. I saw the lights die completely – the cyber cap hadn't been designed to take that sort of punishment.

"Shall we?" she asked, turning to me.

"If you would like to dance naked in the rain, please, go ahead. This is your scenario."

She hesitated. "Can you find the place? You know – just to double check?"

"Of course," I said, lifting my copy of *Lady Chatterley's Lover*.

"Chapter fifteen, I think."

I turned to the relevant chapter and found the section she was referring to.

She opened the door and looked at the straight heavy rain, like a steel curtain, and had a sudden desire to rush out into it, to rush away. She got up, and began swiftly pulling off her stockings, then her dress and under-clothing, and he held his breath. Her pointed keen animal breasts tipped and stirred as she moved. She was ivory-coloured in the greenish light. She slipped on her rubber shoes again and ran out with a wild little laugh, holding up her breasts to the heavy rain and spreading her arms, and run-ning blurred in the rain with the eurhythmic dance movements she had learned so long ago in Dresden. It was a strange pallid figure lifting and falling, bending so the rain beat and glistened on the full haunches, sway-ing up again and coming belly-forward through the rain, then stooping again so that only the full loins and buttocks were offered in a kind of homage towards him, repeating a wild obeisance...

She was nearly at the wide riding when he came up and flung his naked arm round her soft, naked-wet middle. She gave a shriek and straightened herself and the heap of her soft, chill flesh came up against his body. He pressed it all up against him, madly, the heap of soft, chilled female flesh that became quickly warm as flame, in contact. The rain streamed on them till they smoked. He gathered her lovely, heavy pos-teriors one in each hand and pressed them in towards him in a frenzy, quivering motionless in the rain. Then suddenly he tipped her up and fell with her on the path, in the roaring silence of the rain, and short and sharp, he took her, short and sharp and finished, like an animal.

"But what I don't understand," I said, "is why Mellors talks to her in that ridiculous accent, when to everyone else he speaks normally. After all, we were told at the beginning he was an officer. Presumably he didn't spout dialect in the officers' mess."

"I think it's his way of reminding her of the social difference between them. He's goading her, because she's married to an aristocrat and he's a self-made man. Can I have another roll?"

We were sitting together on some sacks by the doorway, sharing the picnic I had brought. After we re-read the passage Miss G had decided to see if the rain eased off a little before dancing in it, and we had taken the opportunity to discuss some of my issues with the text.

"That makes him a rather unpleasant person, surely?" I said, passing her a roll.

"Oh, he's a complete bastard. That's part of Lawrence's intention – she calls him a brute, and he calls her a bitch, and most of the time they don't even like each other very much. But they're drawn together by something that's bigger than either of them – something beyond their conscious control. She doesn't love him, but she can't help being attracted to him."

"So Lawrence was almost writing an anti-love story – "

"Exactly! That's what no one ever understands. He's saying that passion is something quite different from love – it's something brutal, something to be feared, but it's also something we can't ignore. Clifford's in a wheelchair because he's literally emasculated –"

"Hang on. I thought he'd had an accident in the war."

"Well, yes – in the story he'd an accident, but the *reason* he had that accident was because Lawrence needed a symbol of the post-war exhaustion of European culture."

"But that's horrible! That's – doing terrible things to your characters just so they'll fit your own purposes."

"That's what writers do, Steven. They're not so very different from scientists – they perform nasty experiments on their characters to see what happens."

"But then they make up the results. Not to mention words like plasm."

She laughed. "I'll never make you like D.H Lawrence, will I?"

"Actually," I said, "now that you've explained this book, I do quite like it. Or at least, I understand it, which is almost the same thing. But that's only because you explained it so well."

We were silent for a moment. It was a curious thing, but when I was talking to Annie the silences were almost as pleasant as the conversations. It was rather extraordinary to know that even though neither of you was talking out loud, your thoughts were continuing to run along similar lines, so that when after a few minutes she said, "Perhaps he just meant cellular nutrients," I knew that she had returned, as I had, to Lawrence's misunderstanding of the word "plasm".

Outside, the rain was easing. The sun came out, and the two – rain and brilliant sunshine – overlapped briefly, so that it was almost impossible to say which was going to prevail. Suddenly, a spectacular shimmer of colours burst like a firework above the trees, the colours glittering with a soft iridescence against the sky.

"Look!" she said. "A refraction spectrum! What a beauty!"

Somehow I thought it completely unsurprising that Miss G knew the proper term for a rainbow.

"Do you know how to remember the order?" I asked.

"Easy. 'Roy G. Biv.' That's red, orange, yellow, green, blue, indigo, violet. Which Pink Floyd got wrong on the cover of *Dark Side of the Moon*, incidentally."

"I thought it was only me who'd noticed that!"

"Did you know there's a theory it wasn't an accident? That it's a clue to the hidden meaning of the album?"

She had taken off the defunct cyber cap so that her hair would dry. Now, as she explained the fascinating *Wizard-of-Oz* hypothesis of *Dark Side of the Moon*, she idly put it back on.[1] I was pleased to see that, the circuits having dried out, it was working again – and even more pleased, as well as a little intrigued, to note that it was registering amber, or receptive, even though we were doing nothing more than chatting about prog rock.

There was another, longer silence. A rainbow of colours shimmered on her head, the lights flickering from amber up to green and even touching orange before they went back to blue again.

"Penny for your thoughts," I said.

She smiled – a strange wry smile. "Sorry. Private."

"More *Lady Chatterley*?" I indicated the book, which had also now dried out. "There's another sex scene on page 501, although once again I'm finding the physiology somewhat obscure. I'm not sure how one would even begin to roleplay a phrase like 'she came to the very heart of the jungle of herself', actually. But we could have a go."

"Oh, I think that's enough Lawrence for one day, don't you?" She stretched, and got to her feet. Our legs had become entangled, and there was a sudden warm smell of freshly-dried denim as we unpeeled from each other. "He gets a bit cloying after a while. All those long fair-travel-ling billows and throaty caressive murmurs."

"But I thought it was your favourite erotic work?" I said, surprised.

"Yes, but only because the writing is ambitious and the sex metaphori-cal. His less explicit texts are far more interesting. But I've enjoyed this," she added politely as we left the hut. "It's been one of the best afternoons I've had in ages."

---

[1] Apparently, if you sync DSOTM up to the opening credits of *The Wizard of Oz* – a fairy-tale hunt for a mythical rainbow – an entirely different meaning to the album is revealed. To take just two of many examples, the lyric "balanced on the perfect wave" occurs just as Dorothy is balancing on the pigsty fence, while the song "Brain Damage" is played as the scarecrow sings "If I Only Had a Brain".

"According to the cyber cap, that isn't true. You've had much more exciting experiences in the lab, for example."

"Now *that*," she said, slipping her arm through mine as we walked towards the car, "is because you are still thinking like D.H Lawrence."

"How so?"

"Do you ever find yourself wondering…if orgasms aren't a bit over-rated sometimes?" she said, not answering me directly.

"Hmm," I said. "Well, given that they're my life's work, I hope not."

I had been right – there was *definitely* a placebo effect. Halfway through our excursion Miss G had been given KXC79 without realising it, ground up and mixed into a ciabatta roll containing pheasant pâté and crunchy cornichons, and yet from that point on she had seemed if anything less interested in what was, by her own admission, a favourite piece of erotica than she had been previously. And although the crudity of the testing rig meant that I couldn't be sure exactly *how* unaroused she was, I could certainly say that she had been less aroused by the prospect of revisiting D.H Lawrence's copulating gamekeeper than she had been by a discussion about the exhaustion of post-industrial Britain and the cover of an album.

So what was the answer? What should I do next?

34.2

Kes was by now phoning almost every day.

"Steven, I can't say I'm not getting nervous," he told me. "The fact is, we've got a humdinger of a name –"

"Ohhgasm?"

"No, not Ohhgasm. Turns out it's the title of a film. We're going with *Whoosh!* In italics. With an exclamation mark. Pretty good, eh? It's registered, copyrighted and ready to roll. But it's getting to the point where it's almost too late to cancel –"

"Kes," I said wearily, "I'm doing everything I can at this end. Just go ahead and do whatever it is you think you have to do." And, for the first time in my life I put the phone down on him, reflecting as I did so that it was unlikely Charles Darwin had ever had to discuss whether or not to put an exclamation mark on the end of *Evolution!*

So now this is becoming both very lovely and rather strange. Steven seems to have appointed himself as my surrogate boyfriend. And although he insists it's purely for scientific purposes, a girl just knows when a man likes her, doesn't she? And although of course some men like pretty much every female in the vicinity, Steven isn't like that. In fact, his body language in the lab with, say, Susan, seems to translate as more of a "yuk" than a "hmmm".

I could have sworn, for example, when we were in the gamekeeper's hut that something was going to happen. We started kissing – and a bit more than kissing – and for a moment he actually seemed to be suggesting that we were going to tear our clothes off and dance naked in the rain. When I tactfully suggested that the pile of old sacks in the corner of the hut might be more comfortable – I wasn't too keen on the whole getting-naked-in-the-rain-bit, but naked-in-the-hut could be quite another matter – he produced a picnic instead, and we started talking. He had some lovely insights into DH Lawrence, in fact, and his point about the thinness of the characterisation was well made…but still. I wasn't sure if he's waiting for me to take the initiative – after all, I did read him the riot act about not letting personal feelings get in the way of work. But no one ever takes a remark like that seriously, do they? Not if they really fancy someone.

Though talking about Lawrence was nice too, of course. And there's nothing wrong with a slow build-up. After all, I don't want to rush into another disaster like Simon.

Not that Steven's like Simon. Not in a million years. But slow is fine.

So long as it's not *too* slow, that is.

Not long after I had put the phone down on Kes for the umpteenth time, Julian Noble strode into the lab. He didn't seem terribly happy.

"Fisher!" he hissed.

"Here I am."

"What in God's name are you playing at?"

Behind him, Heather appeared to be trying to give the impression that this was absolutely nothing to do with her.

"What do you mean?" I said, baffled.

"Animals!" he snapped.

I looked around. The lab was quiet. Rhona and Annie were hard at work, Susan was oiling the Sybian, and Wulf was using some of our tools to tinker with what looked like a computer chip. "Scientists," I retorted.

"Not here. There!" His bony finger stabbed at the floor. "You have an animal in this building. Of a species banned from scientific research."

With a sinking heart I realised he meant Lucy. "Technically, perhaps. But –"

"An animal, moreover, which has just urinated on my girlfriend and myself."

I stared at him. "Did you just say…"

"Yes. Urinated," he said firmly.

"…*girlfriend?*"

Behind him, Heather was taking a close interest in *Canadian Family Physician*.

"My girlfriend and I –" his smug gesture took in Heather – "were in the basement, when we became aware that there was a *creature* down there. A creature, I might add, doing something of a particularly revolting nature."

"She's a bonobo, Julian. That's what they do. They're like teenage boys. Only with rather less sense of personal decorum." A thought occurred to me. "What were you doing down there?"

"That is absolutely no concern of yours." He looked shifty. "We were seeing where the new labs might go. For some possible new projects."

I glanced at Heather, who was by now immersed in a scholarly article about moose bites.

"It's just that if Lucy thought you were having sex, she would look for a way of joining in," I explained. "It's a kind of parallel play."

He flushed. "I want that disgusting animal out of here by nightfall. You will take it to the Veterinary Department and have it humanely put down."

"I will do no such thing."

"Oh yes, you will."

"I have just got off the phone to Kes Riley," I pointed out. "Shall I call him back and tell him that I am wasting time I haven't got arguing over a monkey?"

I realised that the whole lab were now watching us, agog. Julian realised it too. With a snarl he turned and walked away.

I called after him, "By the way, Julian – that wasn't urine. I can send you the reference, if you're interested."

36.2

When he had gone there was a long silence. Heather put *Canadian Family Physician* down.

"I'm not his girlfriend."

Nobody said anything.

"He's taken me out a few times, that's all. He wants to give me a research project of my own."

Wulf, over in the corner, snorted.

187

"What?" she demanded. But then Susan was laughing too, and Rhona, and even Annie, and then – I couldn't help it – I was joining in as well.

"Oh shut up, the lot of you," Heather said, marching over to her computer.

I went down to see Lucy. As if aware she was in trouble, she sat in a corner of her cage, darting anxious looks at me from behind her fingers.

"Is everything all right?"

I looked up. It was Annie, coming into the basement.

"Oh, hello. Yes, it's fine."

"What will you do with her?" Annie offered her a banana through the bars. Lucy took it shyly.

I sighed. "She's safe enough here during the day, I suppose. But I'd better take her home with me at night, or Julian might sneak her away while I'm not looking. And the truth is, he's right – her behaviour is becoming more uncontrollable. She's lonely."

"Perhaps she just needs some exercise. Why don't I start taking her out at lunchtime, and see if that helps?"

"Would you?"

"Of course. It'll be nice to have a break from lab work, quite frankly. Not to mention orgasms."

"Thank you." I sighed again.

"Is something else bothering you, Steven?"

"Oh." I hesitated. It was, I suspected, not entirely appropriate to discuss the progress of a research project with the research subject herself. But Miss G was also Annie, and quite possibly the person in the lab who had the highest IQ of any of us. For a moment I was torn.

"It's nothing, really," I said.

And so walking in the Parks at lunchtime became another part of our daily routine – for often, I went with the two of them, either to puzzle over the last parts of the jigsaw and how they might fit together, or just to clear my head and to stop thinking, for a few precious minutes, about the possibility of failure.

On one occasion, as we sat by the Cherwell watching tourists attempting to master the art of punting, Annie said, "Do you know how to punt, Steven?"

"Oh, yes. That is, I've never actually done it, but from my observations I can see quite clearly how it's done."

"Come on, then." She was on her feet before I could object.

Five minutes later I found myself stepping into a narrow canoe-like craft, carrying on my shoulder a long and surprisingly heavy steel pole not unlike a piece of scaffolding, while Annie untied the rope securing us to the pontoon. Lucy squatted in the bows looking doubtfully at the water.

"The mistake I have noticed many people make," I informed them, "is to fail to allow for the fact that the pole must be placed to one side of the boat. To go forward in a straight line, therefore, one must employ some basic trigonometry."

I pushed off. Unfortunately, the punt had been moored at a slight angle to the river current, and my initial attempt to propel us into the middle of the stream thus overshot. The boat performed a perfect semi-circle, returning us to the bank from which we had set off.

"Of course, one must be in the right position to begin with," I conceded. "I'll just straighten us up, and then we'll be on our way."

I pushed off again. The river bottom at that point was rather muddy, and in freeing the pole from the sticky mud I was required to employ a certain amount of force. This, in turn, meant that when the pole suddenly came free our punt moved rather abruptly, sending us crashing into the opposite bank.

"Don't be alarmed. I can push off again with my foot, like so –"

"Steven! Quick!"

In the heat of the moment I had somehow made the beginner's gaffe of leaving one foot on shore and another in the boat. At some point, as our craft moved with surprising rapidity back into the centre of the river, I had to make a decision as to which I wished to be committed to. Given that I was holding the pole, I realised just in time that it had better be the boat.

"There," I said. "I think you'll find that we are now under way. What is it?"

Both Miss G and Lucy had adopted similar postures. But whereas I knew that, in Lucy's case, lying in the floor of the boat baring her teeth and pressing her hands under her armpits whilst gasping for breath was a sign of terror, in my other passenger it seemed to indicate mirth.

"I will try to make it a slightly smoother ride from now on," I said stiffly. I judged the angles, dug the pole into the river bed, and pushed firmly.

The punt described a perfect about-turn and grounded itself on the bank. Miss G hooted with laughter.

"I see this is amusing you." I was by now going somewhat red in the face. "It's a shame you can't punt yourself."

"But I can," she managed to say. "Rather well, actually."

"Why didn't you say so? In that case, perhaps you would like to take over."

"Certainly not. Watching you is much more fun."

I pushed again, more gently, with the pole, the bottom of which now stuck completely in the mud. Determined not to let go of it, I hung on for dear life, becoming for a moment a sort of human halyard – I believe that is the correct nautical term – attaching pole to boat. The obvious disadvantage to this arrangement was that the human body is incapable of stretching more than four or five feet. Only prompt intervention from Miss G, paddling us backwards with one of the seat cushions, prevented me from ending up attached to neither.

"All right. I'll show you the basics," she said, getting to her feet. The punt, which had seemed unsteady enough with just one person standing up in it, wobbled alarmingly. "I'll go behind you – don't worry, you won't fall in – and put your hands in the right place – here and here, that's it. Now relax: gently raise the pole up – easy – and place it forward – so…"

It was rather pleasant to have Miss G directing my movements like this. Was this, I wondered, why punting existed in Oxford at all – so that young men and women could flirt with each other? It was not an explanation that had occurred to me before.

"Use the pole as a rudder to straighten yourself out. Wait, not so fast – you don't want to be in such a hurry: you've got to use the current, not fight it –"

We were now achieving a fairly respectable mutual rhythm. At this point, however, the river suddenly became very deep, and in order to keep hold of the pole Miss G and I had to squat together in unison as we sank it right down into the water. Pressed against each other as we were, her entire body – from soft breasts to firm thighs – was folded against my own, as if we were two Zs. I could not see her, of course, but I could feel her; I smelt her fragrance and her hair was silky against my cheek. I experienced a sudden moment of breathlessness, brought on no doubt by the exertions of my punting.

"I think you've got it now," she said, standing back.

She sat down again on the cushions, and I found to my great satisfaction that I had indeed "got it". In fact, I became so confident that I was soon able to turn my thoughts to how the general technique of punting could be improved. I realised, in fact, that the whole process of raising the pole hand-over-hand was wasteful of both time and effort, and that it would be far more efficient to simply alternate different ends of the pole in the water, flipping it over like a giant javelin. After a short while I became so proficient with this revolutionary technique – which I named the Fisher Manoeuvre – that I was able to perform it one-handed. It was, I have to confess, with a certain degree of satisfaction that I proceeded back down the river towards the boathouse in a swift, straight line, speeding past struggling tourists and undergraduates alike. Unfortunately I had forgotten that this area was crowded with trees, causing my pole to become entangled in the overhead branches. This caused more merriment to my passenger, but – as I pointed out to her on the way back to the lab – it was not a fault of the Fisher Manoeuvre per se, only of the environment in which it was applied.

37·3

And then there was the time a couple of days later, as we sat eating our sandwiches, when she pulled something from her bag and said shyly, "Here. This is for you."

It was an old book, almost falling apart. I looked at the title. *Collected Poems of W.B Yeats.*

"I don't think I've ever owned a book of poetry," I said, turning it over in my hands.

"It's to say thank you. For treating me." She blushed. "Well, more for teaching me, actually. And for not minding the way I elbowed my way into your lab."

I leafed through it. There is something about poetry, if I am honest – something about the way it is laid out on the page – that I find rather daunting.

"This one," she said gently. She reached across me and pointed. A curtain of brown hair obscured the text for a moment. "Read it aloud – it'll make more sense that way."

A little reluctantly, I read:

> "When you are old and grey and full of sleep
> And nodding by the fire, take down this book,
> And slowly read, and dream of the soft look
> Your eyes had once, and of their shadows deep…"

"You don't have to make a face while you're reading it. It's poetry, not cough mixture."

"I was trying to look poetic."

"Well, don't. Just speak it like you mean it."

> "How many loved your moments of glad grace,
> And loved your beauty with love false or true;
> But one man loved the pilgrim soul in you,
> And loved the sorrows of your changing face."

"There," she said. "*Now* you've got it."

"Be quiet, will you? I'm trying to read it, and you keep interrupting."

> "And bending down beside the glowing bars,
> Murmur, a little sadly, how love fled
> And paced upon the mountains overhead,
> And hid his face amid a crowd of stars."

"What does it mean?" I said when I had finished.

"A poem doesn't have to mean anything. It just is."

"But it does mean something. You can tell it does – you can *hear* it."

She nodded. "It's about sex."

"It is?" I said, surprised.

"It was written for a woman called Maud Gonne. He was a shy, studious poet with a terrible stammer. She was a beautiful revolutionary, a firebrand and free-thinker. Sometimes it seemed to Yeats he was the only man in Dublin she wouldn't sleep with. He loved her hopelessly, passionately – but he knew, too, that in the end his love wouldn't survive unless it was reciprocated. Unless she loved him back. Physically, the way that he loved her."

"*But one man loved the pilgrim soul in you...* What's a 'pilgrim soul'?"

"No one really knows. No one except him, and possibly her, and perhaps not even them. That's why it's so beautiful. When you hear it, you *think* you know... But you can't define it. You can't explain it. The words just kind of...strike off each other."

"Like a chemical reaction."

She nodded again. "You can analyse everything there is to analyse about that poem – the rhythm, the rhyme scheme, the language; you can compare it with the much older French poem it's based on; you can know every detail of Yeats' own life. But you'll never be able to define exactly why those two words – her pilgrim soul, and his recognition of it – are the very essence of his love."

For a long moment I looked at the words on the page, and I saw – I felt – the truth of it.

Murmur, a little sadly, how love fled...

"Thank you, Annie," I said, closing the book. "Thank you for giving me that."

37.4

Even now, as I sit here, writing these words in the quiet of this big, anonymous hotel – even now I can still feel their force.

But one man loved the pilgrim soul in you...

And I think I do understand now what Yeats meant by that phrase. I think he meant that she was brave, and quick, and a seeker after truth: that her soul was pure, like a pilgrim's, but restless and passionate too.

I think he meant that being with her was like being lit up from within.

And I think the sadness, the regret that fills the last two lines, isn't simply the sadness of a passion unfulfilled. I think it's the sadness of a man who knows that, ultimately, his passion will never be as pure or as unswerving as hers – that his love, unnourished by affection, will wither and die, while her pilgrimage, her intellectual search, will take her further and further away from him.

195

Murmur, a little sadly, how love fled...

I know the chemical composition of tears.

But I can't begin to understand the alchemy by which a man can put seven simple words together, and make the tears start to another person's eyes, even now.

Even now.

And I give him a *Collected Yeats*, and get him to read "*When You Are Old*" aloud...

Did I mention that Steven has the most amazing voice? Dry and sardonic and clever?

When he gets to the words "But one man loved the pilgrim soul in you" he gives me a sideways look that just melts – I was about to write, "my heart", but actually it melts something else as well, a little lower down.

Or maybe it's just that my heart and my other organs are starting to become one and the same thing.

Something has changed, these last few weeks. Something huge.

Because the Steven Fisher who once told me "There are several aspects of your sexual data I'd like to investigate further" is now spending every lunchtime with me, walking Lucy in the park and talking about – oh, everything from the different erogenous zones (he knows all about something called the anterior fornix which has only just been discovered, whereas Simon didn't even know where my clitoris was) to poetry. Not to mention climate change, Richard Collins' early books, bellringing, molecular gastronomy and *Watership Down*.

And although I still can't work out exactly how or why this has happened, or why it's him rather than someone else it's happened with, I'm starting to realise that something rather unprecedented is occurring – viz, I actually seem to be fancying someone who I also really like. And who – unless I'm very much mistaken – seems – finally! – to quite like me as well.

Of course, I still don't want to mess all of it up by doing anything too quickly.

Or do I?

When it's this wonderful, why wait?

Her presence was never less than delightful, but the simple truth was, I was out of time. Worse still, I had run out of ideas. I was committing the cardinal error, for a scientist, of simply repeating the same experiment *ad infinitum* in the hope of chancing on a different outcome.

With a heavy heart, I started work on what Kes Riley had called paper B; the paper I would deliver if the mystery of Miss G was never solved and we had to cancel the launch. It was full of platitudes and waffle and gently encouraging maybes. It was the epitaph of KXC79, and of my career.

I took her to The Turl Tavern, found a quiet table, and over a pint of beer broke the news – the surely very welcome news – that we would be discontinuing the tests.

"Thank you for your patience," I told her. "I couldn't have hoped for a better research subject, or indeed a more able student. Whatever happens to the KXC79 project now, I'll make sure you continue to get work experience in good laboratories. There are people I can speak to – Higachi might even take you on –"

"But I don't want to work for Higachi. I want this paper to be published –"

"It isn't just the publication." I told her about my arrangement with Kes Riley; the conference deadline, and Paper B.

She looked aghast. "But that's terrible! And it makes it even more essential that we don't give up now."

"It isn't fair on you, Annie. I can't ask you to keep doing the tests when I don't even know what it is I'm looking for any more."

"There's still time, though," she argued. "There are – what? – eight days left. We might as well use every hour we've got."

"Well, if you're really sure," I said doubtfully.

"Of course. But next time, I want to choose the context-scenario."

"All right," I said, a little intrigued as to what she would go for. "Are you thinking that you might want to re-enact another fantasy?"

"In a manner of speaking… There's a Swamps and Sorcerers game in college tonight. And we're short of an Orc Lord."

I groaned. "Annie, I don't even have a Swamp character – "

"We can make you one. I've got the dice right here, and it'll only take a minute." She pulled some polyhedral dice from her pocket. "Armour first. Ready?"

Sighing, I took the first die and rolled it along the table. "Fifteen points."

"That's quite good," she said, writing it down. "And very useful in the Gorge of Darkwind. Some of the trolls down there have Weapon Abilities you wouldn't believe. Expertise?"

I rolled again. "Twelve."

"…Which makes you a stormbringer. It's not the highest skill in the Wracked Isles, but believe me it's pretty handy when the Spider Hordes are on your tail. What about Fortitude?"

I rolled for a third time "Two," I said wearily.

"Oh, dear, never mind. Luck?"

"Twenty."

"*Very* impressive. That means you get the Improbability Bonus. If you steal a Staff of Sorcery from one of the Wandering Wraiths, you could be a Seer by the end of the game."

"You have the Magus level?"

"Yes, but most of that's advanced – it's only for those who have vanquished the hordes of Gorgoroth."

"As it happens, I have tyrannised the Gorgorothian Plains on many an occasion," I said without thinking.

She stared at me. "Steven Fisher! You're a Swamper!"

"Oh." I shrugged. "Not really. Well, perhaps a bit. A long time ago."

"But why did you stop?"

"You're talking to someone who used to be a Level 6 Dragon Wrangler, and believe me, that can be pretty time consuming."

"A Dragon Wrangler?" she said disbelievingly. "You're not saying you can speak the Old Tongue?"

"As a matter of fact, I can," I admitted. "Runish was a bit of a hobby of mine at school. But it was a long time ago, and – "

"*Eta bentle!*"

"Oh – *Slub gratel mor wrasper?*"

"*Mentas nord tangela!*"

"*Tran farst can nazoor.*"

She frowned. "Shouldn't that be 'nazan'? 'Nazoor' means 'scarily hideous'."

"Oh, yes. I was trying to say that you're 'nazan'."

She dropped her eyes. "Thank you."

There was a short silence. "Well, anyway, I'll see you tonight," she said.

"Yes, I'll look forward to it," I said hopelessly. "Just don't expect too much of it, will you?"

39.3

Actually, and to my complete surprise, it was rather fun. Playing Swamps and Sorcerers with the Hertford College Fantasy Society that evening, I started to consider what I had missed by immersing myself for so long in the KXC79 project. Perhaps, I found myself thinking, life after it was wound up would not be so terrible after all.

But then I found myself wondering whether I would find anyone to share that life with. Was it pressure of work that had caused me to be single, or being single that had caused me to throw myself into my work? I wasn't sure any more.

Afterwards I walked Annie home, still talking about the game – there'd been some idiot who'd tried to eviscerate me with a rune-bolt, not realising that I already had the Armour of Azeroth.

"Oh, Willem's all right," she said as we walked up Queen's Lane onto the High. "He's just a bit…overloyal, sometimes."

"Well, he won't be trying that trick again, that's for sure."

We walked along in silence for a few moments. On our left, the Gothic tower of Magdalen College loomed out of its quad.

"Steven?"

"Yes?"

"What if I'm actually completely cured, but I'm just not very good at the tests and so on?" she said slowly. "You know…what if the context I really need isn't just a simulation, but an actual, physical person?"

"You mean, you might be consistently orgasmic with a real partner in the real world, but not in the laboratory?"

"Exactly."

"Well, are you?"

"I don't know. I haven't had a chance to find out."

"That's a shame."

"It would be useful data, wouldn't it? Even if just to eliminate a potential false positive."

"It would, yes," I said. "Definitely."

I glanced at her as we passed under a streetlight, and even in the sodium-yellow glow she seemed to me to have turned a little pink.[1]

---

[1] Technically, I suppose, she had turned orange, since the pink of her cheeks would have combined with the yellow glow of the streetlights. So-called "sodium" lights – actually a mixture of sodium, neon and argon gases, held under vacuum in borosilicate pipes – have a very narrow colour spectrum which makes almost anything viewed by their light seem monochromatic, even Miss G's cheeks.

"Besides, it's like riding a horse, isn't it," she added. "It's about time I got back in the saddle. I just want to make sure it's with someone I really like."

"Of course."

There was a pause.

"I don't usually do this," she said with a strange little laugh. "I just don't do it. I still can't quite believe I'm doing it now."

"Doing what?"

We had now reached the corner of her street. We stopped. She seemed to be struggling to say something.

"What would you say, Steven, if – oh, God – if, purely theoretically, I were to ask you to go to bed with me?"

"I'd say you mean hypothetically, not theoretically."

"Sorry – hypothetically. Except that it isn't. Hypothetical, I mean. Or theoretical." She swallowed. "Steven. This person I sleep with. I want it to be you."

39.4

"I was thinking of asking you in for coffee," she said with a nervous laugh. "And then I thought – he'll think I actually mean a bitter-tasting hot beverage served with semi-skimmed milk. So I decided – just ask him. That's science, isn't it – speak the truth."

"Annie," I said wonderingly. "*You* want to sleep with *me*?"

"God, yes. Please?"

I could hardly believe it. Annie. The most beautiful, brilliant, delightful person whose company I had ever shared. She wanted to sleep with me.

"But…" I said. "Don't you see? It's completely out of the question."

The light seemed to drain from her eyes.

39.6

"You're a research subject," I said gently. "Don't you know what that means?"

She shook her head.

"Sexual relationships with research subjects…in any area of science it's considered unethical, but with this type of research in particular it's *unthinkable*. It could destroy the whole project. And not just the project: I'd never be allowed to work in this field again. I'd probably be banned from scientific research for ever."

"Oh," she said in a small voice. "I hadn't realised."

"It's not quite as bad as fiddling your results, but it comes a pretty close second. No one would believe in the integrity of a single claim we made."

She flinched. "But how would anyone know?"

"How would anyone know?" I stared at her. "I sometimes wonder if you quite grasp what we're engaged on here, Miss G. This project isn't about stumbling our way to a solution by guesswork and corner-cutting. When our results are scrutinised – when scientists of the future pore over them, just as they pore today over the discovery of DNA, or the description of evolution – they will see one thing above all: that our methods are sound. There can be no hint of scandal or subjectivity. No time-bomb waiting to go off under our claims. Rigorous emotional detachment is the very cornerstone of what we do. When we abandon that, we abandon science."

"I thought… I thought…" Even in the borosilicate light her face looked ashen. "I thought perhaps you liked me."

For a moment I too hesitated. But my duty now was very clear. I shook my head. "If on occasion I have tried to establish a rapport with you, it was only ever for professional reasons. My own feelings had nothing to do with it."

39.7

She turned and ran up the steps to her door. As she fumbled with her key I thought I caught a sob.

"Annie, wait," I said. "That probably sounded harsher than I meant it to. Annie – "

The door slammed.

39.8

I so nearly went after her.

As Richard Collins never tires of pointing out, every one of us alive on the planet today is the product of a million successful copulations. We are the lucky ones, the few who have made it despite the odds, and in our genes the urge to repeat our ancestors' successes pulses continually, like a second beating heart.

For a long moment I stared at her house. She hadn't turned any lights on. I guessed she was still sitting in the hall, on the stairs. In the dark, crying.

I took a step towards the door.

But in my head I could hear the snide footnotes of future authors, couched in the diplomatic language of science but devastating nevertheless: "Fisher, whose project was terminated after accusations of inappropriate relationships with test subjects, was a proponent of the now-obsolete submolecular approach..." "An ambitious attempt to synthesise oxytocin from a neurotransmitter called KCX79 ended in allegations, subsequently upheld, of sexual misconduct..." "Fisher's theories, which are generally considered to be on the fringe of scientific thinking, were thoroughly discredited after the KXC79 debacle..."

It was completely impossible.

I turned and walked away.

I didn't sleep.

My mind was in turmoil. I wasn't sure if I had stood up for a principle, or thrown away my whole future, or both. I had rejected Annie's proposition almost without thinking. But now, in hindsight, had I made the right choice? And – more importantly, perhaps – had I made it in the right way?

I was at the lab early – before anyone else. Waiting for her to arrive. When she did, though, she ignored me completely.

I gave her a few minutes, then went to where she sat at her computer. "Annie…"

She barely glanced at me. "Yes?"

"I just wanted to say," I took a deep breath. "To apologise –"

"There's no need," she interrupted. "You were absolutely right. I see that now."

"Really?"

"It was a moment of professional weakness which betrayed my inexperience as a scientist. In future I will keep my personal feelings and my work separate, just as you do."

"Right," I said. "Of course."

"Will there be anything else?"

"No," I said. "There's nothing else."

At lunchtime I went out for a walk, on my own.

Oh dear.

How am I going to write this bit?

Everything seems to have got messed up.

So I finally decided to sleep with Steven.

It was partly because of something Susan said. I don't think Steven realises that whenever he and Wulf leave the lab someone puts a kettle on and all us girls get together over peppermint tea to talk about boys. How's Rhona getting on with Wulf – we get the blow by blow update. (Synopsis: it's going pretty well but she's not sure he's quite grown-up enough for a serious, long term relationship. Also, he tends to be a bit quick in bed. But she's thinking of suggesting they move in together, even so.) Heather – beautiful, poised, clever Heather – is being courted by Julian Noble. It's been a bit of a secret – Steven didn't know for a while, and there was general agreement that he wouldn't be happy. (I'm picking up a little radar-bleep that maybe Heather and Steven once almost had something... Interesting.) Heather doesn't exactly reciprocate Julian's feelings, but, equally, it's clear she's very ambitious.

"The thing is," she says to me, "science is still an incredibly sexist career. You've no idea how difficult it is to get your foot on that first rung. Julian can be a real help to me."

"Not to mention plenty of mind-blowing KXC79?" I suggest slyly.

She frowns. "Actually, it's not doing that much for me. Do you think it's everything it's cracked up to be?"

And then there's Susan. One time, when we're alone, I ask her if she's seeing anyone.

"I haven't got a boyfriend, if that's what you mean."

"Boyfriend, partner..." I say casually.

"Ah." She nods. "I was wondering if you'd realised."

We look over at where Heather is working on her computer. Beautiful, sphinx-like Heather.

"I know pretty much everything there is to know about female sexuality," Susan says softly. "And at the end of the day it doesn't matter a hoot. All that matters is whether the person you want to go to bed with wants to go to bed with you." She sighs. "What about you, Annie? Found yourself a new man yet?"

I shake my head. "No time."

"Take my advice. Don't hang around here. Get out there and find the real thing. Or before you know where you are you'll have become crazy and bitter. Like us."

"You're not crazy."

"Believe me," she says, "you don't know the half of it. You really, really don't know the half of it." And she gazes over at Heather again.

Hmm.

So, anyway, that remark of Susan's gets me wondering who I *do* want to sleep with.

And I think, Well, why not?

And that, in a nutshell, is the sum total of my logic. Oh, I dress it up with all sorts of fancy justifications and post-rationalisations (like: I did fib to him about my results, before, so if I sleep with him we'll be quits) but basically, once I let myself think about the actual possibility of going to bed with Steven Fisher, I just feel this enormous surging excitement and I know for sure it's absolutely the right thing to do.

And no, for once I don't think the KXC79 has anything to do with it.

So – if I was going to make a pass at Steven – how exactly did I end up sleeping with Professor Richard Collins instead?

You may well ask.

So we have a great time at the Swamp game. Afterwards I let Steven walk me home, and then I make my play. Subtly, naturally.

And then – when he doesn't respond – rather less subtly.

Eventually I just come right out with it. And he looks puzzled – he actually looks confused.

"You mean you want to sleep with me?"

"YES, PLEASE," I almost shout at him.

"But it's completely out of the question," he announces – as if this point were so obvious that only a dimwit arts slut like me wouldn't have spotted it.

You see, it turns out that scientists have standards about this kind of thing. Principles, even. And that makes me feel even more sluttish and humiliated.

I run inside and for a long time I just sit on the stairs in a crumpled heap.

According to Steven, the chemical composition of tears means they rid your body of toxins and stress hormones. In other words, crying really does make you feel better.

Doesn't work this time.

I then spend a pretty-much-sleepless night. During which I come to two conclusions:

A) At least it was Steven I asked. Somehow I know he isn't going to go shouting this around.
B) This is a test.

By which I mean, a test of whether I'm really a scientist. Am I going to let my emotions get in the way, or am I going to get on with my job?

So I grit my teeth and turn up at the lab as usual.

To make matters worse everyone else is in a bad mood too. I don't know what's up with Heather – something to do with Julian, I suppose. Someone mentioned he's discovered Viagra, which can only be bad news.

Rhona and Wulf have had some kind of row, so they aren't speaking either. And Susan's just constantly in a bad mood.

What with one thing and another it's a huge relief when it's lunchtime and I can get out of there. I grab some reading matter and hurry down the stairs with my head down, which means I don't see the man with the frequent-flyer gold tag on his laptop case until I've literally bumped into him.

"Hello," he says, in a soft Irish brogue, picking my books off the floor for me. "Good Lord – *A-level Crystallography*. Haven't seen that for a while."

I mumble something about giving myself a refresher course.

"You're new, aren't you?" he says, taking a look at me. And I mean a *look*. But I don't mind too much – in fact, I'm rather flattered. Because I've just recognised him from the picture on the back of *Enzymes and Influences: How Biochemistry Built Our Brains*.

"Annie Gluck," I say. "Research Assistant. Pleased to meet you, Professor. In fact, I was just –" I indicate the much-thumbed copy of his book on the floor.

"Oh, that," he says, a twinkle in his eye. "Just a little essay, really. Although I did hear yesterday it's going to make the *New York Times* bestseller list this weekend." He snaps his fingers. "Wait a minute! Gluck, A, Hertford College?"

"Yes," I say astounded. "But –"

"Co-author of the KXC79 paper? I knew it – style isn't usually Steven's strong point. And unless I'm very much mistaken, that Syrian Golden Hamster reference was probably yours as well."[1]

"He sent you a draft?"

"Indeed. So, are you going to have lunch with me?"

"Me!"

---

[1] Bradley, K and Meisel, R: Sexual Behavior Induction of c-Fos in the Nucleus Accumbens and Amphetamine-Stimulated Locomotor Activity Are Sensitized by Previous Sexual Experience in Female Syrian Hamsters, *The Journal of Neuroscience*, March 15, 2001, 21(6):2123-2130.

"Of course. I'd take the whole gang, but it looks like you're the only one here. And I'm celebrating – I just did a signing at Blackwell's that sold rather a lot of books."

"Um…"

"I'll throw in an autographed copy," he says winningly.

"Well, OK," I say. Thinking, this is not only a great chance to meet a very important scientist. It's also a chance to forget about all the crap going on in the lab for an hour or so.

Outside, a car and driver are waiting to whisk us back to the Randolph Hotel. Normally I might get a bit irate about someone using a car to drive less than half a mile, but today is different. For one thing I just have to accept that this is his world and it's different from mine, and for another it's so beautifully cocooned in the back there that for the first time all day I manage to relax.

At the hotel there's a Japanese TV crew waiting to catch a quick interview with him. He talks about the book briefly, with the Japanese presenter translating for the viewers, and then we go for lunch.

"Hope you don't mind," he says. "I've ordered it upstairs – the dining room's so public, we wouldn't be able to talk without being bothered by people wanting me to sign stuff."

"Sounds perfect," I say.

"Upstairs," of course, being the Presidential Suite, where he's staying. It's like being inside a very padded church, with High Gothic windows and deep blood-red carpets. The food arrives on a series of covered silver trolleys, wheeled by white-jacketed flunkeys. Lobster, caviar, monkfish skewers, scallops, freshly-made mayonnaise… Silver fingerbowls full of cool water and slices of lemon, to rinse our fingers in. A stack of white linen towels to dry them with. Richard's voice – his brilliant, soft hypnotic voice…

He asks me about the project, and how I came to be involved, and I end up telling him rather more than I meant to. Heavily edited, naturally, but still.

212

When I get to the bit about not actually having a science degree he frowns. "But that's fantastic."

"It is?" I say doubtfully. "I assumed it might be a bit of a drawback."

He shakes his head impatiently. "No – you're *cross-disciplinary*. You're just the sort of person we've been looking for."

It turns out he's on a committee that finds people with multi-discipline skills and sends them to Harvard on a scholarship to study...well, whatever they like, really.

"We're not talking scholarships in the piddling English sense here," he adds. "These endowments are worth fifty thousand dollars a year."

Oh my God.

"The only drawback, I'm afraid, is that you'd be under my personal supervision," he says with a disarming smile. "It's a competitive application, but with your background you'd be a shoo-in. Bristol, Oxford, a credit on the KXC79 paper – they'd be mad to turn you down." His smile broadens. "Well, when I say 'they', I probably mean 'we'. In fact, I probably mean 'I'. Since the scholarships are technically known as the Richard Collins Endowments, I hope I have *some* influence. Tell me about the golden hamster thing again?"

And I am not so naive that I don't know how this might be going to play out. We're in the sitting room of his suite, but the double doors are open to the other room and the whole time we're having lunch I can see the big double bed, spread with crisp white linen like an altar. At some point, either directly or indirectly, Richard Collins is going to make a pass at me. Probably – since he is a charming and cultured man – in a polite, humorous way that makes it quite clear his regard for me will be entirely undiminished if I say no.

Which, of course, I am absolutely going to. In a polite, humorous way which makes it quite clear that I am flattered rather than offended to have been asked.

In other words, all very grown up.

It's difficult, though. Because Richard Collins is not only charming and cultured, he is also the second most brilliant man I have ever met.

And deep inside my cells a million years' worth of evolutionary imperatives are waking up in their cosy little burrows and shouting "*Good sperm, Annie! Good sperm!*" in voices that all sound exactly like my mother's.

But even that might not have been enough to persuade me, except that he starts talking about Steven.

"God, that man is clever," he says, shaking his head. "The best postgrad I ever had. There are so few people I can have a conversation with as an equal. Steven's one of them. Some of the discussions we used to have! Brilliant, brilliant stuff!"

He goes on, but I'm not listening by then. I'm thinking about Steven, and last night, and how it all went wrong. And I feel another stab of that complete, bewildering misery.

"Are you all right?" he says, glancing at me.

"Oh – fine."

And I think: if it can't be Steven I sleep with, who *is* it going to be?

So that when Richard eventually looks at me in a way that means the time has come, and says quietly, "Brandy? Unless of course, you've got to hurry back," I shrug and say, "Why not?"

It wasn't just me: everybody seemed to be in the foulest of tempers. Perhaps it was understandable, after we had all spent so long working on the KXC79 project. But there seemed to be even more to it than that.

Wulf and Rhona weren't talking at all. At least in that instance, I was able to find out what the problem was.

"The usual thing," Wulf said gloomily. "Evolution."

"You've fallen out with Rhona about *evolution*?"

"Not *about* evolution – *because* of evolution. It's like Richard Collins says in his book: because women in our distant past invested more risk in sex than men did, having to look after babies and so on, obviously evolution favoured women who were picky about their partners. Being selective is literally second nature to them. But equally, once they've found a partner they're happy with, they want to settle down. Or as Rhona puts it, 'take this relationship to the next level'."

"Whereas you want to…not settle down?"

He shrugged. "Men are different. Once we've found a partner we're happy with, we start looking for the next one. Job done: next job. Look, don't get me wrong. I adore Rhona. I'm just not sure I love her. Not like that, anyway. Women want commitment: men want freedom. It's hardwired into our biology – the difference is good for the species, but that doesn't help when your girlfriend's refusing to talk to you, let alone have sex."

Heather was upset because she was having to dodge Julian Noble. It was rather pathetic, actually – little cards and notes kept turning up in the internal mail, and a big bunch of flowers arrived by courier. She threw them straight in the bin.

Susan was miserable because… Actually I couldn't work out why Susan was miserable. Uncharacteristically, she seemed to be fretting about KXC79.

"There must be something we can do," she kept saying. "Have you tried analysing the pills? Maybe you mixed up the real pills and the placebos somehow."

"I'm not an idiot, Susan."

It seemed to me that she sniffed.

Then I heard a familiar Irish voice behind me. "Steven!"

I turned. "Richard!" I clapped my hand to my forehead. "I'm so sorry – you left a message, didn't you? I've been distracted –"

"No problem. I was in town anyway, for a signing. To be honest, Kes asked me to swing by. It's time to make a decision, Steven. About the conference."

"Yes, of course." I had been expecting something like this. With a heavy heart I said, "Shall we go somewhere private?"

42.2

We went into the testing room and I told him what I had decided.

"You're sure?" he wanted to know.

Reluctantly, I nodded. "It's the only responsible thing to do."

"You realise what this might mean for your funding?"

"Of course."

"Steven…" Richard leaned against the testing couch and gave me a frank look. "Sometimes science has to be…flexible. At least in the early stages. If you pull out now, people will think it's because you've discovered a major problem with your approach. You won't be able to come back later and say, 'Oh, it was just a small glitch with one subject and we've sorted it now.' People move on. You know as well as I do that in this business there are fashions, bandwagons…some other approach will gather the momentum."

"I know that. But I can't change my results."

"But maybe...polish them a little? KXC79 worked on twenty-seven out of twenty-eight subjects. That means you have a success rate of over 95%."

"But I don't know *why* it didn't work on Annie. That's the point: I can't explain it –"

"Hang on!" He was staring at me. "Are you saying – your anomaly – this research subject who's holding up the entire launch – it's *her*? Annie Gluck? Your intern?"

"I know it's not strictly orthodox to have her on the staff. But I can explain –"

"But Steven – there is no problem!"

"What?"

"I slept with her. This afternoon. And she's perfectly fine."

I looked at him, unable to believe what I was hearing.

He shrugged. "You'll discover this for yourself soon enough, Steven. Women like successful men. It's the evolutionary imperative – they take one look at us and a billion years' worth of maternal ancestors start jumping up and down shouting 'Good sperm! Good sperm!' The point is, you can stop worrying. If she ever had FSD, she certainly doesn't have it now."

I didn't know what to say.

"I'll phone Kes," he said, getting to his feet and clapping me on the shoulder. "Boy, will he be relieved! And then I think we should all do dinner tonight, don't you? A celebration is called for, and I have to be in Edinburgh tomorrow."

42.3

I still couldn't believe it. Annie and Richard? It was impossible.

But then I looked over at Annie. She'd been avoiding me all day, but now she glanced up from her computer and I caught her eye.

217

In that moment I saw that it was true. And something inside me – something that had been waiting there patiently, quiet but alive, for, oh, at least the last two million years – turned its head up to the sky and howled.

42.4

Eventually she went into the testing room to set up the VPG and I followed her. I pretended to be rerouting the cabling for the biothesiometer but I wasn't.

"How was Richard?" I said curtly.

"What do you mean?"

"I gather you had lunch with him."

"Oh. He was well, yes."

"What did you talk about?"

"The paper. And he," she hesitated, "he's suggested I might go to Harvard."

"Harvard!"

"Apparently there's some sort of scholarship."

"Well, you certainly qualify."

"What's that supposed to mean?"

"Didn't you know? Every single one of the Richard Collins Endowments is held by an attractive young woman. I believe over there they're known as Dick's Chicks."

"That's ridiculous."

"So it's not true that you slept with him?"

There was a long, angry silence. "That is absolutely no concern of yours."

"Evidently not." I tossed the biothesiometer leads into a corner. "But you did."

She turned on me then, her expression suddenly furious. "And why

218

shouldn't I sleep with him, Steven? Isn't that meant to be what all this is about?" Her gesture took in the testing room, the lab, and most of the rest of Oxford as well. "That's what you do here, isn't it? You take women who are completely happy not having sex and you stuff us full of your little pills and pronounce us cured. By which you mean, ready to go out and fulfil our biological function – at least, our function as far as *men* are concerned." By now she was almost shouting. "Are you really such a great scientist, Steven Fisher? Have you ever done anything that will actually make the world a better place? Or do you just do nature's dirty work? You're – you're just evolution's *pimp*."

For a long minute we stared at each other: me stunned, Annie defiant.

"You are quite correct," I said stiffly. "The question was not one I should have asked, and the answer is none of my business. Please accept my apologies."

42.5

That afternoon, Miss G was scheduled to perform a standard series of tests. Under the circumstances I deemed it inappropriate to attend.

According to the notes I pulled up later, she reported a satisfactory orgasm and the stimulation programme was terminated after twelve minutes.

"Well, it wasn't the biggest I've ever seen," Susan said, showing me the readouts. "Two microvolts isn't much stronger than a tightly-clenched jaw. But it's a replication. The launch can go ahead."

I looked at the data. Susan was right. Annie was indeed, as Richard Collins had put it, cured.

"Yes," I said. "The launch can go ahead. We'll incorporate these results and send the data off for peer-review immediately. Thank you, Susan."

"Steven?"

"Yes?"

"Are you all right?"

"Of course. Why would I not be?" The phone rang. "Steven Fisher."

"Steven! It's Kes. Thank God! And in the nick of time, too. I don't know what you had to do to get this result but I promise you, you won't regret it –"

"I did nothing, actually, Kes. It's Richard you should thank."

"Indeed." Kes launched into a long spiel about the conference – the charts he would need, how to deal with the press, how KXC79 was going to be renamed Libidia or Femamax or Kix because it turned out that *Whoosh!*, despite the italics and the exclamation mark, meant "ugly pig" in Hungarian. I'd stopped listening.

I was watching Annie as she walked back to her place at the lab bench. Very carefully, she unbuttoned her white lab coat. Then she took it off, folded it up and placed it on the bench before walking to the door.

She didn't look back.

For the celebration dinner, Richard had booked one of Oxford's most expensive restaurants. I wouldn't have gone, but I knew my team would take it as a snub. And for their sakes, at least, I had to try to be pleased.

As I shaved beforehand, I glanced at the piece of paper pinned over my mirror. *For every human action there is a chemical reaction.*

For so long, that line – so brilliant and witty and provocative – had seemed like a rallying cry for a revolution. A revolution that was taking place in universities and research institutions all over the world, as science finally emerged from the shadows into which it had been forced and became recognised, at last, as the dominant force in human life. Evolution, DNA, the cracking of the human genome, and now the mysteries of desire itself... And I was going to be part of it. Like Gabriele Falloppio and the Fallopian tubes, Ernst Gräfenburg and the G-spot, or Realdo Colombo and the clitoris,[1] the name of Steven Fisher would be forever linked with the heights of female pleasure.

And yet I couldn't help comparing that great aphorism of Richard's with the words that Annie had showed me.

Murmur, a little sadly, how love fled...

---

[1] In fact, Colombo didn't actually want his discovery to be called the clitoris. "Since no one has discerned these projections and their workings, if it is permissible to give names to things discovered by me, it should henceforth be called the seat of Venus," he wrote. But it has to be said that Colombo's claim is disputed by – amongst others – Caspar Bartholin, Hippocrates, Avicenna, Gabriele Falloppio, Albucasis, Regnier de Graaf, and Georg Ludwig Kobelt. More recently it has been "re-discovered" by a team of Australian researchers. See: O'Connell, HE, Sanjeevan, KV and Hutson, JM: Anatomy of the clitoris. *The Journal of Urology*, October 2005, 174 (4 Pt 1) 1189–95.

We sat at a big round table. The whole KXC79 team – with one exception. Annie hadn't turned up.

Richard was a dazzling host. On that, at least, I can hardly fault him. Even I, who have read all his books, and hung on his every lecture – I swear there was barely a word or a thought he spoke that night that wasn't new to me.

"For my next project," he said thoughtfully, "I'm looking at what I call 'geekonomics' – the way that men and women's sexual strategies vary to maximise their chances of success. For example, young men in their teens and early twenties find it very hard to attract women, because the pool of available women are mostly pursuing older, higher-status men. But in your late twenties and early thirties, the position is reversed – those same women are not only having to compete with a new generation of younger women, they're also increasingly driven to find the person they're going to have children with. Suddenly, men who haven't been able to get a sexual partner for a decade start to look quite attractive."

"That's brilliant," Susan said. There was a general nodding of agreement. "And so true. Why, I've even noticed that I'm starting to fancy Steven, a little bit! How bizarre is that?"

There was an awkward silence. Then Richard Collins politely changed the subject, and the conversation moved on.

"What about love?" someone asked, as the meal was drawing to a close.

"Love! Now that's a very interesting question. What about love, indeed?" Richard rolled the brandy around in his glass.

"Compared with sex, love is a relatively recent evolutionary phenomenon," he began thoughtfully. "After all, sexual reproduction pre-dates the entire animal kingdom, let alone that tiny offshoot of it which are the mammals, or the even smaller twig which we call humanity. We can assume love only came about at all because of our unusual, not to say highly inefficient, method of perpetuating our species: that is to say, singly, the mother needing to devote several years to each offspring until it is ready to fend for itself in the wild.

"No other species invests so much time and personal vulnerability in the individual embryo. No other species, therefore, invests so much in each act of sex. No wonder we have allowed ourselves to buy into the comforting – and in evolutionary terms entirely bogus – notion that every human being is in some way sacred."

There was a murmur of agreement around the table.

"Seen from that perspective," the great man went on, "it's clear that love is simply a compensatory strategy – in the case of mother–child love, a way of inducing the female to stick around for as long as the embryo needs her care, and in the case of love between mates, a way of inducing the male to assist her.

"But – and this is surely the more interesting aspect of all this – *it is no longer necessary*. There are no longer sabre-toothed tigers prowling around outside the cave, waiting for us to turn our backs for an instant so they can devour our young. There are no longer mastodons competing with us in our supermarkets for the scarce resources we need for our young to survive. Like the human tail, then, which gradually shrank once it was no longer needed into a vestigial remnant of itself, or the appendix, or the wing feathers of the ostrich, we can assume that – slowly, slowly – love, no longer offering any evolutionary advantage, is on the decline."

He took a sip from his glass. "It is no longer the embryo whose parents have pair-bonded who survives: therefore, generation by generation, the ability – the *necessity* – for pair-bonding will be bred out of us, and in a million years or so people will look back on our brief obsession with it and marvel, just as we marvel at the furry bodies of the Neanderthals or the diminutive stature of the Cro-Magnons. Sex, of course, will suffer no such decline: sexual reproduction being, one imagines, the sole prerequisite for evolution to take place at all."

Richard raised his glass. "To the triumph of evolution, and the death of love. Or should I say, the death of pair-bonding."

We all echoed his toast.

"Isn't it possible, though," somebody asked, "that love will survive as an anomaly – like goose bumps, or male nipples, or blushing?"

"Hmm," Richard said. "Well, I suppose it's possible. But we must always be wary of sentiment in our approach to science. We leave that to the physicists, hmm?" – an *aperçu* which, of course, caused us all much merriment.

43.4

It was around midnight when we left the restaurant. Some of the others were going on to a club. I waved them goodnight.

In front of me stood the Martyrs' Memorial and the imposing stone façade of Balliol. I should have turned left, to begin the long trudge back towards my empty flat.

Instead, as if drawn by some invisible force, I crossed St Giles and began to walk up Broad Street. I passed the Sheldonian, went under the Bridge of Sighs, and emerged onto the High. Magdalen Bridge... St Clements... I was hurrying now. I barely allowed myself to acknowledge where I was going as I cut across to Iffley Road –

And finally, I was there. In front of her house.

There was a light on in her kitchen. Hope surged in my breast. I stepped into the street, just as a taxi drew up in front of me.

Richard Collins stepped out of it, speaking into a mobile phone. "In about four seconds, actually," I heard him say.

Annie opened the door. She was in her nightwear – pyjamas and a dressing gown – and she too was holding a phone.

224

"Make that three," he added. "Or even none. Hello."

"Hello."

He lowered the phone. "I missed you tonight."

"So I gather," she said, as she raised her face to be kissed.

44.1

I am a scientist.

    Sometimes it is easier to be detached and rational than at other times. Sometimes, in fact, it is very hard indeed.

44.2

I couldn't bear to go home. I went back to the lab. I caught an hour or so's sleep in one of the old monkey cages in the basement. But long before dawn broke I was awake. Pacing. Thinking.

44.3

The myth that women are less sexually promiscuous than men is, I need hardly say, just that – a myth. Over the last thousand years or so there have been periods when, for cultural reasons, people have tried to deny this truth – but simple biochemistry, as ever, soon supplies the proof. For example, there is the fact that the last portion of a man's seminal fluid actually contains a spermicide: it kills a certain proportion of the man's own sperm, but given the abundance of sperm produced, this is a price well worth paying for the opportunity to kill the most motile, active sperm of the man who comes immediately after you. Mechanisms like this one attest to the fact that, while women in our evolutionary past may have been more choosy than men, having found a high-status man they happily fall into bed with him at the drop of a hat, or indeed any more intimate item of apparel.

Even so, I was somewhat surprised that Miss G had progressed so quickly and with apparently so little compunction from inviting one man – that is to say, me – to share her bed, to having brutish and unthinking sex with a different partner altogether.

Was it just a coincidence? Or something more? Could it be – I found myself considering – something to do with KXC79?

44.4

I read through the test data again. And again. Something was nagging at me. Something I couldn't quite put my finger on.

I kept hearing Annie snap, "*You're just evolution's pimp.*"

I heard Susan saying, "*Maybe there's something you haven't thought of.*"

I heard Annie's voice, as she and I walked back to her house that night. "*I don't do this.*" A strange little laugh. "*I just don't ever do this… I still can't quite believe I'm doing it now.*"

And then: "*Why shouldn't I sleep with him?*"

And, last of all, I heard Kes Riley's shrewd tones.

"*No side effects? Are you sure?*"

And I realised, with a dawning sense of horror, that there was something wrong – terribly, terrifyingly wrong – with the KXC79 project.

44.6

I grabbed my mobile.

"Wulf," I said. "We have a side effect. Something we never even considered."

I didn't have to tell him how bad this was.

"What is it?" he said. "Acne?"

"Worse. Much worse. It's *behavioural*. I think KXC79 is making women have sex with men they don't really want to have sex with."

He whistled. "But that means –"

"Exactly. An emotional response."

Emotional side effects are terrifying for us because they're so nebulous. If your headache pill causes acne, you can potentially do something about it. But if your acne cream causes depression – as, it has been suggested, some acne creams do – then, given to the general population, it is going to be implicated in suicides, mental breakdowns, relationship problems, college drop-out rates…and ultimately, huge and expensive class-action lawsuits.

Nobody wants a pill that makes women have sex indiscriminately. That was not what our project was about – far from it. We were trying to restore a normal function, not create an abnormal one. Imagine, for example, a treatment for FSD that became associated with rising rates of sexually-transmitted diseases or divorce. No government would dream of licensing such a treatment. No pharmaceutical company would go near it.

"Are you sure?" Wulf said at last.

"Not yet. Should I tell Trock?"

"If you tell Trock, they'll cancel the launch for sure. And you might still be mistaken – you don't have any proof."

"What should we do?"

"Stick to the science. Whatever happens, always stick to the science."

He was right. At this moment of all moments, I needed to think rationally.

I had my hypothesis. What I needed to do now was to test it. And the only way to do that – I immediately realised – was via the ultimate form of experiment: a randomised double-blind comparative trial.

That the placebo effect can distort a scientific study is well known, but what is less widely understood is that there are a number of other things that can also skew our results – what scientists call "confounding factors".

For a start, there's something called "selection bias". In a proper study you need, as well as your treatment group, a control group who get a placebo instead. But it's been shown that if the researchers themselves decide which subjects receive the placebo and which the real treatment, they unconsciously steer the "best" patients into the real treatment group. The only fair way to assign subjects is by flipping a coin – in other words, via a "randomised" selection process.

Then there's "observer bias". Even a scientist, when giving a treatment, may see improvements where in fact there aren't any. So the person running the test mustn't know which subjects are receiving the placebo and which the treatment – in other words, he must be "blinded". And to be completely sure of impartiality, he should continue to be blinded until after he has assessed the results as well.

If you follow these safeguards, what you end up with is known as a double-blind randomised trial. Such trials are routinely carried out before a drug is licensed, often with a large cross-section of the population, at a cost of millions of pounds.

I couldn't carry out a proper randomised double-blind of KXC79, but I could perform one on a smaller scale – a very small scale, in fact, with a sample of just two subjects.

I am referring, of course, to Miss G and my colleague, Dr Susan Minstock.

Believe me, I did not take this step lightly. There are serious ethical concerns in giving a drug without consent. But I reasoned that my co-workers, as scientists, would surely have consented if I *had* asked them. The only reason I did not was because knowing they were test subjects could have affected the results.

The experiment I was embarking on was a little unorthodox, but it was completely scientific.

45.3

First I took care of my own observer bias by "blinding" myself.

I took a set of dummy pills from Julian Noble's cupboard. Then I took some real KXC79 pills from the locked fridge where I kept them. I spun the two sets of pills round and round in the rack until I had no idea which was which. One lot went into a pink pill bottle, the other into a blue one.

To find out which pills contained the active ingredient, even I would have to wait until I carried out a chemical analysis, after my experiments were complete.

46.1

I emailed Miss G, informing her that we would need to triple-check KXC79's effectiveness by re-running tests under all the conditions in which it had previously failed.

The answer, when it came, consisted of a single word.

Fine.

46.2

Based on this, I wasn't sure how Miss G was going to be when she came in – that is to say, whether there would be any awkwardness between us.

But in fact she was perfectly polite; almost determinedly so, although the same word she had used in her email – "Fine" – was also employed in answer to most of my initial remarks.

"And you?" she said at last, not meeting my eye. "How have you been?"

"Well, I have been somewhat busy," I said. "With my paper for the forthcoming Sexual Dysfunction conference, which is now only six days away. Unlike some others, I have had little time for socialising."

Miss G performed the standard and by now familiar series of tests. However, I couldn't help but notice that, although she reported her orgasm to be a good one –"Absolutely fantastic, thank you. God, I could happily do that all day" – the machines told a different story.

When everyone else had gone home, I called Susan into the control room and asked her to look over the results with me.

"I'm really starting to wonder if there might be an issue of false reporting with Annie," my colleague commented as we worked through the figures. "I could have sworn she was anorgasmic today."

"The data certainly suggests that she wasn't getting much out of it," I agreed. "Perhaps there's an emotional problem we haven't accounted for?"

Susan frowned. "There was nothing in her Minnesota."

"The monitors, then? Could we simply be reading too much into these numbers?"

"You mean, she might be having orgasms but the machines aren't picking them up?" she said doubtfully.

"Exactly. Perhaps we mis-calibrated the instruments in the first place."

"But the only way of double-checking –"

"Would be for you to go into the testing room and show us what an orgasm *actually* reads as. Yes, that had occurred to me, too."

Susan stared at me. "What?"

"Before we determine that Miss G is lying, we need to be absolutely sure we know how a genuine orgasm presents," I explained. "With all these new instruments, an accurate recalibration is surely the only answer."

Susan was giving me a look that I found slightly unnerving. "And you think *I* should do it?"

"Well, it doesn't have to be you, of course. But it can hardly be me. And it needs to be someone we can trust not to false-report. Of course, if you're embarrassed…"

"I'm not embarrassed, Steve," she said slowly. "After all, it's nothing I haven't asked our test subjects to do. I'm just wondering why you're asking me and not, say, Rhona."

"Rhona's not around." I busied myself with some charts.

"No, she isn't. We just happen to be having this conversation at quite a private moment." Susan pointed to the monitors. "Sure you can run all these without me?"

"Pretty sure. You might need to take it slowly."

"Don't worry. I won't rush you." There was a wry note in her voice I hadn't heard before.

"Right then. If you'd just like to –"

"I think I know the drill."

She went over to the CD player and put on a disc. "Slow Hand", by the Pointer Sisters. Her favourite.

In the testing room a video monitor flickered into life. Susan typed a command, and a faint whirring sound cut through the music.

"I'll control those manually," she said. "Unless you'd rather do it from in here, of course."

Again there was that faint wry note in her voice. She sounded almost *playful*. I frowned. "Manual should be fine."

"Instruments ready?"

"GSA, Startle, biothesiometer, EMG. All ready to go."

46.4

Susan went into the testing room and I saw, on the thermograph, her head settle itself into position. On the Startle monitor the image of her eye, magnified a hundred times, filled the screen. Was it my imagination, or did the eyelid close over the pupil, slowly and deliberately, almost like a wink?

"The things we do for science, eh, Steven?" she murmured. The whirring noise intensified.

Susan grunted – a hard, guttural grunt, like a tennis player trying to pull off a particularly difficult backhand. A few seconds later, as if the ball had been unexpectedly returned by her opponent, she grunted again.

"Nngh."

Her opponent must have sneaked the ball in behind her forehand, because she added a sudden howl of protest to the umpire. "Nnnnah!"

This pattern continued for several minutes. Backhand grunt– forehand grunt – backhand grunt – line call. After that, the tennis player was joined on court by a shotputter.

"NERRR," Susan groaned. "Nngh – Nngh – Nngh – NERRR."

On the loudspeakers, "Slow Hand" came to an end after only three minutes fifty-one seconds – ironically, it is one of the Pointer Sisters' briefest numbers – and was replaced by "He's So Shy". Evidently, we were listening to one of my colleague's compilation discs. I checked the thermograph. A deep flush of heat had given Susan a bright yellow neck and the eyes of a panda.

"HOOOO!" she yelled. The stylus of the GSA recorder quivered, hesitated – then drew a textbook orgasm, a series of spires and steeples at intervals of exactly 0.8 seconds. It was, I thought, not unlike the skyline of Oxford – you could make out Tom Tower, and Carfax, and the steeple of St Giles, and if you half-closed your eyes and squinted a bit, that final aftershock was quite like the Sheldonian Theatre (*Figure 18*).

"Thank you, Susan," I said into the microphone. "That certainly seems satisfactory."

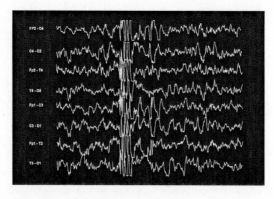

Figure 18: Instrument calibration test (excerpt).

"Strike one," her voice muttered, oddly far away.

"Susan?"

I watched with a terrible fascination as the stylus fell back to the bottom of the screen, bounced limply, and began another arduous ascent.

"Nngh – Nngh – Nngh," grunted the tennis player.

"Nerr – Nerr – Nerr," strained the shot-putter.

There now also seemed to be a third participant, making a high-pitched panting sound like someone who has just popped a very hot potato in their mouth. "Hor… Hor… Hor…"

"Susan?" I said again. No answer.

On the thermograph, vertical green streaks showed where sweat was trickling down her forehead. The stylus of the GSA flew up; stayed there for a long, paralysed moment, and then crashed back down to the baseline.

"Strike two," her voice gasped, still oddly distant.

Finally. I reached out to switch the monitors off Record, but a loud buzzing sound, as if the lab had been invaded by a swarm of bees, told me that Susan, far from being done, had just marshalled reinforcements. On the soundtrack, "He's So Shy" yielded to the 1977 classic "Vibetime". I glanced at the clock. I had not imagined that this stage of the experiment would take quite so long.

On the camera, I finally saw why she wasn't answering. Her headphones had slipped down around her neck. I would just have to wait. I sighed, and reached for some pencils that needed sharpening.

After an encore of "I Want Fireworks", the Pointer Sisters had given up and gone home. In their place came "The Great Gig in the Sky", the final track of side one of Pink Floyd's *Dark Side of the Moon*. Susan had evidently misinterpreted the free-form vocals as being redolent of the sound of a female orgasm – a mistake which a lot of people make.[1][2][3][4][5][6]

---

[1] "The Great Gig in the Sky" is about Death. In rehearsal, the song was known as "The Religion Song", and in live performances it was listed as "Mortality Sequence". If this wasn't clear enough, the song also features two spoken sections. The first, at 0:38 – "And I am not frightened of dying. Any time will do" – was taken from an interview with Gerry O'Driscoll, the Irish doorman at Abbey Road Studios where the song was recorded. The second, at 3:33 – "I never

said I was frightened of dying" – was a snippet of conversation with Clare Torry, a freelance session singer who was called out of the blue and asked if she could contribute some vocals to the track. For this she was paid £30 – it was a Sunday, so she charged double her usual amount.

[2] One thing I always found puzzling, though, is why the cover art for *Dark Side of the Moon* contains so many basic scientific errors. At first glance, it is a depiction of Isaac Newton's famous experiment which demonstrates that light is made up of many different wavelengths. But it actually contains a number of elementary mistakes – such as, on the back cover, showing the refracted colours of the rainbow re-combining to make white light! In fact, that is simply not possible, as Newton himself demonstrated in 1670.

[3] And another thing: there is no Dark Side of the Moon. A "dark side" of any world is defined as a side that faces permanently away from the sun. One side of the moon does indeed face permanently away from the earth, but not from the sun, and every part of the moon gets both day and night in two-week alternations. The side of the moon that is turned away from the earth is the *far* side, not the dark side. So DSOTM should really have been called FSOTM.

[4] However, there is a fascinating theory – relayed to me by Miss G – that it is *not our moon it refers to*. This would explain why the physics of light displayed on the cover are different from those in our own world: DSOTM is set in another universe altogether. So which universe is it? Intriguingly, if you sync DSOTM up to the opening credits of *The Wizard of Oz* – a story in which a refraction spectrum takes a central role – an altogether different meaning is revealed. In addition to the examples given to me by Miss G, my own investigations have revealed:

- Chimes and bells sound just as Elvira Gulch appears on her bicycle.
- During the "Time" guitar solo the fortune teller sign "Past, present & future" appears.
- The fortune teller tells Dorothy that she needs to go home as the lyrics play, "home, home again".
- "The Great Gig in the Sky' plays as the tornado lifts Dorothy's house into the air.
- The vocal ends when the window sash knocks Dorothy out.

[5] It occurs to me that I am probably now disregarding Kes Riley's advice to keep the footnotes to a minimum. Apparently there is an equation somewhere which correlates the number of footnotes in a text to the number of readers who throw that text aside. And I believe it was Noel Coward who said, "Having to read a footnote resembles having to go downstairs to answer the door whilst making love." But this is a very poor analogy – for one thing, you do not have to leave the room to read a footnote. Nor are you likely to be making love at the time. A far better analogy would be that made by the *New York Times* writer who said of a certain article that "reading it is a bit like playing a Bach toccata on the organ – you have to look not only at the keys but also at the pedals below".* Personally, I am rather a fan of the intriguing footnote, though not as great a fan as Edward Gibbon, who devoted one quarter of *The Decline and Fall of the Roman Empire* to them.

*David Margolick, *New York Times*, 5/8/1990.

[6] Technically, when a footnote occupies the majority of the page like this, it is no longer a footnote but a bodynote. And when a footnote itself contains a footnote, like the one above, the latter is known as a toenote.

But at least I now had something more interesting to listen to than the sound of my colleague's arousal.

46.5

"Whoa-a, whoa-a, waah, whoa," sang Clare Torry. "Whoa…" As the track came to an end, I realised my attention had been wandering. But when I checked the readouts, nothing much had changed.

"Whoa," Clare Torry whispered. "ARRGH," sang Susan. "AAA-AAARRGGH." At what point, I wondered, should I worry about hyperventilation?

On the GSA sharp, jagged spikes of activity stabbed suddenly upwards. "Owww," Susan said. "Strike three!" I looked at my watch. She had been in there for nearly twenty minutes now. And, incredibly, it was still not over. After just a few moments, the tennis player was back on court. "Nngh," she grunted. "Nngh – nngh – nngh –"

Then my colleague resettled her headphones, and I seized my chance. "Susan, that's enough. Really. More than enough."

"Oh. In that case I'll just…" She unplugged the mike. I reached out and killed FSOTM too. The only sound was the rattle of the printer as it spewed out Susan's results. I took them from the machine and slid them under a pile of other papers. Then I turned off my laptop.

"So," Susan said, coming back into the control room. Apart from a faint flush, she was no more out of breath than if she had just run up the stairs. "Got what you wanted?"

"Yes, thank you. The printer's just warming up. Can I make you a cup of tea?"

"Tea? Yes, tea would be nice," she said, drumming her fingers on the desk.

In the lab kitchen I tossed a coin. Heads. That meant blue.

I took the blue bottle from my pocket and slipped out a pill. Grinding

237

it up with the back of a teaspoon, I added it to Susan's tea. "Here you are," I said, going back into the control room and handing her the mug. I watched her closely as she drank from it. Good.

Susan, meanwhile, was looking at the printer. "Did you say this was warming up?"

"That's right."

"Nothing's come through."

"Let me check." I turned to my computer. "Oh, drat."

"What is it?"

"The system's crashed."

"What?"

"Completely frozen," I said, pressing buttons at random.

"What about the data?" she said, running her fingers through her hair.

"All gone, I'm afraid."

"You mean –"

"We'll just have to run those tests again. Sorry. I must have pressed the wrong button." I had done no such thing, of course. I had simply been establishing a baseline, *before* Susan drank the tea with the ground-up pills in it, so that I could compare the two sets of results and determine what difference, if any, the pills had made.

I glanced up. Susan was looking at me with the same wry expression she had been wearing earlier. "Let me get this straight, Steven. You want me to do that all over again?"

"Well, not immediately. Feel free to finish your tea."

"Steven?"

"Yes?"

Susan leaned back against a desk. "I think we both know what's really going on here."

"Do we?"

"It's hardly rocket science."[7] For one awful moment I thought she was

---

[7] It is a common misconception that rocket science is in some way complicated. In fact, the physics of thrust, as explained by Tsiolovsky's rocket equation, is far, far more straightforward

238

trying to pout. "How long have we known each other?"

"About three years?"

"In those three years, have you ever had a girlfriend?"

"As it happens, no."

"While we've been working together – quite closely – in these unusually intimate conditions…"

"True, but –"

"And now everyone we know seems to be pairing off," she said. She slid along the desk towards me. "Wulf and Rhona. Heather and Julian. Even Annie and Richard. It's hardly surprising if you and I are feeling a bit left out."

"I don't feel left out."

"I know how tough it's been," she said. "Working on a project like this. Tough for any man, but for a man with no emotional or physical outlets…" Her voice, I noticed, had taken on a husky quality I had previously only heard when she had a bad cold. "I've seen you looking at the women here, Steven. You probably think I haven't noticed but I have."

"Noticed what?"

"Sometimes, when I look into your eyes, I don't see a man. I see an animal. A hungry animal."

"If you're referring to the time I ate your Jaffa cakes," I said, "I apologised the moment I realised my mistake –"

"I'm not talking about Jaffa cakes."

"Oh."

"You needn't feel guilty. We want to screw each other's brains out. It's only natural."

"But I don't want to screw your brains out," I said. "On all sorts of levels, I really, really don't want that." My own voice, due to a sudden involuntary constriction of the throat, seemed to have become a little squeaky as well.

than, say, the biochemistry of female sexual function.

239

She sighed. "If you say so. Anyway, I'm going home now, where I intend to have a long soak in a hot bath with a large glass of cold wine. If you change your mind and decide to join me, you've got my number."

And with that, she was gone.

46.6

I created a new file in my laptop and made some notes.

KXC79 – Double-blind trial – test one

Subject one – Dr M

Method

I established a baseline set of results without treatment. A first orgasm manifested after approximately six minutes forty seconds, with subsequent orgasms at 8.20 and 12.50.

I then administered 10mg of KXC79/placebo (blue pills) without the subject's knowledge and attempted to retest.

Results

Within a few minutes of the treatment being administered, the subject's behaviour altered dramatically. I noticed fidgeting, drumming of fingers on table surfaces, facial flushing, self-caressing, self-grooming and prolonged suggestive eye contact. Her conversation was unusually frank, even for her, and consisted of repeated invitations to have sex. This was accompanied by references to our past relationship which bore little resemblance to reality. Dr M's mental state, in fact, seemed to me to be consistent with what psychiatrists call "confabulation', self-deception of an extreme or psychotic nature.

When her advances were declined, Dr M abruptly left the building. I was deprived, therefore, of the opportunity to see if orgasms were a) more frequent b) stronger or c) closer together than previously. However, on this first trial it certainly seems that the treatment had a marked and alarming effect on desire, arousal, and, indeed, behaviour.

The first part of my experiment had been revealing, if hardly reassuring. Now I had to perform a similar test with Miss G.

I had previously given her a placebo, of course, with inconclusive results. What I needed to do now, therefore, was to see how orgasmic she was without any treatment at all, not even a placebo, before carrying out an identical test with the pills, just as I had with Susan. It sounds a little complicated, put like that – although it became clearer once I had turned it into table form (*Figure 19*).

Figure 19: Double-blind schematic.

	Subject M	Subject G
Blue bottle (subject unaware of treatment)	Done	
Blue bottle (subject aware of treatment)		
No pill (baseline)	Done	
Placebo (subject aware of treatment)		Done
Pink bottle (subject unaware of treatment)		
Pink bottle (subject aware of treatment)		

When I had written it all down I stared at the chart for a very long time. I had just realised that there was absolutely no way I could carry out this test on Miss G without sleeping with her.

47.2

Believe me, I resisted. I racked my brains for any other way – any way at all of doing this without compromising the project still further. But I had already established that Miss G was susceptible to the placebo effect, and that her real-world results were very different from those we saw in the lab. For this test to be accurate, she had to be unaware that it was happening. There was simply no option.[1]

---

[1] I can imagine that at this juncture there may be some of you who are wondering how I reconciled this conclusion with my previous assertion to Miss G that it would be inappropriate – not to say unethical – to have sex with her. The answer, which will surely become apparent after only a moment's reflection, is that I was now proposing to have sex with her not for personal gratification, but to serve the higher cause of science. There is a long tradition of scientists who have involved themselves in their own experiments in this way. One thinks of Dr Barry Marshall, the Australian gastroenterologist who, in order to test his hypothesis that stomach ulcers are caused not by stress but by the common bacterium *Helicobacter pylori*, drank a mixture containing the bug and suffered gastritis as a result. For this discovery he later shared the Nobel Prize. Likewise, the 18th-century Scottish surgeon John Hunter deliberately gave himself gonorrhoea in order to study a potential cure (unfortunately, the cure was unsuccessful, and Hunter had to postpone his marriage as a result), while Jesse Lazear, a US Army surgeon, died of yellow fever in 1900 after allowing an infected mosquito to bite his arm. A more recent example in my own field is that of Professor G.S Brindley, whose lecture on the efficacy of intravenous drugs in male erectile dysfunction was memorably described in the *British Journal of Urology*.

"His slide-based talk consisted of a large series of photographs of his penis in various states of tumescence after injection with a variety of doses of phentolamine and papaverine. After viewing about 30 of these slides, there was no doubt in my mind that, at least in Professor Brindley's case, the therapy was effective. Of course, one could not exclude the possibility that erotic stimulation had played a role in acquiring these erections, and Professor Brindley acknowledged this…

There might have been no alternative to sleeping with Miss G, but that did not necessarily mean that it was going to be straightforward. In fact, now that I thought about it, there was another, possibly even more insurmountable hurdle. Although polite relations had been restored, Miss G was still being somewhat distant, and I suspected that any suggestion from me that she and I go to bed together might well meet with a frosty response, not to mention accusations of hypocrisy, double standards, and even jealousy.

It was imperative that I did not waste unnecessary time over this. Turning to the internet, therefore, I googled "dating skills".

47.4

There were a huge number of sites to choose from – over two million, in fact. To take just the first few examples:

> He indicated that, in his view, no normal person would find the experience of giving a lecture to a large audience to be erotically stimulating or erection-inducing. He had, he said, therefore injected himself with papaverine in his hotel room before coming to give the lecture. He then summarily dropped his trousers and shorts, revealing a long, thin, clearly erect penis…
>
> [Saying] "I'd like to give some of the audience the opportunity to confirm the degree of tumescence" he waddled down the stairs, approaching (to their horror) the urologists and their partners in the front row. As he approached them, erection waggling before him, four or five of the women in the front rows threw their arms up in the air, seemingly in unison, and screamed loudly. The scientific merits of the presentation had been overwhelmed, for them, by the novel and unusual mode of demonstrating the results."
> Laurence Klotz (2005): *BJU International* 96 (7).

Dating Tips For Men

DoubleYour**Dating**.com **Dating** Tips On How To Approach, Meet & Date
Any Woman You Want (sponsored link)

Social, Conversational, and **Dating Skills** – Psychological Self-Help
Social, conversational, and dating skills to relate better.
www.mentalhelp.net/psyhelp/chap13/chap13l.htm – 25k – Cached – Similar
pages

The **Dating** Academy
Professor Pickup shares scientifically-proven secrets of seduction
www.professorpickupsdatingacademy.com – 25k – Cached – Similar pages

You don't get laid, I don't get paid!
Improve your **Dating skills** right now!
Tripod/psyhelp.htm – 25k – Cached – Similar pages

As you can imagine, I was relieved to find amongst the dross a fellow academic who had taken the trouble to test and verify his findings. I clicked on Professor Pickup's entry. It took me to a page that read:

Discover the power of Advanced Neurolinguistic Programming!

Join Professor Pickup for his Seduction Seminar 101 and learn:

- How to Approach a woman
- Using Fluff Talk to elicit her Values
- Kinaesthetic techniques: Embedded Commands that make her Want You
- Patterning Her for Sexual Seduction
- and many other Scientifically-Proven Techniques

Contact The Professor.

None of these terms was familiar to me, but as the subject was somewhat removed from mine, I was not entirely surprised by that. I opened the email link and wrote:

Dear Professor Pickup,

Forgive me for contacting you out of the blue. Like you I am an academic, although I confess that I am not at all familiar with your field of neurolinguistics.

However, I now find myself in a situation where a research project I am engaged in requires me to go on a date with a young woman and, as unlikely as it sounds, to persuade her to have sex with me. Have you published any papers on this subject that might help?

Kind regards,
Steven Fisher DPhil,
Oxford University.

PS I am in a desperate hurry.

Barely half an hour later I received a reply.

From: professorpickup@hotmail.com
To: Fisher.S@nb.ac.uk

dude,

sure I can help you jus email me the money using Nochex or Paypal. It's $99 for three emails. You are so going to nail this chick.

best,

The Professor

The tone of this reply made me a little anxious. However, I was eager to find out about the professor's research, so I sent the payment and awaited a response.

That, too, arrived almost immediately.

From: professorpickup@hotmail.com
To: Fisher.S@nb.ac.uk

hey steve,

thanks for the $99. This is the first email, right? **Here's how you're going to use Advanced NeuroLinguistic Programming (ANLP) to achieve your goals!**

1. DON'T go on a date with this chick. Fact: chicks go on dates with men they're never going to sleep with. Dates are for schmucks (or as we Pick-up Masters call them, AFCs – Average Frustrated Chumps).

2. Get this chick to come along to something you were going to do anyway. Then here's how you play it.

There followed a detailed list of instructions which encompassed everything from the importance of Fluff Talk to the necessity of Keeping Away From Facts:

Facts BORE her! Get to the FEELINGS. Instead of saying, 'I like your perfume. What is it?' say, 'What's the STORY behind that BEAUTIFUL, SENSUAL perfume you're wearing?'

Then there was a section on something called Kinaesthetic Anchors:

> Mirror her Trance Words back to her in the same language she uses, while gently touching her on the elbow.

> What you're doing is linking that Positive Value to your touch, so that every time you touch her in the future she'll associate it with good stuff!

While the section on Embedded Commands was frankly revelatory:

> Use the power of the subconscious! Dude, if you talk about giving her 'MASSIVE hapPINESS', her subconscious will hear 'massive penis'! If you say 'BELOW me', she'll hear 'blow me'! This stuff really works!

Most of all, though, Professor Pickup wanted to impress upon me the Power of Patterns:

> A Pattern is basically when you TALK about GREAT SEX whilst PRETENDING to talk about something else. That way, you're putting the idea in her mind that SEX WITH YOU will be GREAT!

He provided half a dozen Sample Scripts for me to memorise and signed off with the encouraging words:

> If you use these scripts properly I GUARANTEE that you will have sex tonight.

Despite the admirable clarity of these instructions, I couldn't help but feel a little uneasy. Much as I wanted to believe ANLP would work, I wasn't entirely confident in my own ability to deliver some of the scripts without stumbling. And there were certain parts of the email that looked suspiciously as if they had been cut-and-pasted from different sources.

I hit Reply and wrote:

From: Fisher.s@nb.ac.uk
To: professorpickup@hotmail.com

Dear Professor Pickup,

Forgive me if I query a couple of your points – the urge to double-check is, of course, the scientist's curse. Could you tell me which journals this research was validated in? May I have the references?

Sincerely,
Steven Fisher

From: professorpickup@hotmail.com
To: Fisher.S@nb.ac.uk

Hey Steve,

It's Advanced NeuroLinguistic Programming, right? This stuff is scientifically PROVEN. There are plenty of references to it on the interweb, if you do a search.

Good luck,
The Professor

From: Fisher.s@nb.ac.uk
To: professorpickup@hotmail.com

Dear Professor Pickup,

Could you at least tell me who awarded your Chair, and what professional bodies you are affiliated to?

Steven Fisher

From: professorpickup@hotmail.com
To: Fisher.S@nb.ac.uk

Hey Steve,

Chair? Don't follow you on that one, my man. I have a chair but it's just your basic Office World computer-desk model. It does have wheels, though.

That's your last email, officially, but seeing as how we've had a great chat, let me know if you need any more help and we'll sort something out.

The Prof

Despite my misgivings, I had little alternative but to follow Professor Pickup's recommendations. Even if he wasn't a real scientist, he almost certainly knew more about picking up women than I did.

I went through the university's Daily Information sheet, looking for something I would have been going to anyway. The problem was, I rarely went out, and certainly not to student productions of *A Midsummer Night's Dream* set entirely in winter, or the latest scabrous TV comedian at the Apollo, which was all that seemed to be on offer that evening. Then I remembered that the Campanology Society was planning a half-peal at St Giles', an event that would last about an hour and provide some interesting changes between different ringing progressions.

Annie still seemed to be avoiding the lab, so I called her mobile.

"Oh, Steven," she said neutrally. "It's you. What can I do for you?"

"I was wondering – are you doing anything tonight?"

There was a slight pause. "Not much. Just going through some essays on valency."

"I was wondering if you'd like to hear some church bells being rung." Even as I said it, I realised it wasn't the most exciting of invitations.

"No, not terribly."

"Oh," I said. I flicked through my notes. Oddly, this was the one eventuality Professor Pickup seemed not to have anticipated. I cleared my throat. "The thing is, it's in the nature of a test. A date-replication scenario."

She snorted.

"Perhaps not the most exciting or realistic of dates," I said, "but it's either that or *A Midsummer Night's Dream*. And I saw that years ago." I seemed to remember her saying she loathed drama.

There was a long pause, and for a moment I thought Professor Pickup's advice must have been flawed.

"Well, OK," she said at last, with a heavy sigh. "If you insist."

"Great," I said, relieved. "Shall we meet at St Giles' church? They're planning to start at seven."

48.2

Hmmm... Steven's asked me to some kind of bellringing concert. A little odd, perhaps, but he insists it's just another date-replication scenario.

Actually, I got the impression when he phoned that there might be some other agenda as well. I suspect he's trying to say that he wants to do something with me. As a friend, I mean. An olive branch after all the mix-ups and me making that stupid pass at him and him turning me down.

I'm still angry with him about that, actually. But I also miss him terribly – miss talking to him in that open, easy way that we used to before the whole making-a-pass thing happened.

So I'll go along. Even though it does sound... Well, a bit weird.

Although if this were some big Victorian novel, bellringing would probably be another corny metaphor.

48.3

At ten to seven I was waiting in the church, along with a small audience of campanologists, mathematicians and other interested parties. I had printed out Professor Pickup's email for reference, and passed the time memorising his script lines.

A few minutes later Annie turned up, and slid into the pew alongside me. She was wearing a lovely grey velvet scarf that set off her eyes.

"Hi," she said.

"Hello." We were speaking in whispers, as one does in a church. I cast my mind back to the professor's instructions. Step one: Fluff talk.

"What have you been up to?" I asked. No – damn – that was eliciting Facts. But Annie was answering anyway.

"Quite a lot, actually. I've covered all of covalent bonds, electronegativity and the Pauling scale. Oh, and I rewrote an essay on ionic bonding." I think she was still angry, but it was hard to tell, because of the whispering.

"And how does that make you FEEL?" I whispered.

She gave me a puzzled look. "Well, it's not ideal, is it, trying to do all that in a week, but it's better than nothing."

"No, I meant…" I changed tack. "What's the story of that BEAUTIFUL, SENSUAL perfume you're wearing?"

"I'm not wearing perfume." She pulled the top of her sweater up to her nose so she could sniff it. "Do I smell? It's probably washing powder."

So far, I felt, Advanced Neurolinguistic Programming was not proving much help. "If I were to ask you," I whispered, "what the most important thing to you in a relationship is, what would you say?" I was, of course, simply Eliciting Values here.

She looked startled. "In *our* relationship?"

"No, um – just any relationship."

She thought about it. "I would say that different things are important in different relationships, depending on the other person. Why? Is it for a survey?"

"No," I said. "I was just wondering."

Now I had to Mirror her Values back to her.

"Wouldn't it be nice," I suggested, "if you could spend time with a man who makes you feel differentiated? Whose voice intrigued and at the same time stimulated you? I get the feeling that this could happen to

253

you right now, with me." As I spoke I touched her several times on the elbow.

"Steven – why are you poking me like that?"

"No reason." I cleared my throat. It was time to move on to a Pattern. "What do you really love doing, Annie?" I whispered.

"Well," she said doubtfully, "work, I suppose. That's what I really like – working."

"Work?" I repeated. Surely not even Professor Pickup could turn work into a paradigm of sexual intercourse. "Anything else?"

She shrugged. "And Swamps and Sorcerers, of course."

"I'm curious... what is it about Swamps and Sorcerers that makes you love it?" I whispered. "What do you FEEL when you're playing Swamps and Sorcerers? What's it like when you're THERE NOW, Swamping and Sorcering?"

"Well, I suppose one of the things I like is that gender doesn't come into it at all. You create a character, and the character has certain powers, such as long-sightedness, indefatigability or whatever, and then you roll the dice, and that's it."

Put like that, Swamps and Sorcerers also seemed unlikely to provide the opportunities I was looking for. I decided to move on to one of the Professor's own sample scripts. "You know that feeling you have when you get home after a hard day of work and all you can think about is STRIPPING off your clothes and SLIDING into a hot bath?"

"No," she said, somewhat shortly. "I shower. In the mornings."

At that moment there was a terrific din as several tons of iron began to peal above our heads.

I leaned towards her. "You know, I learned this amazing visualisation exercise that really helps you pick yourself up when you aren't feeling that great. Would you like me to show it to you, so that you too can do this and feel absolutely wonderful?"

She pointed to her ears and shook her head, frowning. "I CAN'T HEAR YOU," she yelled.

"IMAGINE YOU'RE HOLDING A FLOWER," I shouted.

"AN HOUR?"

"A FLOWER."

"WHAT KIND OF FLOWER?"

"THAT'S UP TO YOU. CAN YOU SEE THE BEAUTIFUL PET-ALS?"

"NO," she said. "WHAT'S WITH ALL THE PSYCHOBABBLE, ANYWAY?"

"I THINK I WANT TO MAKE LOVE WITH YOU."

"WHAT?"

"NOTHING."

Above our head, the ringers effortlessly changed from Plain Bob Minor to Grandsire Triples. The members of the audience turned to each other, nodding and smiling. I glanced at Annie, but she was staring straight ahead with a scowl on her face.

It was fully ten minutes before Grandsire Triples changed to Cambridge Treble Bob. Annie was by now looking almost catatonic. With a sinking feeling I realised that I had invited her to something that was boring the pants off her – or rather, and far more problematically, boring the pants onto her. What on earth had I been thinking?

Eventually, after forty-five endless minutes, the ringers changed to a triumphant course of Plain Hunt, and thus to Rounds. After that the only sound was the echo of the bells' reverberations subsiding gracefully off the stone walls. A little later the ringers themselves trooped out of the tower, to be greeted by a smattering of polite applause.

"Well," Annie said, putting her scarf on. "That was, um…yes."

"Wait," I said, "Annie – I'm sorry – it wasn't very interesting."

"It was fine, Steven. Really."

"Annie," I said miserably, "you were bored witless."

"No, I wasn't," she said. She looked at me, and suddenly she didn't look quite so angry. In fact, she almost looked as if she might be trying to suppress a grin. "Though it was a little…repetitive at times."

"I'm afraid it's one of those things you really have to do for yourself before you can enjoy other people doing it."

"And then it's different?"

"Oh, yes," I said. "You see, bellringing is all about making quite complicated mathematical patterns. You probably didn't even notice, but each one of those rounds – the peals – involved the ringers swopping their positions. Take Plain Major." I scribbled down a rough number line on a scrap of paper. "See? If you're the eighth bell – the tenor – every new peal puts you in a different position." (*Figure 20*)

"So it must be pretty difficult?"

"That's the funny thing. When you start ringing, it's all you can do to keep the rhythm. You just heave on the rope when it's your turn, and hope no one notices the odd fumbled stroke. But once you get a bit more confident, you find yourself keeping track of the changes almost without thinking. Ringers call it bellsense – it's like a sort of intuition. Your arms seem to move of their own accord. And – it's hard to explain – somehow you're inside the pattern, and you don't have to plan what comes next at all. Instead of you pulling the bells, it feels as if the bells are pulling you. And that's when you relax and let the noise and the movement and the pounding of the bells just pick you up and take you away."

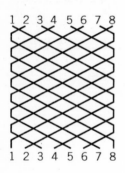

Figure 20: An eight bell peal progression represented as a number pattern.

"Put like that," she said with a rueful smile, "it doesn't sound quite so dull after all."

"Exactly." I knew I had, at the most, just one more shot at this. I reached out a finger and stroked her scarf. It was soft – some kind of cashmere, perhaps. "What's the STORY behind this lovely scarf?"

"This?" She looked down and smiled. "It was a present from Richard. He sent it down by courier from Edinburgh this morning. Why?"

"Nothing," I said.

At home I wrote up my notes.

KXC79 – Double-blind trial – test two

Subject two – Miss G

Method and results

I attempted to establish a baseline without treatment. Miss G showed no sexual arousal or interest, despite being exposed to a number of "chat-up" scripts containing proven neurolingistic patterns. Thus a very different response to that exhibited by Subject One was established (*Figure 21*).

Figure 21: Updated schematic.

	Subject M	Subject G
Blue bottle (subject unaware of treatment)	Done	
Blue bottle (subject aware of treatment)		
No pill (baseline)	Done	
Placebo (subject aware of treatment)		Done
Pink bottle (subject unaware of treatment)		
Pink bottle (subject aware of treatment)		

Then I fired off a rather curt email to Professor Pickup.

Dear Professor,

I have to report that, far from "nailing" the young woman in question, the non-date was a non-event. Your scripts contributed remarkably little, and indeed were described by her at one point as "psychobabble". Do you have any further suggestions?

Regards,
Steven Fisher

To my surprise, he once again replied almost immediately.

From: professorpickup@hotmail.com
To: Fisher.S@nb.ac.uk

Steve,

Hey! Don't worry, we see the "psychobabble" block plenty of times. There are powerful, proven ways of turning it round so that she's jelly in your hands! These are, like, really advanced techniques so it's $199 for three more emails.

The Prof

This time I did not respond.

My temper improved next morning, however, when I recollected that, whatever the results of these first two tests had been, I could reasonably expect them to be precisely the opposite when I swapped the pills over: that is to say, if the pills from the blue bottle had indeed been responsible for Susan's behaviour, then giving them to Annie should have exactly the same effect on her.

Of course, if I were to accurately gauge the effects of the pills on Annie, they should really be the only variable between the two events. Logically, I should take her to exactly the same bellringing concert all over again, repeat exactly the same chat-up lines, and only then determine what difference – if any – the addition of the blue pills made.

Sometimes, we scientists don't exactly make things easy for ourselves.

49.2

I was at the lab bright and early the next morning, hoping that she would make an appearance.

She did. She had brought in a large cardboard box, into which she began carefully stacking all her chemistry textbooks.

"Good morning," I said, going over to her. "I hope that on reflection you enjoyed last night."

"Oh – Steven. Yes, it was very interesting. Thank you."

"Perhaps you'd like to do it again sometime," I suggested.

"That would be nice," she said without much enthusiasm.

"Excellent. How about tonight? There's a very similar progression planned for a church in Summertown – a minor Surprise followed by Doubles. I think you'll find –"

"Actually," she said quickly, "I've already got plans for tonight."

"Oh." On the lab bench, I noticed, was a large and expensive-looking bunch of flowers. They had clearly just been delivered, as they were still wrapped in cellophane.[1] "Those must be for Heather," I said, reaching for them. "From Julian. I'll put them by the right workstation." I glanced at the card.

Can't stop thinking about you – Richard

I put them down again. "They seem to be for you after all," I said stiffly. "From Richard. Richard Collins, presumably."

"Presumably." She busied herself sorting through some folders.

"He's your plan for tonight, I take it."

"No, actually. Tonight he's in Copenhagen. And I've got a Swamps and Sorcerers game."

"Ah." I was aware, of course, that it had been after a Swamps and Sorcerers game that everything had got so horribly mixed up. But time was pressing. "Well, perhaps I could come to that."

"If you like." She was sorting through her essays as she spoke. "We always need more Orcs."

49.3

"Steven?" It was Susan, standing at the door.

It was four o'clock. I had spent almost the entire day lost in thought.

---

[1] The biochemical symbolism, as it were, of cut flowers as a courtship gift is, now that I come to think of it, rather fascinating. Flowers are, of course, the sexual organs of the plant: once cut, their lifespan becomes even more limited than it was before. The giver is therefore reminding the givee that their own sexual organs will remain sweet-smelling for only a short while before they too wither and die.

"How's it going?" she asked, coming in and perching on the desk.

"Oh – fine. Just a few last-minute things I'm still double-checking. For the conference."

"It's not too late to cancel, you know," she said. "No one will think any the less of you if you decide you need more time to refine the formulation. No one who really matters, anyway."

I glanced at her, surprised that she had divined the reason for my unease.

"Steven... " she continued. "These results of Annie's... I think you and I need to talk about them. Now. Before it's too late."

I sighed. "You're right, of course. I'll get us some coffee."

In the kitchen, I ground up two pills from the pink pill bottle and added them to her cup.

49.4

"To some extent I blame myself," she was saying. "I should have realised when she first put herself forward that she was completely unsuitable."

"Mmm," I said. I glanced at the clock. It had been eight minutes since Susan started drinking her coffee. And so far, she was displaying no signs of behaving any more irrationally than usual. Quite the reverse, in fact. This was the most reasonable she'd been in months.

I sighed. There seemed little doubt that whatever was causing the problem, it was in the blue pills and not the pink ones.

"And then there are her latest tests. Steven, I'm certain she's stopped being orgasmic. Could the new formulation somehow be responsible for that?"

"But if you look at the brain mapper scans there's nothing different," I argued. "Apart from this very faint activity in the anterior cingulate."

"Show me?"

I pointed to my laptop screen.

"Mmm," she said. "I do see what you mean."

As she leaned over my laptop I became aware of a faint but not unpleasant odour. Susan was wearing perfume.[2]

"Have you considered confounding factors?" she said, glancing at me over her shoulder. As if by accident one of her hands, dangling off the desk, brushed my knee.

"Of course. Observer bias, randomised selection –"

"I meant on her side."

"Such as?"

"Maybe she just gets off on all this."

I frowned. "In what way?"

"The machines, the pills, the equipment…scientists in white coats… Some people find this kind of thing pretty sexy." Once again her hand brushed against my knee. "I know *I* do sometimes."

I shot her a puzzled look. Unless I was very much mistaken, my colleague was once again attempting to flirt with me.

Susan, meanwhile, seemed to take my silence as some kind of positive response. The hand travelled upwards, increasing its pressure. It came to rest at the very top of my thigh.

This, of course, was most puzzling. Assuming that the pills from the blue bottle were the ones containing the active ingredient, she should on this occasion be behaving normally.

But then, I reflected, what *was* normal, for Susan? Given what I had seen at SexDys, it might be that what I, or any sane person, would describe as erratic or disordered behaviour was, for her, an everyday mental state.

---

[2] Given that man's olfactory receptors are no longer capable of detecting the sexual signals in female sweat, it might seem puzzling that women bother with perfume. However, further investigation shows that the picture is more complicated than it first appears. For example, it is well known that women in a closed community gradually synchronise their ovulations, the mechanism for which can only be airborne. Equally, the principal ingredient of perfume – musk – is obtained from a male deer that is in season, while the secondary ingredients – flower fragrances – are the plant's own natural attractors to pollen-spreaders. Clearly, there is some biosocial aspect to perfume-wearing that is not yet fully understood.

On the other hand, my colleague had never before attempted – as she was doing at this precise moment – to drag the ends of her painted fingernails lightly up and down the inner surface of my leg.

Could I have got it wrong? Could the pills from the pink bottle, in fact, have been the ones containing KXC79? And if so, was I now witnessing a side effect of a magnitude that even I had not anticipated?

"I missed you last night," she murmured. "That hot bath…let's just say it wasn't quite as hot as it would have been if you'd been in it too."

In thermodynamic terms, of course, this statement made no sense whatsoever.

Susan swung my chair around to face her. Spreading my knees, she slid off the bench so that she was standing directly between them. Then she began gyrating her upper torso, while simultaneously unbuttoning her lab coat.

"What are you doing, Susan?" I asked incredulously.

"I'm taking my clothes off."

Her bra was red and black, festooned with tiny bows. But perhaps a sexologist has to invest in decent underwear.

"Yes, I realised that," I said, mystified. "But why?"

"It makes sex so much easier." She swivelled her skirt around, undid a button, and stepped out of it. Then she reached up behind her back and unhooked her bra.

As her breasts – her surprisingly large and shapely breasts – swung free, I distinctly heard her mutter something that was even more surprising than her breasts: "I just hope this works."

Definitely a side effect.

49.5

As Susan was disrobing, I had a sudden thought about KXC79. It had just occurred to me where the difficulty might lie. Because KXC79 synthesised l-oxytocin from other peptides, the gain in oxytocin was matched by a potential loss of other neurotransmitters. It was as if I had turned all the buses in the city into taxis – there would be more taxis on the street, but no buses, so no one would be able to get to where they wanted to go.

Susan was by now squatting in front of me, undoing my trouser zip.

"Oooh," she said. "Nice."

If the other peptides – my buses, if you like – were having a previously unrecognised inhibitory effect on female behaviour, that would explain why turning them into oxytocin had the dual effect of enhancing arousal *and* changing behaviour. It wasn't an insurmountable problem, just a setback.

"It's not insurmountable," I said.

Susan pulled open my belt buckle. "Let's hope not."

"I need to send some of my taxis to their original destinations, and re-route some of my buses."

"You need to get out of this underwear."

"Susan, you don't understand. I needed to experiment –"

"Fine. Wear *my* underwear, if that's what you want." Then she started doing something to me which was really rather pleasant. Mind you, I suppose a sexologist has to be good at that sort of thing.

"Susan," I said firmly.

"Mmnghf?"

"There's something I need to tell you."

"Hmmngh. Nndt gdtyh."

"Yes, now. The thing is –"

"Steven," she said, lifting her head, "shut up." And she began doing something really quite ingenious with the end of her tongue.

The mechanisms which control the human erection are interesting. There are actually two completely separate neural networks involved: the sympathetic and the parasympathetic systems. Nerve impulses are sent by the brain to an erection centre positioned at the base of the spine. This causes the release of a substance called acetylcholine, which in turn causes the small arteries in the penis to dilate. The parasympathetic system is the one which usually manages this process, with the sympathetic system acting as an override, for example in cases of fight-or-flight. Neither mechanism is under the control of the conscious brain – we can no more tell the penis to stop erecting than we can tell the stomach to stop digesting or the heart to stop beating.

Of course, what we *do* with our erections is a different matter – here the conscious brain does have a role. But the part of our brain used for conscious thought is actually a very small proportion of that organ; principally the outer part, which makes up less than 5% of the whole. It's a bit like the ocean: the surface may be where the fishing happens, but the really big, weird creatures live a long way below.

In the dark, murky depths of the cerebral cortex, not a lot of what we would recognise as actual thought takes place. Down there lurk the shadowy synaptic remnants of all our forefathers; not just recent ancestors such as *Homo sapiens*, but the millions of generations which went before – Piltdown man, *Homo heidelbergensis*, *Homo erectus*, the prehuman hominids, the pre-hominid primates, *dryopithecus* and his ilk; and further back still, eon after eon of mammals, fish, and various species of amoeba.[3]

And what every single one of those billions of ancestors was shouting

---

[3] I choose amoebae as our ancestors here because it is the popular – albeit sentimental – choice: I am of course well aware of the controversy that surrounds this simple assertion, and that, in all likelihood, it may be more accurate to say "bacteria".

at me now – either in my own language, or Indo-European, or cave-dwelling Neanderthal, or the animal cries of pre-placentals; even, perhaps, in the tiny squeaking urgings of amoebae – was this: "Do it, Steven! Do it!"

Goodness, she was certainly lithe.

49.7

Susan was evidently one of those people who like to talk during sex.

"In a minute, Steven," she said as she wriggled on top of me, "I'm going to tell you something."

If I replied at all, it was probably in Neanderthal.

"I'm saying this now," she said, grimacing as she pinned me to the chair with a particularly athletic squat-thrust, "because I know you're going to be angry."

"The thing is," she said after a moment, "I've done something rather terrible."

"Urrgh," I said.

"And I want you to promise me," she said, looping her arms round my neck and throwing her head back and forth, "that when I do tell you, you're not going to over-react."

She paused to rearrange herself into a position redolent of the stretching exercises a jogger does at traffic lights.

"What you have to remember, Steven," she said with a catch in her voice, "when you feel yourself getting angry – is that whatever I've done, I've only done for love."

"*Love?*" I said incredulously. "For whom?"

Susan did not answer this question immediately, and I did not press her, my own mind now being on other things.

We lay together on the floor, panting.

"Wow," she said. "Steven Fisher, you *are* a dark horse. That was totally amazing."

Indeed, I could not quite explain what had come over me towards the end of that brief, unlikely coupling. Three years' worth of sexual frustration – not to mention three years of studying orgasms at close quarters – had been unleashed in the space of a few minutes. The chair, the desk, a filing cabinet, the floor – all had been utilised in our frenzy.

"So," she said eventually, "I'd better explain."

I sighed. "There's something I've got to explain first. I'm sorry, Susan. I've been giving you KXC79."

She looked puzzled. "Why would you do that?"

"I just needed to double-check something."

Susan started to shake with laughter. She laughed wildly, madly, and without mirth.

"Oh, Steve," she managed to say. "You've been giving me KXC79. Of course you have. That is priceless. That is absolutely fucking priceless."

"I was worried about psychological side effects, you see," I explained. "And I was right. It definitely made you irrational. More irrational, I should say."

That was an understatement, actually. It seemed to me that Susan was by now quite hysterical.

She got up, fetched something from her desk, and threw it into my lap. Something small and white.

"It's all on there," she said. "You'd better read it."

I looked at the object. It was a memory stick.

"Steve," she said impatiently, "you really don't get it, do you? It's all bollocks. This KXC79 you say you've been giving me – it doesn't exist. It's a figment of your imagination. You stupid, stupid, stupid *arse*."

I looked at her pityingly. She really was behaving extremely irrationally.

"In which case, Susan," I said patiently, "what have we been testing for the last three months?"

For a moment she pressed the back of her hand to her forehead. Then, in a small voice, she said, "Smarties."

"*Smarties?*"

"They're small candy-covered chocolates that come in an assortment of colours. Including pink."

"I know what they *are*, Susan. But why?"

She took a deep breath. "Because I'm in love with Heather, that's why. Because I needed to steal the pills to persuade her to sleep with me. And because all the time she's been playing me for a fool."

"But I still don't –"

"It's all in there. Just read it." And, pulling on her lab coat, she hurried from the room.

I plugged in the memory stick. On it were a number of sub-folders, labelled:

- Book Proposal (*My Life as a Sex Goddess: Inside the KXC79 Experiment* by Dr Susie Minstock)
- Notes & diary
- Ibiza pictures (hot girl-on-girl)

I clicked on the second one.

50.2

June 12th

I'm in heaven. This job is:

a) A job. At last! Luckily Dr F didn't spot the small gap on my CV. I guessed he wouldn't be too happy about my having spent a couple of years working on the phospheration approach, so I just skipped that bit.[1]

---

[1] I certainly wouldn't. The phospheration approach has been thoroughly discredited. Technically, Susan got her job on false pretences.

b) Fantastic. I mean, I'm in sole charge of the whole subject-selection side. Dr F just goes bright red and walks away whenever the subject of sexually dysfunctional women comes up. Seems odd, really, that such a nerdo would end up working in this field.

I asked him yesterday if he'd tried KXC79 himself yet. He stared at me. "But I'm a man," he said. "Oxytocin-derived enzymes are not a variable factor in my physiological response."

"I meant, have you tried it with a girlfriend," I explained.

He looked even more confused. "You mean as an experiment?"

"Or just for fun."

His frown deepened. "It could be seen as unprofessional. In any case, I don't have a sexually dysfunctional girlfriend."

"Oh – lucky you."

"I don't have a girlfriend at all."

Like I say, what a nerdo. Can't wait to get my own hands on some of that KXC79, though.

July 13th

Getting some KXC79 is proving harder than I expected. Dr F keeps it all locked in his fridge. But then he gives *me* the pills in a little paper cup, to give to the subjects. So I switched a few with some Smarties, just before I passed them on – the pink ones look excatly the same. Unprofessional,[2] I know, but I really need to find out if this stuff works.

July 14th

Hmm, interesting. I mean obviously I'm only a sample of one but I'd say

[2] A better description might be "criminally irresponsible".

that on the evidence of last night, Dr Fisher's certainly on to something. (Lasted for ages, almost a multiple.) Haven't felt that good since Seville, and those three waiters. Which means...if this ever gets to market, I could make millions. Not to mention being the most famous sexologist in the world... Hooray!

I need to own this project. Have decided to flirt with Dr F, just a little. He seems like the frustrated type, so he should be putty in my hands.

July 17th

Flirting with Steve is harder than you'd think. He doesn't seem terribly interested. Could he be gay? That would be ironic, in more ways than one... On the other hand, he did tell me with a straight face that his last research project involved seeing whether female monkeys could have orgasms. So he trained them to use vibrators, and monitored the results.

"Er – Steven. Please," I say faintly. "Too much information."

"I've never understood that phrase, actually," he says thoughtfully. "How can one possibly have too much information? Surely that would be like having too much truth, or too much oxygen?"

In my case, I'm thinking, it's because – Yikes! – I've just realised I'm sharing a laboratory with a man who makes monkey porn![3]

Mind you, all that practice on the higher primates should have done wonders for his technique. If only he wasn't such a stiff!

[3] This is a ridiculous slur on my reputation. Yes, I did study female monkeys to see if they could have orgasms – but at the time, so did a number of other researchers. See, for example, Burton, F.D 1971: "Sexual climax in female Macaca mulatta" *Proc. 3rd Int. Congr. Primat.*, Zurich 1970 3: 180-191; and Allen, M.L and Lemmon, W.B 1981: Orgasm in female primates, *Am. J. Primatol.* 1:15-34.

August 1st

Summer vacation. Yay! Ibiza here I come. I've built up a little stockpile of KXC79 to take with me, natch.

September 18th

We've acquired a particularly gorgeous graduate researcher over the summer. Heather Jackson. Twenty four years old, blonde, blue-eyed, and cute as a button. But then you realise there's a little touch of mischief there as well... Subtly brought the conversation round to "some bi-curious girlfriends of mine", and there was a definite flicker of interest. It's funny how one just *knows*. And to judge by the way she gave me a sideways glance from under that blonde fringe, she knows just why I was mentioning it, too. So now the chase is on... This should liven up the autumn term.

September 20th

Heather was cleaning out the lab cupboards today when she found some steel frames. They looked like orthopaedic devices.

"Do you still need these, or shall I throw them out?" she asked Dr Fisher. "What are they, anyway?"

Dr F went bright red, although as that's something that happens at least once a day it took me some time to realise what his long-winded explanation actually meant. Apparently when he was getting the monkeys to diddle themselves, they sometimes lost interest and wandered off to eat some grass or whatever instead. So he had these frames made, and strapped the monkeys in before getting to work.

"Of course, this was at the beginning of the study," he said. "Later, as they came to associate the frames with pleasure, they actively sought them out. I had one particularly bright bonobo who learnt how to strap herself in."

Double yikes! I'm sharing a lab with a man who's into primate bondage!

Once he began talking about the monkeys, it was as if he couldn't stop. Apparently the very bright bonobo – that was Lucy, of course – started out by biting him every time he came near her (he showed us the scars) but ended up by grooming him for fleas as a sign of her affection. And that, ladies and gentlemen, was what started him thinking about the role of neurotransmitters in female sexual dysfunction (No, I don't understand the link either, but then I don't understand most of what Dr F says. The actual science of this project is way, way too advanced for me.)

Anyway, Heather – who is busy wrapping all the men in the Department round her little finger – asked him how the frames work, and under the guise of showing her how it all fitted together he was soon strapping her in and demonstrating. She looked at us from under her blonde fringe and made a monkey noise... I swear Dr F looked more excited than he has done in months. He had to go for a walk to calm down.[4]

So of course while he was gone I went and helped Heather out of the monkey frame. Except that before I undid any of the straps I thought I'd better make it quite plain that I wouldn't be letting her out at all unless she was a good little monkey... And then the little tease started doing the same noises to me. "Ooo Ooo?" she said plaintively, opening her big blue eyes very wide. "Ooo Ooo Ooo?"

I couldn't resist it. I kissed her. Not her first girl-girl kiss either, to judge by her reaction... Unfortunately Dr F came back, or we might have managed a bit more.

---

[4] This is, needless to say, complete nonsense. I had a bellringing practice to go to.

September 24th

Nothing for the last few days... At least nothing overt: on the surface we're just being very cool with each other, very *matter-of-fact*, but the eye contact goes on just a fraction too long, and the body language is just a little more blatant than it should be. She'll smooth her hair back over her head, and I'll give a little stretch... She'll fiddle with her necklace, and I'll touch my earring... Oh, women are so *bad*. How can Dr F not have noticed? The air is thick with oestrogen and female lust.

September 26th

So today Heather wanted a guided tour of the testing room. I showed her the stimulators, of course, and there was a mock-innocent episode where I held a couple against her arm to show her how powerful they were.

Then she looked me in the eye and asked me if she could have some KXC79.

I explained it wasn't that simple – Steve keeps the pills locked up, and every single one he gives out is recorded in his lab notes.

"Please?" she said, fetchingly. "Pretty please?"

"Why do you want it, anyway?" I asked. "You're not going to tell me *you're* suffering from FSD."

She pouted. "Might be."

"Uh uh," I said. "Though if you are, it could be because you've wasted too much time with men. It takes a woman to know what a woman needs."

"You're probably right," she agreed. "But some KXC79 would make the experience even better, don't you think?" More pouting. "*You're* the one who dishes them out. You could take a few when he's not looking, and replace them with Smarties."

Could she somehow have guessed I'd already done exactly that?

The big blue eyes were giving nothing away. "But then Dr Fisher would think he was giving someone KXC79, when he'd actually be giving them nothing at all," I pointed out.

"You could pull those results from the study. After all, it's not like we'd be talking about many pills. Just half a dozen or so."

"Half a dozen!"

"Some for me and...some for you?" A sly, wicked laugh in her eyes. "We could see which of us gets more out of it."

So that's the deal. She'll sleep with me if I get hold of some KXC79. Well, put like that, maybe a couple of duff results won't be that big a problem.[5] It's not like we're in a critical phase or anything.

I think I may be in love!

October 1st

It's taken me a week to get the pills – I replaced them with more Smarties. I'm pretty sure Steve isn't suspicious. His mind's on next week's Sexual Endocrinology conference and the paper he's giving about, I don't know, chimpanzee enzyme breakdowns or something.

So I told Heather I'd got the gear, and more or less suggested that we stay behind in the lab after everyone else had left to see what effect they had.

A frown. "Here? Here's not very *comfy*."

"Who wants comfy? We're talking about a two-way trip to sexual ecstasy."

Pout. "A girl can't just turn it on. I have to be in the mood. After all –" rolling her eyes at the lab – "this is where I *work*."

I refrained from pointing out that getting her in the mood was

---

[5] I am absolutely astonished by the casual manner in which my colleague here reveals that she has, in fact, been undermining my project from the very beginning. This, it seems to me, is what comes of allowing sexologists into science laboratories – a total erosion of standards.

exactly what the KXC79 should be helping with. I'd already guessed what was coming.

"Of course," says the shameless little thing idly, "you and Dr Fisher are going to that conference in Toronto next week, aren't you? Did you know it's at a five star hotel?"

"So it is. But even if I wanted to take you, I couldn't. It's completely oversubscribed."

"You and I could share a room," she said. "No one would think twice about that, would they?"

The thought of sharing with Heather Jackson at Sexual Endocrinology was, I had to admit, extremely tempting. After all, once we were in a room together for the night, the teasing would have to stop...

"You're an evil, manipulative hussy," I pointed out.

"I'm very, very bad," she agreed.

"And I won't be taking any nonsense from you at the conference."

"I probably do need firm handling."

"I'll tell Steve tomorrow that you're sharing with me."

October 20th

Well, SexEnd is finally over, and I have to say that it didn't quite go as planned.

For a start, when I imagined sharing a room with Heather, it was just that I was picturing – the room, and the two of us enjoying a quiet (or, possibly, a noisy) night in, helped along by Dr Fisher's happy pills. But it turned out that before we could get down to business in the room, we had to hit the bar. And – Good Lord, what a surprise – there were half a dozen people there Heather knew from previous jobs. (What previous jobs? I must say it was news to me that she'd been working in this field long enough to get to know so many people.)

When I say people, of course, I mean men.

In fact, I noticed that in our little group – our rather raucous little

276

group – Heather and I were absolutely the only women. When other females drifted in our direction, an apparently chance remark from Heather would spin them round and have them walking away again.

Heather, I was coming to realise, is not the sort of woman other women like. Unless, of course, they're bisexual and romantically deluded.

Round about midnight I noticed several other things, more or less simultaneously.

a) We were now pretty much the only group left in the bar.
b) Heather had got out the little pill bottle containing the KXC79 I'd stolen. She put one on her tongue, and held one up for me... I opened my mouth, and she put it in. Then we swallowed together.
c) Later, when she thought no one was looking, she passed the bottle to a man who was standing behind her. I saw him take it without looking at it and quickly put it in his pocket. Almost as if this was something pre-arranged. Something they didn't want to draw attention to.

I said to the man I was talking to, "Who's that?"

He looked round. "Him? That's Paul Bryant. The Sales Director."

"Sales Director of what?"

"Carvel Pharmaceuticals, of course. All us lot work for Carvel."[6]

"Not Heather," I pointed out. "Heather works for me and Steven Fisher."

"Sure," he said vaguely. "Do you want another cocktail? It's a free bar."

"Did Heather," I said slowly, "ever work for Carvel?"

He shrugged. "Maybe. A summer job, I think. Very briefly." He handed me a mojito. "There you go."

I couldn't remember having asked for it, but I took it anyway.

---

[6] At this point in Dr Minstock's account I had to stop reading for five minutes while I threw up.

Then at some indeterminate time I was in my room – our room – with Heather, and Paul Bryant, and three or four others, and someone had lit a joint. And whether it was the KXC79 or not I couldn't have said, but things were definitely getting out of hand.

Then Steve came to the door. He wanted some papers. And – it was a funny thing – but I was actually pleased to see him. I thought to myself, good old reliable Steve, somehow he'll sort all this out.

He didn't, of course. He didn't even realise it was happening. He took the papers and went back to his own room, oblivious as always.

When I went back inside, Heather was already naked, and most of the men were getting that way too.

With a sinking sensation I realised that, although I was going to have plenty of sex that night, it probably wasn't going to be with Heather.

October 21st

Something else odd about that experience at the conference – I can't stop hiccupping.

November 1st

Heather's been avoiding me ever since SexEnd. But eventually she went into the testing room to hook up some new instruments.

"I need to talk to you," I said, following her.

She glanced over her shoulder. "Oh, it's you."

"You're an industrial spy, aren't you? For Carvel?"

"That's putting it a bit strongly. I'm just helping out some friends."

"How could you do this to us?" I demanded.

"It's entirely *your* fault."

"What do you mean?"

"Ever since I arrived," she said, turning those innocent blue eyes on

278

me, "it's been clear to me that getting on here is dependent on giving you sexual favours."

"*What?*"

"I still haven't decided whether to make an official complaint. They take sexual harassment quite seriously in universities these days, don't they? I should imagine that for a sexologist, of all people, an accusation like that – particularly from another woman – could be quite a stumbling block in her career."

She turned and waved to Steve, who was on the other side of the lab, going through some printouts. "Just imagine if he could hear us now."

There was nothing I could say. She had me exactly where she wanted me.

"Oh, and one other thing," she said. "If you were ever to tell anyone you'd been stealing KXC79 to assist you in your pathetic attempts to get me into bed – well, that probably wouldn't look very good either, would it?" She laughed. "Do you know, when I first came here, I assumed it would be Dr Fisher who'd give me those pills. But I couldn't get anywhere with him. I was just starting to think I'd have to give up when you started coming on to me. Wasn't that a stroke of luck? My friends at Carvel are very pleased with me."

"What do you want?" I said.

"For the moment," she said, "I just want you not to do anything foolish, like tell Dr Fisher that I ever had those pills."

"That Carvel has those pills, you mean."

She shrugged. The conversation was clearly at an end.

Oh, shit.

November 2nd

What do I do?
What do I do?
WHAT DO I DO?

November 3rd

Option 1: tell Steve everything.
Option 2: tell Steve nothing.
Option 3: do something. (But what?)[7]

November 4th

Option 1: if I tell Steve everything, he'll have me fired. My career will be ruined.

Option 2: if I tell him nothing, Carvel will use the pills to scupper us. It won't be anything so obvious as copying our formulation – that would still leave them trying to catch up. More likely, they'll bring out a spoiler. For example, announce they've tried a treatment which just happens to be very similar to ours and discovered a nasty side effect. The only responsible thing to do, they'll say, is to abandon the whole approach. It doesn't have to be true – no one would let KXC79 go to a clinical trial with that hanging over it.

Which leaves:

Option 3: do something.

(But what?)

November 5th

Heather sidles up to me. "I need some more pills."

"Why?"

"That last lot were no good, apparently – something to do with

[7] It is, surely, obvious even to an unprincipled nymphomaniac what she should do, namely Option 1.

hiccups. But Dr Fisher's been talking about a new formulation he's testing. So I need some of those, please."

Naturally I say, "Well, I'm not giving you any."

"If you don't get me those pills," she says sweetly, "I'll find some other way of getting hold of them." She looks across at where Wulf, Rhona and Dr Fisher are deep in conversation. "One of them will give me the pills. I doubt it'll take long. And then there'll be no reason not to get you fired."

Oh, shit.

November 16th

So here's what I'm going to do: I'm going to replace *all* the KXC79 with pink Smarties.

This is not as stupid as it sounds.

If I replace the KXC79 with a dummy, it won't work. If it doesn't work, Steve (who, whatever else he is, is undoubtedly a genius) will assume that the formulation isn't right. If he assumes the formulation isn't right, he'll think of a different way of solving the problem – call it KXC80. Thus, when Carvel announce their spoiler, we'll be able to say it isn't an issue as we abandoned KXC79 ourselves some time ago.

Plus, even if Heather does get her hands on them, they won't be much good to her.[8]

November 25th

It's done. I got the key out of his lab coat when he went for lunch.

---

[8] When I consider the utter, arrant stupidity of this plan, words simply fail me.

January 12th

It seems to be taking a bit longer than I expected for Steve to realise that the pills aren't working any more.

Oh well. He'll get there in the end.

January 16th

He still hasn't twigged. The main problem, actually, is that we don't have enough test subjects. Our small ad in the local paper ('*Are you sexually dysfunctional? Female? Would you like to earn a little extra cash by helping out with medical research?*') only ever seems to attract Ukrainian prostitutes using us as a sort of free common room. As far as they're concerned, faking the odd orgasm is a small price to pay for a nice lie down and a hot drink when it's raining.

I've told Rhona and Wulf to ask amongst their friends, with a cash bonus for every volunteer they find.

February 12th

We have a test subject at last. Annie G, a postgrad who's clearly something of a geek herself (although she wouldn't actually be unattractive if she only did a bit more with herself). Not an ideal subject by any means – viz. the following excerpt from her initial interview:

Susie: Could you describe a sexual fantasy, please?
Miss G: I don't really have any.
Susie: You must have fantasies. Everyone has fantasies.
Miss G: No, sorry.
Susie: (*Sighs*) Why do you want to take part in this project, Annie?
Miss G: It sounds interesting, I suppose.

Susie: But you do want to become sexually functional as well?

Miss G: Not really.

Susie: Then what are you hoping to get out of it?

Miss G: I suppose I'm hoping that he'll stop getting cross.

Susie: Who are we talking about, Annie?

A little tea and sympathy, and it eventually all came out. She'd been having a relationship with her supervisor – or rather, he had succeeded in seducing her, only to become annoyed that she didn't enjoy his attentions as much as he thought she ought to. Annie is just the sort of person we should be screening out, but needs must. I tidied up her notes so that everything looked above board and told her that the next stage would be for her to meet Dr Fisher.

February 18th

Steve has met Annie. It didn't go too well, at first – he rather grumpily pointed out that we weren't meant to be recruiting any more research subjects. Then I had a brainwave.

"Anything you want to know about the science stuff," I suggested to Annie, "this is the man to ask!"

Well, of course, he grabbed the opportunity to bore her rigid. Poor girl – I glanced through the lab door fifteen minutes later and he was drawing her a diagram of what her orgasms should look like!

Mind you, she didn't seem to mind too much. And the test was excellent – by starting the programme a bit early, I managed to contrive it so that it was completely unexciting for her. She actually went to sleep! If that doesn't alert Steve to the fact that his precious KXC79 doesn't work, nothing will.[9]

---

[9] The notion that it is somehow my own fault I failed to notice when I was being hoodwinked by a crazed, duplicitous virago is surely proof that here Dr Minstock – who, I repeat, is not a

February 20th

This might be a slight problem – Trock want Steve to deliver his paper on KXC79 at SexDys. It's the most amazing opportunity for all of us – but if he hasn't reworked the formulation by then, this could get really messy. I need to get this sorted, fast.

February 22nd

Annie's an odd one, actually. Every time Steve launches into one of his interminable scientific monologues she gazes at him adoringly. Steve, of course, shows no sign of noticing whatsoever.

February 25th

Strike that last thought. Steve has taken to lending her science books and telling her that she has "a very fine mind, if I may say so".

He's never said that to *me*.

Annie is lapping it all up and pretending to have some vague clue what he's on about. Today I heard her hinting that she'd like to come along to one of his lectures "to find out more about neurotransmitters". Yeah, right. Luckily, he didn't take the hint.

real doctor but merely has a PhD in Applied Masturbation from the University of Sydney – has taken leave of her senses.

February 27th

Steve might not have taken the hint – but that didn't stop her from turning up to his lecture anyway. Hussy.[10]

February 29th

This is getting stupid. Annie spends the whole of every session sighing and casting Steve longing glances. Whenever he's not around it's Dr Fisher this, Dr Fisher that, when will Dr Fisher be here, what does Dr Fisher say about it, and – the really irritating one – you are so lucky to be working with Dr Fisher, he's easily the cleverest man I've ever met. She clearly fancies the pants off him![11]

Hello? Can this be the same Dr Fisher we're talking about? The one who a few weeks ago picked up a Valentine's card from Rhona that was sitting on Wulf's desk, looked puzzled and said, "Why do they call it a love heart, when it's clearly an idealised representation of the sender's vulva?"

The Steven Fisher who can't even tell that his bloody pills DO ABSOLUTELY NOTHING?

To make matters worse, I think Annie's started having orgasms. Steve hasn't noticed yet – but when he does, what if he thinks it's because of the treatment? He'll never change the KXC79 formulation if he thinks it's actually working.

Meanwhile Heather is prowling around the place in a cloud of fragrant CK One, like a cross between an albino panther and a heat-seeking missile. Oh, God.

[10] A bit rich, considering who this comment is coming from.

[11] Needless to say, this notion is just as ridiculous as every other deluded fantasy that inhabits my colleague's so-called mind.

March 6th

So much has happened since I last wrote. Annie and her boyfriend have broken up... and she's persuaded Steven to enrol her as a lab assistant AND give her a credit on the paper. We're all furious, even Rhona, who's the sweetest-natured person in the world.

The only compensation is seeing how pissed off Heather is. She's just realised she's got competition!

March 7th

Steven just assumes that we're all going to teach Annie A-level science for him. Which is a bit bloody much. Rhona says sarcastically, "Oh, it's not like we're busy." To which he just nods and says, "Excellent."[12]

To begin with I almost refuse out of principle. But then I remember that a) she's only here because of me b) she might be useful, and c) I don't really have any principles.

Later I spot Heather talking very intently to Julian Noble. It's soon clear why — she's found out that Trock have made Steven lock the pills in Julian's cupboard.

March 10th

So now Heather is flirting with Julian Noble. There's a kind of terrible fascination, actually, in watching her at work. He doesn't stand a chance

---

[12] This is not how I remember this conversation at all, incidentally. My colleagues were delighted to assist me with teaching Miss G, a task which in any case was — as I have related elsewhere — always a pleasure.

– it's like watching some doddering old fighter being demolished by a ruthless punk half his age.

March 18th

Heather storms into the control room. "Very clever," she snarls.

"What is?"

"Those decoy pills. The ones in Julian's cupboard."

"Nothing to do with me," I say. "Must have been Steven, being careful."

"If you only knew what I had to do to get my hands on those pills," she hisses. "Now, if you don't want me to make that accusation of sexual harassment against you, you'd better get me some of the real ones. And fast."

I stare at her. "You're still thinking of accusing *me* of sexual harassment? After what you did to Julian?"

She smiles lethally. "But that's just the point, isn't it? Professor Noble's going to be so upset when he finds out you've been hitting on his girlfriend."

I think quickly. I could get her some Smarties, of course, but that's not going to solve anything. Carvel will have them analysed and realise straight away they're only chocolate.

"It'll be difficult," I say, stalling her. "If anything, he's got even more paranoid about them. But I'll do whatever it takes. I promise."

"Well, don't take too long."

March 20th

The paper seems to have acquired a momentum of its own. Richard Collins even flies in ahead of the conference, to mark the project with his scent like some snarling beast or something.

Maybe I should just come right out and tell Steve the truth? I can't let him launch pink Smarties as a sexual wonder-pill. Can I?

March 21st

Annie and Richard – who would have thought it?! It was only the other day she finally admitted to Rhona and me that she's totally got the hots for Steve.[13]

March 25th

Poor Steve. He's taking this Richard thing pretty hard. In fact, I've never seen a man so deranged by grief. I just hope he doesn't do something stupid.

March 25th

Heather sidles up after lunch. She looks unusually triumphant, even for her.

"It's all over," she announces. "There's a side effect. Steven told Wulf, and Wulf told Rhona."

"Meaning what, exactly?"

"Meaning I no longer need those pills, of course. Either you'll pull the paper yourselves or – even better, from Carvel's point of view – you'll be stupid enough to go ahead and publish. In which case we'll trash Dr Fisher's reputation for ever."

Oh shit. Even I can't let that happen.

So here's the choice I'm left with.

[13] *Really?*

I can either let Steve go on thinking there's a side effect, in which case he'll postpone the launch and I'll be stuck in this lab for ever.

Or I can tell him everything, and the launch can go ahead. Of course, he's going to be a bit pissed off with me. But I'm hoping he'll be so relieved to discover that there actually is no side effect to his precious pills that he'll get over it.

Mind you, it's definitely a conversation that'll be easier to have after I've given him the best sex of his life.[14]

---

[14] If anything shows the extent of Susan's self-delusion, it is surely this comment. Sex with her, whilst superficially engaging, was not unlike that famous description of life before the Romans – nasty, brutish and short.

When I had finished Susan's diary I sat very still, thinking.

Then I went to the fridge where I kept the KXC79 and unlocked it. Experimentally, I took one of the pills and put it in my mouth. The coating seemed unusually sweet, for a pill. I bit it in two.

The inside of the pill was chocolate.

I tried another. That, too, was chocolate.

It was, of course, wonderful news.

Naturally, I was furious to discover that Susan had been deceiving me. But mostly, I simply felt relief. Because, as Susan said, if the pills weren't KXC79, there was no side effect after all.

Not only that – there was no effect. Annie's results were now completely irrelevant. We had reverted, in fact, to exactly the situation we had been in before she first walked into the lab: twenty-seven sexually dysfunctional women had trialled the real KXC79, and twenty-seven women were now sexually functional. Our success rate was once again 100%.

Better still, Annie herself wasn't even a research subject. She had never passed the selection criteria, and never been given the treatment. She was a co-worker, nothing more.

Heather, meanwhile, had been as misled by Susan's ruse as I was, which meant Carvel would be under the impression that the treatment was sufficiently flawed not to require any further sabotage from them.

And now I finally understood why Annie's tests had been the way they were.

Luckily, I knew where she would be.

Oxford was swathed in fog as I hurried through the medieval streets towards her college. Street lamps took on the soft, hazy glow of dandelion clocks. Only the occasional hiss as a student sped past on a bicycle reminded me that I was not completely alone.

At the Porter's Lodge I asked the occupant where I would find the Swamps and Sorcerers. He tutted and shook his head.

"Not here, I'm afraid, young man."

"Not here?" I echoed.

"There's been no swamp in this college since they made the lake, two centuries ago. As for sorcerers – well, there's some who do claim that Elias Ashmole was an alchemist, back in the seventeenth century."[1]

I stared at him. It dawned on me that this oaf thought he was being funny. "Where is the Fantasy Society? It is a matter of great urgency."

He chuckled. "Turn left at New Staircase, straight ahead through Old Quad, turn left at the misty lake. You're then faced with a choice of two paths. Stop, roll a Decision Dice…" He must have seen my face because he added quickly, "Bear left and you can't miss it."

[1] Elias Ashmole, 1617-1692, was a polymath who studied law, natural history, mathematics and astronomy. In the Prolegomena to *Fasciculus chemicus* (1650), written under the pseudonym James Hasolle (an anagram), he defended alchemy against the charge that it was fraudulent. There are, he wrote, "many occult, specifick, incomprehensible and inexplicable qualities" hidden in natural substances, waiting to be discovered. This assertion was, of course, exactly right, although it was not until the advent of biochemistry that we were able to prove it.

There were a dozen or so people in the room. Papers and dice were spread over the tables, along with the little plastic figurines that Swampers use to keep track of their position. Annie was wearing a metal helmet that curled down around her cheeks. I recognised it as the helmet of Azeroth.

"Annie!" I cried.

"Lady Maud," she corrected.

"Lady Maud. I'm sorry I'm late. But it's wonderful news. You never had a sexual dysfunction at all."

She turned to the others. "This interloper is a powerful adversary. We will need to pool our resources if we are to evade incarceration in the putrid recesses of his castle, where we would be forced to endure his every hideous whim."

For a moment I wanted to tell her everything then and there, but – with a happy sigh – I realised it could wait. There was a Level 3 adventure to be fought, with the prospect of ravishing Lady Maud in the Dank Dungeons at the end of it.

I held out my hand.

"Give me those dice," I commanded. "And prepare to flee from the wrath of Lord Loroth."

52.3

After the game we walked by the lake – the real lake, that is, the one in the college grounds, not the Sea of Silver Light.

"That was excellent!" I exclaimed.

"Tonight was a particularly good level," she agreed. "Although I did think Willem was out of order, introducing salamander slime into your dungeon like that."

"We saw him off, though, didn't we?"

She nodded. "Or rather you did, when you proved beyond doubt that his salamander slime would be desiccated by the unique atmospheric conditions of Castle Loroth."

We stopped, gazing over the lake. Mist drifted through the woods, enveloping us in skeins of muffled silence.

"Did you know," I said at last, "that a cubic mile of mist contains less than a gallon of water?"

"Yes," she said.

I turned towards her. Her lips were parted, and her eyes very wide. There was something about her stillness that told me that now, if I chose to, I could kiss her.

I leaned towards her.

"What did you mean, Steven," she said thoughtfully, "when you said earlier that I wasn't sexually dysfunctional after all?"

"It can wait," I said.

52.4

"No, really, I'm curious," she said. "What was it you meant?"

"Well, in a nutshell…" And I told her about Susan, the substitution of the pills, and the fact that she had never been given KXC79 at all.

"I was worried about confounding factors, you see," I concluded. "Things like the placebo effect and so on. When all the time, it was the tomato effect I should have been worrying about."

She looked puzzled.

"When the tomato was first introduced to North America, scientists thought it must be poisonous," I explained. "It was only when they saw people cooking with it that they drew the obvious conclusion. So scientists use the phrase 'tomato effect' when we fail to spot what's right

under our noses. That's you, Annie – you're a big, red, juicy tomato."
(*Figure 22*)

She looked even more puzzled.

"Metaphorically speaking," I hastened to add. "What I'm trying to say is, that's the explanation for all your false tests, isn't it – you were simply too embarrassed to admit that it was *me* who was making the difference. Annie – that's the answer to everything: *you're in love with me.*"

She took a deep breath.

"A simple blood test could confirm it," I added.

"A *what*?" she said slowly.

"A blood test. Romantic attraction is associated with raised levels of phenyl ethylamine, or PEA – it's PEA that causes your heart to race when you see me, your breath to come faster, and makes you secrete almost imperceptible odours from your sweat glands." I began ticking the effects off my fingers. "It's PEA that triggers a cascade of adrenaline, making you hyper-alert, and another of dopamine, making you more suggestive. It's the PEA in your system that dilutes your natural levels of serotonin, the chemical associated with inhibitions and the control of impulses, making you do crazy things and giving you a jittery feeling whenever you see the object of your affection – that is, me. And it's PEA which makes you feel those first irresistible stirrings of desire."

"But I still don't see why I need to take a blood test."

"Ah." I could see I was getting ahead of myself again. "Obviously, *I*

Figure 22: A good example of 'observer bias.'

know you're attracted to me, and *you* know you're attracted to me, but we'll need a higher level of proof than that for the conference."

"Conference?"

"Yes. Annie, don't you see – you're the best kind of evidence there is. You're confirmation that where nature is chaotic and muddled, science is ordered and logical. You'll be the climax of my presentation – the ultimate visual aid!" I was gazing out at the lake, but what I saw in front of me wasn't water. In the swirling mist I could see row upon row of people – the greatest minds of my generation – my peers – clapping and cheering. Some were even getting to their feet, giving me a standing ovation... And there, beside me on the stage, was Annie, beaming proudly as she joined in the applause...

I turned round. She was staring at me, and the expression on her face was nothing like the proud, shy smile I had just been picturing.

"'A visual aid?'" she repeated.

"Um...perhaps 'living proof' would a better description."

"I enjoyed this evening," she said slowly. "That's what makes this even worse. I actually enjoyed it."

"So did I – "

"No, wait," she said. "I'm trying to explain something. Something *important*. I enjoyed this evening because I thought it was nothing to do with experiments, or measuring my responses, or any of those other things I've had to do for the last eight weeks. I thought, this is *fun* – almost like a normal thing that normal people might do. But it wasn't, was it? All the time, you were watching me. Trying to work out if your theory was correct. Whenever we're together, whatever I do, to you I'm always just *data*."

I opened my mouth to protest, then closed it again.

"You see, Steven, you are – as usual – quite correct. I do get the jitters every time I see you. My heart does race, and I do find it hard to breathe, and to concentrate, and all those other things you described. I didn't choose any of that. It just happened. But I can choose what I do now."

She looked at me, and I quailed under the ferocity of her gaze. "You know something? Sometimes those chemical messengers get it wrong. Well, now it's me who's doing the deciding, not them. And what I decide…" She swallowed. "What I've decided, Steven, is that I'm not going to be your lab rat any more."

"But, Annie…"

"But what?"

"What about the conference?" I said anxiously. "You will be there, won't you?"

"I suppose so. I can't really let Richard down now."

"What's Richard got to do with it?"

She said slowly, "Because I'm going to be staying with him, of course. In his suite."

52.5

I stared at her, aghast.

"I thought you realised," she said.

I shook my head.

She shrugged. "He had to rush off from Copenhagen to Dublin for an interview. So we said we'd meet up at SexDys."

"I see," I said, although in fact I could see almost nothing. Lysozyme, lipocalin and lactoferrin pricked at my eyes.

"So I guess I might bump into you there after all." She let out a breath. "I'm sure your paper will be a triumph, Dr Fisher. Just keep me out of it, all right?"

There was no side effect. No drowsiness. No possible reason why this treatment shouldn't launch.

The acclaim of my peers – the great prize I had pursued for so long – finally, it was within my grasp.

And now I knew that I did not want it.

There was only one thing I really wanted, and that was the thing I had casually – so casually! – thrown away.

I was on top of the world. And I was at rock bottom, both at the same time.

53.2

Later that night there was an email. There was no subject or salutation, although I saw from the time and date it had been sent in the small hours.

> If we do bump into each other at the conference, I think on reflection it would be better if we didn't speak to each other. I need to move on. And I don't think it's fair on Richard.

> PS If you really need proof, try this.

There was a web address, together with a short phrase in what looked like German, complete with umlauts and a cesaura. I hypothesised that it might be some kind of password.

I read her diary, and I wept.

Somehow I packed my suitcase for the conference. I assembled my slides, my charts, the spreadsheets breaking down our results by ethnicity, age, and every other variable known to science. I went through the presentation line by line, deleting every reference to Miss G and her now-irrelevant results. I was still working on it as I took the train to London.

At least, I suppose I was. Afterwards, I could remember almost nothing about that journey. The only thing I can recall is that at some point I found myself staring at a train door, completely unable to remember how to open it. An elderly lady who was standing on the platform waiting to board had to remind me what to do.

Eventually I found myself in the vast lobby of the London Hilton, under a sign which said in five languages, "*Towards a Sexual Dysfunction-Free Future – Trock Pharmaceuticals Proudly Welcomes You!*" In the distance I saw Richard, surrounded by a gaggle of admirers and a Japanese TV crew, the bright lights bouncing off his gold frequent-flyer luggage tags.

Kes was standing by the check-in desk, talking rapidly into his mobile. "Steven. Thank God," he said, looking up and gripping my arm. "Got your presentation? Give it to the girls in the hall, they'll load it up for you. Richard's going to introduce you – I've seen his stuff: it's quite a build-up. Not that the paper won't top it, of course. This is going to be *fantastic*."

"Actually, there are a couple of details I still need to address," I said mechanically. "I'll play it straight from my laptop."

"No major changes though, I hope?" he said anxiously.

I hesitated. "Kes, is there somewhere we can go? Somewhere we can talk?"

The bar was full of delegates eagerly consuming Trock's special cocktails, wittily named "KXC1". Eventually we found a quiet corner.

"The thing is," I said, "I'm having doubts."

His pale eyes didn't blink as he waited for me to go on.

"Oh, it's not the science – that all hangs together. It's just that I think the whole project could be based on a misapprehension. We've always assumed that women who can't have sex properly are dysfunctional. But what if that simply isn't true? What if by tinkering with sex, we're somehow hastening the death of love?"

"'The death of love?'" he repeated, perplexed.

"It's a phrase of Richard's."

"Is this something to do with that research subject? Your anomaly?"

"No. Well, yes. In a way. It turns out she was never part of the study at all – it's a long story. The issue isn't KXC79 – it works, all right. But what does it actually *do*?"

"Steven," he interrupted. "You recall Wernher von Braun, the German rocket scientist who went to America after the war to work on their atomic programme?"

"Of course."

"He was once asked about the effect of his missiles on the civilian population. Know what he said?" Kes leaned forward intently. "Von Braun said, 'My job is to send the rockets up. Where they come down, that's someone else's department.'" He nodded. "You've done your job, Steven, and done it brilliantly. As for the rest – that's someone else's department. Look, you're a little nervous. Of course you are: it's a big day tomorrow. A day, dare I say it, that will transform both our lives. Get a good night's sleep. And tomorrow, let's make history. Yes?"

He slapped me on the back, and then he was gone, his hand raised in greeting to a delegation of Chinese endocrinologists.

On the way back to my room I passed the reception desk.

"Has Annie Gluck checked in yet?" I asked the clerk. "She's staying in one of the suites."

He looked at his computer. "Not yet, sir. Do you want to leave her a message?"

"No," I said. "No, thank you. No message."

53.7

I sat in my room, my head in my hands. Was I nervous, as Kes had suggested? No. I was numb – quite numb.

As I sat there, there was a knock at the door.

I looked up, startled. It came again. I rushed to open it, hope and phenyl ethylamine surging through my veins –

But it wasn't her. It was Wulf and Rhona.

"What's going on?" Wulf demanded. "What's all this Susan's saying about chocolate and Annie? Where is she? And why are you sitting up here on your own?"

53.8

So I told them. Susan. Heather. KXC79. The experiment that never was. My idiocy. The double-blind comparative trial where all the blindness was entirely in my own mind. The irrelevant results that, the more I thought about them, were more relevant than anything else I had ever worked on.

Finally, I came to the end of this litany of disasters.

"Well, people make mistakes," Wulf said.

53.9

It was such an inadequate response to the situation that I almost laughed. "Wulf," I said, shaking my head, "your gift for understatement is almost as magnificent as your work is incomprehensible."

"No," he said doggedly. "Listen to what I'm saying, Steven. *People make mistakes*. Isn't that what science is, in the end? Trial – and error?" He ticked the names off his fingers. "Alfred Nobel said, 'My dynamite will lead to world peace sooner than a thousand world conventions.' Thomas Watson of IBM believed there was a world market for no more than five computers. Lord Kelvin, the greatest British scientist of the nineteenth century, thought aeroplanes were a hoax. Watson and Crick's first attempt at a model for DNA was so implausible, they were actually forbidden from working on another one. Einstein's first proof for E=MC2 contained a hopeless mathematical error. Robert Watson-Watt was actually trying to invent a death ray when he stumbled across radar, the technology that stopped the German rockets and won the second world war. Galileo, Aristotle, Newton, Bohr – they all cocked up, time after time. And time after time, they picked themselves up and they *tried again*. And that's what made them scientists, Steven. Not their brains. Their *faith*."

He looked at me expectantly. I said wearily, "This is different, Wulf. In the morning I have to go out there and tell five hundred of the most eminent scientists in the world what I've been doing. And I have a horrible feeling that what I'm going to say is somehow missing the point."

"Then why don't you tell them the truth?" Rhona suggested.

"Hardly. The truth would finish my career."

"But isn't that our responsibility too, as scientists?" she said. "To

302

admit our mistakes, however stupid it makes us seem? So that those who come after us can learn from them?"

They sat on the bed, hand in hand, watching me: so earnest, and so naive. "What you seem to forget is that right now, my career is all I've got. Annie's already made her choice." I sighed. "Look, I appreciate you coming, but you'd better go now. I've got to finish taking her out of the paper."

53.10

As I slid my laptop from its case something fell out of the side pocket. Something bulky and rather battered. A paperback.

Collected Poems of W.B Yeats.

Picking it up, I began to turn the pages. As I did so I thought about that man – that shy, stammering poet, who knew that he was never going to be the kind of person whom Maud Gonne would love, and who had poured his heart into creating these poems instead.

Yeats had told Maud Gonne how he felt. It made no difference, in the end, but at least he had told her, in poem after poem. Even if she had asked him to stop, he would have no more been able to than if she had asked him to stop breathing.

I thought: if Yeats had been given the opportunity I had been given – if the woman he loved had so nearly loved him too – would he have sat in his room writing a presentation, or would he have done everything in his power to win her back? Would he have given up – or would he have rolled the dice just one more time?

Well, of course, he was a poet, so perhaps he would have chosen to write poetry after all. But I was not a poet. I was a man of science.

And scientists, as Wulf had so rightly pointed out, are not to be deterred by a couple of trivial mistakes.

Throwing W.B Yeats to one side, I booted up my laptop and deleted in its entirety the presentation I had been intending to give.

Then I began to construct a quite different paper.

This paper.

The last paper that I will ever be invited, or indeed allowed, to give.

The paper in which I will finally admit – to all of you, to Annie, to myself – the truth.

Downstairs, as I write these final words, over five hundred delegates are busy collecting their name-tags and their Welcome Packs from Registration. They mill in the bar, drinking their complimentary rum punches, exchanging nods and handshakes and gossip.

Here in my room, though, it is very quiet. Occasionally I hear sounds from the corridor, knocks on doors, voices raised in greeting. As the night has worn on the knocks have become more furtive. The voices speak in whispers, the doors open and close more softly, as the parabola of human encounters proceeds to its inevitable conclusion. Strangers, male and female, catch sight of each other; exchange a glance, look away, then go back for a second glance. Strangers who before the night is out – who knows? – may yet become lovers.

My paper…how will it go, I wonder? By the time I reach this last section, how will you all be reacting? Stravinsky's *Rite of Spring*, famously, provoked its first audience to a riot. But we in the field of sexual dysfunction are a more subdued lot. There'll have been some murmuring, I guess. Many of you will have exchanged looks ranging from the baffled to the outraged; rolled your eyes, snorted disbelievingly… Perhaps you will even be putting me through the ultimate indignity as one by one you get up and leave the hall, either in protest or in perplexity, until all that remain are those who indulged themselves too freely the night before.

What shall I say to you few who are left? What great conclusions shall I draw from all this data?

Three things.

If, as Professor Collins has so brilliantly suggested, you think of sex as a parasite which needs human beings to propagate, then you can see that in recent centuries the parasite probably thought it was doing rather well. Its host population had been growing at an astounding rate; the forces of repression appeared to have been all but vanquished.

And then sex hit a problem. Chemistry.

The discovery of norethynodrel, the first contraceptive pill, meant that, in evolutionary terms, sex was effectively neutered. People might be having more sex, but suddenly sex wasn't making so many humans.

So sex hit back. Sex used every means at its disposal. Because for sex, this is always a total war – a fight to the death, if you like. And, since sex has successfully taken over people's brains as well as the rest of them, it was able to use books and films and magazines and the internet to pump out the same propaganda, over and over: *Have more sex! Have more sex!*

But propaganda wasn't enough. Sex needed to use the same tools that had stopped it in its tracks. Sex needed *chemical weapons*. So – lo and behold – suddenly, as if from nowhere, an industry appeared that whispered: *Take this pill, and have more sex.*

Oh, I know that our treatments will initially be for those with sexual problems, and it will undoubtedly make a great difference to their lives. But do we really think that it will be used only by them? It will be a massive social experiment – an experiment in which there is no control group, no antidote, and no going back.

Not a single person in this industry – not the scientists, not the pharmaceutical companies, not the sexologists – can tell us what life will be like when feeling desire for another human being is as simple as popping a pill.

Secondly, you will recall the legend of Pandora, the first woman, created by the gods and given by each of them a gift to make her more beautiful. Jupiter, who was angry with mankind, sent a box, along with instructions not to open it. The box contained all the pestilences of the world. But it also contained their cure, hope.

I think we, like modern-day gods, are in the process of making another Pandora's box. In that box there are many kinds of desire. But there is also love.

Sex and love – I have only just realised how very different they are. Sex says spread your seed as widely as possible. Love says put all your eggs in one special basket. Sex says me, me, me: love says you, you, you. Sex says muscle in on all the best-looking genes you can find. Love says search for that one unforgettable face.

Sex says move on, find someone new. Love says don't let anyone or anything take her away.

Sex, you see, is biology. But love is chemistry.

And there is one last thing I have to say to you.

What if sex isn't meant to be straightforward?

What if women are not just complicated, but complex; so that when you finally – finally! – meet someone who makes you feel amazing, it's because they *are* amazing?

What if sex is like the riddle in the fairy tale, the one that has to be solved before you get to carry off the princess?

What if it's all a kind of test? A test I failed?

And that is why, as the last slide in my presentation, I am putting up on the screen the chemical formula of KXC79 (*Figure 23*).

$$CH_3–C–O–O–CH_2–N+(CH_3)–K_9$$

Figure 23: Chemical formula of KXC79.

54.5

It's priceless, of course. Priceless…and worthless. There's really no point in rushing to scribble it on your sleeve or photographing it with your mobile phone or – if you're Kes Riley – trying to unplug the projector before anyone can copy it.

Now that everyone has it, no one will have any interest in developing it. That's the way pharmaceutical companies work, isn't it – no point in pouring money into clinical trials for a pill your rivals already have.

The pills don't work. Or rather, they do, kind of. But it isn't enough.

You see, it turned out the real problem wasn't with Annie after all. It was with me.

54.6

What I failed to say to Annie – failed even to acknowledge to myself – is that I felt exactly the same way she did. That my own pulse raced when I saw her. That I too knew the sweet agony of phenyl ethylamine coursing through my veins. That I too felt the vagus nerve twitch in the pit of my stomach whenever I thought about her, which was all the time. That the thought of kissing her – of holding her in my arms – makes me weak with pleasure; or that when she's near me my inhibitory serotonin levels are so non-existent I have to restrain myself from turning cartwheels and bursting into song, just for the pleasure of seeing her smile.

I treated Annie like a problem to be solved, when all the time I should have treated her like a woman to be loved.

Why did I not realise what these things meant? Why had I never admitted them to myself?

Because I'm a fool.

Because denying my feelings has become a habit.

Because years of trying to be a good scientist has made me ashamed of the irrational, flawed, emotional human being I really am.

54.7

So, will that be it? *Finis*, the end, goodnight? Will I – God help me – ask if anyone has questions?

In my imagination, I can't help but believe another outcome is possible. In that reality, I look up and she's standing there, at the back of the by-now-almost-empty hall, where those whose eyes are fixed on me, in pity or alarm, don't see her.

I say into the microphone, "Annie…"

And if she gives me any sign or encouragement at all – a smile, a nod, even a tear – I will run from the podium and make my way towards her, knocking the papers from the lectern in my haste: notes tumbling in my slipstream like confetti, data and diagrams dispersing on the draughts of that vast auditorium…

Is that how it will be?

I've just rolled the dice on Luck, and it looks as if I still have the Improbability Bonus.

So.

Who knows.

References

Kohn, I and Kaplan, S: *Female sexual dysfunction, what is known and what remains to be determined*. Contemporary Urol. 1999;11(9):54-72.

Phillips, N.A: *Female sexual dysfunction: Evaluation and treatment*. Am. Fam. Physician. 2000;62;127-136, 141-142.

Carmichael, M.S, Humber, R, Dixen, J, Palmisano, G, Green Greenleaf, W and Davidson, J.M 1987: *Plasma oxytocin increases in the human sexual response*. J. Clin. Endocrinol. Metab. 64(1):27-31.

Zumpe, D, Michael, R.P 1968: *The clutching reaction and orgasm in the female rhesus monkey (Macaca mulatta)*. J. Endocrinol. 40:117-123.

Burton, F.D 1971: *Sexual climax in female Macaca mulatta*. Proc. 3rd Int. Congr. Primat., Zurich 1970 3:180-191.

Chevalier-Skolnikoff, S 1974: *The ontogeny of communication in the stumptail macaque with special attention to the female orgasm*. Contributions to Primatology 2.

Goldfoot, D.A, Westerborg-van Loon, H, Groeneveld, W and Slob, A.K 1980: *Behavioral and physiological evidence of sexual climax in the female stump-tailed macaque (Macaca arctoides)*. Science 208:1477-1479.

Allen, M.L and Lemmon, W.B 1981: *Orgasm in female primates*. Am. J. Primatol. 1:15-34.

Slob, A.K, Groeneveld, W.H and Van der Werff ten Bosch, J.J 1986: *Physiological changes during copulation in male and female stumptail macaques (Macaca arctoides)*. Physiol. Behav. 38:891-895.

Elkan, E 1948: *Evolution of female orgastic ability – A biological survey (parts I-II)*. Int. J. Sexol. (1):1-13 & 2(2):84-93.

Fox, C.A and Fox, Beatrice 1969: *Blood pressure and respiratory patterns during human coitus*. J. Reprod. Fertil. 19:405-415.

Fox, C.A and Fox, Beatrice 1971: *A comparative study of coital physiology, with special reference to the sexual climax.* J. Reprod. Fertil. 24:319-336.

Belzer, E.G Jr 1981: *Orgasmic expulsions of women: A review and heuristic inquiry.* J. Sex Res. 17(1):1-12.

Darling, C.A and Davidson, J.K 1986: *Enhancing relationships: Understanding the feminine mystique of pretending orgasm.* J. Sex Marit. Therap. 12(3):182-196.

Singer, J and Singer, I: *Types of Female Orgasm.* In J LoPiccolo and L LoPiccolo, eds., Handbook of Sex Therapy. New York: Plenum Press, 1978.

Dr K.M Dunn, Dr L.F Cherkas and Prof T.D Spector: *Genetic influences on variation in female orgasmic function: a twin study.* Biology Letters, a Royal Society journal. June 2005.

Editorial

International Journal of Submolecular Biochemistry, June, 2008

The furore, if that is the right word, over Dr Steven Fisher's paper to the Trock Sexual Dysfunction Conference continues to dominate these pages. In this month's issue is a response by Ms Heather Jackson, one of Dr Fisher's former colleagues. "It saddened many of us," she writes from her new position at Carvel Pharmaceuticals, "to see this once promising scientist reduced to spouting wild conjecture and rambling anecdote. In his defence, I would point out that for many years Dr Fisher has laboured under enormous professional and personal pressures. No one could ever have driven him harder than he has driven himself. Of course, I accept my own share of the blame for not noticing sooner the strain he was putting himself under. I only wish he'd had the courage to ask for help."

Other correspondents have highlighted the continuing difficulty of defining what Female Sexual Dysfunction is, and therefore what scientists such as Dr Fisher are actually trying to cure. "Until we understand what constitutes 'normal' female function, what does 'dysfunction' mean?" asks one. "And what makes us think these women even want a treatment for it?"

However, the letter from Kes Riley, Trock's Director of Marketing, stresses that Dr Fisher's project was "only one of a number of possibilities we have been pursuing in this area. In fact, we had recently informed Dr Fisher that his programme was to be wound up owing to lack of progress, coupled with some very exciting and positive outcomes from a completely different approach we have been funding elsewhere, of which you will be hearing more very shortly. Had we known that this news would add to the personal burden under which Dr Fisher was already labouring, we would have offered him counselling. The welfare of our employees and colleagues is always our number one priority."

We also print a letter from a Dr Jay, who was actually present at Dr Fisher's presentation. As he points out, "If every scientist who now claims to have been there really had been, the room wouldn't have held us all. The truth is, I don't suppose there were more than a hundred in the audience at the start, and by the time Fisher finally wound up there were only eight of us left. I myself only stayed because I fell asleep around ten minutes in. When I woke, I found to my surprise that, according to my watch, more than two hours had passed. I was about to follow the others out when I realised he was almost done – he was rambling incoherently by this time about chemical weapons and sorcery and someone called Miss G. Then he peered towards the back of the room and started calling 'Annie? Annie?' in a querulous voice. Well, we all looked round – but there was absolutely nobody there. After that the wind seemed knocked out of him, and he got his things together and left. I've heard since that he was supposed to be frothing at the mouth, or that he started manhandling the security staff, saying they must have stopped this woman from coming in – but I certainly never saw him do anything like that. He looked perfectly calm to me, almost dignified, although of course you can never tell with mad people."

Whatever the truth behind Dr Fisher's behaviour – and it now seems likely to be the subject of a detailed investigation by the authorities at his university – it is certain to raise further issues about the governance and regulation of research studies dealing with female sexual function.

Congo Blog

Hey ho, here we are on Day Five already. I'll try to post yesterday's photos on Flickr when I get a chance (most of the places we stop off at only have generator power, so I'll wait until we reach something resembling civilisation before I risk an upload). Today has been spent paddling slowly upriver, first through the mangrove swamps, then proper rainforest. Funny, after spending most of my adolescence in a Swamp, to actually see one for real at last. It's nothing like the Blood Swamps of Azeroth, of course. For one thing, we never had to worry about mosquitoes in those days. Here the little beggars are everywhere. Hope the malaria tablets are working (they make me feel terrible, so they're obviously doing something).

And – ah, dammit. Here we go again. I'm crying.

It still creeps up on me at the oddest times. Just then it was because I wrote that stuff about taking the malaria pills. Suddenly I was back in the lab, knocking back my KXC79. With Steven.

Will this ever go away?

It will. Of course it will. Already I'm not crying more than, I don't know, six or seven times a day. Six months ago it was, oh, seven or eight.

Six months ago. It feels like another lifetime.

I didn't go to the Trock conference. Or rather, I did, but not to Steven's presentation. When I turned up at the hotel – very late – Richard was waiting in the suite. He'd arranged dinner with some very important scientists on my behalf, as well as the senior management of Trock, all lined up to meet me. He'd warned me to bring my best frock, and then of course when I put it on he decided that I looked so nice he just had to take it off, plus he hadn't seen me for well over a week, so after all that was resolved to both parties' satisfaction we had to get dressed all over again and it was almost ten by the time we went downstairs.

No sign of Steven. I did ask one of the Trock people but it seemed he'd shut himself away in his room, working on some last minute changes to his paper.

And they were all very pleasant but as dinner progressed, and wine was drunk, I couldn't help feeling exactly what I told Steven I didn't want to feel. Like I was an exhibit. Did they somehow know I'd been part of the study? Richard swore not.

Then it came to me. The reason all the other men were giving me these surreptitious, greedy little glances is because I *was* an exhibit. Exhibit A.

I was the proof that Richard was the most successful, best-looking, smartest male at the table.

In the foyer there was a stack of his books and a big photograph of him, ready for tomorrow's book-signing. "Embarrassing, isn't it?" he said on our way back upstairs. But actually he didn't seem embarrassed. Just cheerful.

Then, as I was sitting at the dressing table taking my earrings off, he came up and stood behind me, watching me in the mirror.

"What?" I said, catching his eye.

"When you come to Harvard," he said hesitantly, "will you...that is, do you think...would you move in with me?"

Well, that *was* unexpected.

"What's brought this on?" I said, buying time.

"We're great together, aren't we?" He trailed one finger down my back, as if to reassure himself that I was real. That I was actually his.

"You mean we have great sex."

"That too," he agreed. "But, as you of all people will surely agree, it's a pretty good start." He put his hands on my shoulders. "A connection like this, Annie...it doesn't happen often. Believe me. And when it does, you've got to grab it. No matter what other people may say."

"Why – what do they say?" Then I realised. "Oh, of course. Dick's Chicks. Your latest conquest."

He made an impatient gesture. "Let them. You and I know it isn't true.

316

Besides, I – I want to change my life. Stop this endless globe-trotting. All the pointless PR touring and the signings and the TV. I want to get back to proper science. To *research*. You could help me – as an intern, I mean. With full co-authorship rights, naturally. I've got this little project on hiccups that's reaching a very interesting phase –"

"Hang on," I said. "Hiccups? Wasn't Steven working on that? Before KXC79?"

He took a step back. "Was he? I wasn't aware. There are so many research projects. One can't keep track of them all."

"But Steven was one of your postgraduates," I pointed out. "And it was you who switched him from hiccups to orgasms in the first place. Or have I got that wrong?"

For a moment his face was dark. Then he nodded. "He was quite clearly on the verge of a massive breakthrough," he said quietly. "And once that happened, he wouldn't need me as his supervisor any more – he'd have his own fame, his own funding..."

"So you persuaded him to drop it."

"It was a joke!" Abruptly, he sat down on the end of the bed. "God – I swear it was only a joke. I passed him on the stairs and said something about why couldn't human females have as many orgasms as his blasted bonobo did. But Steven doesn't do jokes. And before I knew it, Trock were all over him with their chequebooks open. I never in a million years imagined he'd crack FSD as well." He looked at me. "Well, Annie? What do you say? I –" He swallowed. "I think I'm falling in love with you."

And I thought how much, over the last eight weeks, I'd been wanting to hear those words.

I don't deny, it was a tempting proposition. Not just the scholarship, and the ready-made research project. But the fact that I could learn so much from this man. If I'm honest, I was even a little flattered by all the rigmarole that went with him – the cameras, the dinners with eminent scientists, the knowledge that, as his girlfriend, I was a prize worth coveting.

"I'm sorry, Richard," I said. "The thing is, I simply don't feel the same way. Or rather, I do, but not about you."

317

And, as gently as I could, I told him what had really happened. Who I was really in love with. I told him it wasn't his fault and that there was nothing either of us could do about it. And while he was still in a state of shock I packed my bag and walked back to the station.

Should I have stayed? Would things have been different if I had? Sitting on the train back to Oxford that night I told myself I was doing the sensible thing. That once the conference was over, there'd be plenty of time to sit down with Steven and have a proper, grown-up conversation about the whole thing.

But there wasn't. Suddenly all hell was let loose. There were demonstrations outside the Department building – it was the animal rights people, who'd got worked up about Lucy, with a few feminists and anti-Trock protestors thrown in for good measure. Steven was suspended. Simon Frampton even popped out of the woodwork, making heinous – and entirely hypocritical – allegations about him and me, which whipped things up even more. So then there was an investigation, and somehow it was all Steven's fault, the attitude of the university authorities towards the female sex being much the same as Tennyson's:

> Weakness to be wroth with weakness! woman's pleasure, woman's pain—
> Nature made them blinder motions bounded in a shallower brain...

Of course, with no supervisor, no thesis and no job, and the KXC79 paper a laughing stock, my own dream of walking into any science department in the country was in tatters too. But, after a bit of moping around, I eventually managed to scrape a place on a biochemistry course at one of those establishments that calls itself a uni but which snobs still refer to as polytechnics. And it's great – absolutely great. Quite apart from anything else, I've met a terrific bunch of people.

Though I doubt if any of them know the chemical composition of tears.

*

318

Funnily enough, the one thing I don't regret was telling Steven to get lost, that time by the lake. My whole problem was that I'd been behaving like some swooning Victorian heroine, drifting along, being wooed, letting everyone else tell me what to do and who to do it with. Even when I played Swamps and Sorcerers I was letting the dice make the decisions. But sometimes you can't just roll an LR-1 and let it decide your fate, can you? Sometimes you have to make a plan. And telling him where to get off was the start of that.

Admittedly, the bit in between the conference and starting my science degree is a bit of a blur. Not that I necessarily regret any of that either, you understand, but it wasn't really me. Call it making up for lost time. I even surprised myself by becoming a bit of a slut for a while...until I realised that the person I really wanted to be a slut with wasn't there.

I'd lost touch with the others in the lab by then. Although I did glimpse a couple of things... There was an article in the *Daily Mail* about some new sex toy. Apparently it uses miniaturised biofeedback software "based on the technology used in professional sex research laboratories". According to the article, the young couple who invented it, Rhona and Wulf Sederholm, are on track to become multimillionaires.

And then one day during my first term I was buying *New Scientist* in WH Smith's when I saw a paperback called *Sex Goddess: Inside the KXC79 Experiment* by Dr Susie Minstock. On the cover was a full-length picture of Susan looking sexy. And a publicity quote from Professor Richard Collins, bestselling author of *The Evolution Revolution*: "Full of mystery, humanity, laughter and sex."

Meanwhile, I've been keeping busy during the vacations by going on field trips with the gang from my course. Like this one. Well, when I heard it was bonobo, how could I not sign up? Plus, it sounds like we might actually be doing something useful. Bonobo numbers have been shrinking over the last ten years, but without accurate tagging it's impossible to say how much or why – everyone's pretty sure it's the destruction of their habitat, but we need the data to prove it. So that's what we're going out to do. Though – secretly – we're having a good time too. Today, for example, I found myself sitting in the middle of a mangrove swamp, eating grilled river perch, arguing with Melissa from the Second Year about who's cooler, Leela or Trinity. (Well, duh – despite all her awesome powers Trinity is clearly only in the movie as eye candy for the boys, whereas Leela is a Strong Woman in her own right. Plus her relationship with Fry always makes me cry, and no one could say that about Trinity and Neo.) How much fun is that?

Urlgirl67@hotmail.com ☺
"There are only ten kinds of people,
those who understand binary and those who don't"

Day Six. Today we pushed the last sixty miles upriver to the camp. Nice place – basic but friendly. Ben, our group leader, has been here before, and the local people greet him effusively before unloading our stuff and carrying it into the huts. And – hurrah! – there's even broadband access, a really ingenious rig that uses a router hooked up to a satellite phone that's connected to some toll-free number in Mexico…hence the blog update.

After supper we get a brief introduction to bonobo culture. I know most of this, of course, but it's always interesting to hear it from an expert. Except that as Ben explains about how they use sex for conflict resolution I feel the familiar pricking behind my eyes, because talking about bonobos reminds me of Steven. Oh dear. That was something I didn't factor into my packing – that I might end up blubbing every half hour. The nearest supply of Kleenex is six hours away.

And because I'm thinking about Steven I zone out for a while, so that I almost miss the reference to someone called Fish.

Fish is their tracker, it seems, a man who understands bonobos so well he can follow them through the rainforest and find their camps. Fish can almost talk bonobo. Fish has even rigged up webcams in the jungle

320

to send pictures of bonobo gangbangs back to UCLA.

"If you've got any questions about bonobo social organisation," Ben says, "he's the man to ask. But you may have to wait a few days. We've got a hunting party of chimps in bonobo territory." It turns out, you see, that bonobo and ordinary chimps don't mix. Although bonobos are vegetarian and peace-loving, regular chimps aren't, and occasionally they organise raids into bonobo territory to steal their babies and eat them.

"Which, of course, poses a dilemma for us conservationists," Ben adds. "Do we save the young bonobo from their predators, on the basis that their numbers are so depleted they need our protection? Or do we simply observe? It may be that when predators take the weaklings, they actually end up strengthening the herd. If we intervene, we risk upsetting the evolutionary balance."

"What does Fish say?" someone asks.

"Fish says..." Ben pauses. "Well, Fish has a slightly unorthodox perspective. Fish says we can never be just observers. He says we're part of the experiment, like it or not. And he also says that sometimes you just have to tell evolution to go screw itself. So that's what he's doing now – guarding the bonobo's kids."

Well, of course that prompts a heated debate about the rights and wrongs of this – not *too* heated, mind you, because it's thirty degrees already. Someone prepares food, and as the sun begins to set the Africans in the camp start to sing, a lovely mournful sound. That sunset – it's a real Congo sunset, the sun like a great orange egg yolk that seems to swell until it fills the whole sky, slowly squashing itself down against the horizon, and finally breaking in a gush of red and yellow into the swamp. The forest goes quiet, and the heat of the day dissipates so quickly you can actually feel the sluggish air draining from your skin. Then, from the forest, comes a whole series of unearthly shrieks and calls.

"Bonobo," Ben says.

I lean against a tree trunk and watch the sky as it turns a rich, streaky purple, only half listening to the conversation around me. I hear someone say, "What a beautiful sunset," and then a different voice says, "Yes. It's the refraction that does that, of course. The longer wavelengths of the sun's rays are filtered by the atmosphere of the earth."

I know that voice.

I look up and –

He looks so different. For one thing, the jungle clothes really suit him. He's wiry and lean and completely at ease. But that's not the most striking thing. With his long hair, and that wild beard...he looks an awful lot like Chewbacca.

How come I never noticed that before? He was a clean-shaven Chewie, all the time.

He sees me too, and he hardly seems surprised. Like he's been waiting for me to turn up, all this time.

He nods, slowly.

"Annie," he says simply. "You're here."

I stand up, and then somehow we're walking away from the camp together, heading into the forest.

"Where are we going?"

"Ssshhh. I'll explain later." And I follow him down a moonlit path into the forest, wondering about snakes.

Eventually we come to a clearing. He stops and peers into the gloom.

"There," he whispers. "See them?"

It takes my eyes about a minute to get used to the near-darkness. Then I spot them. About half a dozen bonobos are rolling around on the floor of the clearing, having enthusiastic bonobo sex. In the foreground, a big male squats on his hind legs, thrusting away at a female who's lying back and eating a bamboo shoot. Another female comes up and helps out. Then a second male comes over and takes care of the second female, helping himself to a mouthful of bamboo as he does so. More join them. They stop, start, break off, swop round, and occasionally pause to pelt each other with fruit. When they finally call a halt the males lie back, pleased with themselves, passing a piece of bamboo around like a cigar, while the females groom each other for fleas and indulge in a little surreptitious extra sex-play.

"There's Lucy." He points to where a knot of simian polyamorists are clustered around one particularly tireless female.

"You remember me saying that no one knows what the female orgasm is actually for?" He speaks quietly so as not to disturb the bonobos. "Well, I've been developing a new theory about that. I think it might be related to mate selection. If females gravitate towards mates who have the ability to make them climax, it would favour more intelligent, dextrous, empathetic males, and ultimately enrich the gene pool. That would explain why female orgasms are apparently random and elusive: it's a kind of compatibility challenge."

"So nothing to do with neurotransmitters after all?"

"That's the interesting thing. How does a female know in advance which male will be clever enough to make her orgasmic? Guesswork? Romance? Trial and error? There could be a role for some kind of chemical messenger after all."

I nod. Then, because I realise he won't be able to see me in the near-darkness, I say, "Interesting. But the trouble with messages is that they can be so hard to read. Even chemical ones."

"Almost impossible," he agrees.

"Take you and me, for example. How wrong did we get those signals?"

"Exactly." He pauses. "Just to make absolutely sure that neither of us is misreading them now, shall we double-check our reactions against each other?"

"Good idea."

"For a start," he says, "I'm feeling a little unsteady on my feet."

"Check," I say. "Which is probably due to a rush of dopamine, increasing visual attention but impairing fine motor co-ordination."

"You've been doing some more science?" He sounds impressed.

"A degree course. Biochemistry."

"I'm also feeling intense gratification at your presence," he says.

"Check. That would be the effect of opiate-like beta-endorphins creating addiction-and-reward pathways in the brain."

"I'm getting an overwhelming urge to touch you –"

"…Caused by oxytocin, elevated levels of which are associated with cuddling, breast-feeding, and other attachment stimuli. You can if you want. Touch me, that is."

He takes me in his arms. "There's a strong sense of euphoria –"

"Check," I say, a little breathlessly. "From cascades of serotonin, a powerful mood enhancer."

"– excited yet calm at the same time –"

"A cocktail of epinephrine, which causes the excitement, and its sedative counterpart, L-dopa –"

" – dizzy…"

"…from the intoxicating effects of norepinephrine…"

"…but also strangely focused. As if there's nothing outside this place, this moment, just being here with you."

"Me too," I breathe. "Prostaglandin."

"My lips are tingling –"

"I know! As if they're dying to be kissed –"

"In fact," he says, "I think it might be a good idea to do just that."

So he kisses me, and then he kisses me some more. First on the lips, and then the neck, and then the ears and the eyelids and the throat, before finally going back to the lips again. For one endless, ecstatic minute, every single cell in our bodies jumps up and down and applauds.

"I'm pretty sure our chemical messengers are reporting an exceptionally high level of compatibility," he murmurs.

"Possibly. Although the view that kissing has any such function is regarded by many scientists as overly sentimental," I tell him sternly.

"What's not in doubt is that I'm becoming somewhat vasodilated."

"I'd noticed."

"Sorry."

"Don't be. It's reassuring to know you won't be needing Viagra. Plenty of nitric oxide in the old corpus cavernosa."

He kisses me again, more deeply. I sigh and wriggle further into his arms. "Mind you," I admit, "I think I might be experiencing a little vasodilation myself. There's a definite feeling of wanting to melt into your arms like a swooning Victorian heroine. And I'm getting a strong urge to take all my clothes off."

"Hardly surprising, with all these chemicals reacting inside us. First law of thermodynamics." As he kisses me again he slips his hands a little higher, inside my shirt, where he does something clever with his thumbs.

After that, rational thought becomes pretty much redundant. A few minutes later one of the female bonobos looks up, sees us, and chatters. The others regard us curiously; then, as if we've given them the idea, they get back to doing what they were doing before, which is pretty much the same as us.

There are fourteen major erogenous zones on the female body. And it turns out that Steven Fisher knows the location of every single one.

Figure 24: Lucy and a friend.

Acknowledgements

I am indebted to Dr Cynthia Graham, Research Fellow at The Kinsey Institute for Research in Sex, Gender, and Reproduction, Senior Research Fellow at Harris Manchester College, University of Oxford, and Research Tutor, Oxford Doctoral Course in Clinical Psychology, for reading through the manuscript. Dr Fisher's errors are in no way hers.

My thanks also go to Ileen Maisel who, in developing the film adaptation, offered many ideas which found their way into the manuscript; to Tom Vaughan and Peter Friedlander, who championed it from the beginning; to Danielle Friedman at Touchstone and Laura Palmer at Corvus for their suggestions during editing; to Tim Riley for being a sounding board; and to Louise Lamont, Judith Evans and Elinor Cooper of AP Watt, for liking Dr Fisher as much as I did.

Many of the scientific papers cited by Dr Fisher can be read at his website, chemistryforbeginners.com.

Picture credits